The Reluctant Tourist

To Marty & Greta,

Best wishes,

Ron

The Reluctant Tourist

Ronald Barnett

Writer's Showcase
San Jose New York Lincoln Shanghai

The Reluctant Tourist

Writer's Showcase
an imprint of iUniverse.com, Inc.

For information address:
iUniverse.com, Inc.
5220 S 16th, Ste. 200
Lincoln, NE 68512
www.iuniverse.com

ISBN: 0-595-18320-4

Printed in the United States of America

Preface

"Daddy, tell us a story." That is what my sister and I would tell our father as he tucked us into bed each night. The stories were always about London, Siberia, China or Japan. We never thought to ask him questions. Each story was exciting and we took it for granted that fathers of our friends told them similar tales.

We realized, as we grew older that these were true stories of a great adventure he had experienced. It was not until after his passing that I began doing research into the overall historical period in which his stories took place. It was then that his saga began to be more meaningful and exciting.

Why and how he went to Siberia was told to me by his sister in London. The book is well researched on the little known period of history during the Allied Intervention into Russia and Siberia after the Russian Revolution, during 1918 and 1919.

The book is a historical novel based on the true story of a young deserter from the British Army during World War I. The British and Russians were both at war with Germany when the Conventions with the Allies Act became law in Britain in 1917. It provided that any Russian subject living in Britain, of draft age, could join the British Army or return to Russia and join the Russian Army.

The material was researched in the Soviet Union; the Public Records Office, London; the London Borough of Tower Hamlets Central Library, London; The Public Archives, Canada; City of Vancouver Archives, Canada; Provincial Archives, British Columbia; Archives of the Hoover Institute, Stanford University; University of California at Los Angeles Research Library and Law Library.

Prologue

Morrie looked out the window of the huge jet flying at 38,000 feet over the Atlantic. His eyes were fixed on the inboard engine pod as the illumination of the strobe light bounded off of it at regular intervals. It was early October 1959. He had been away from London for over forty-one years and repeated over and over to himself what he would say to his sister, Flora, and to his father. Morrie really couldn't believe that his father was ninety-one years old and had lived to see him return to England.

Morrie never got over the feeling of being a fugitive, although World War I had been over since 1918. He was unaware that an amnesty had been enacted by Parliament many years ago. He was also an American citizen, but the fear had remained in his belly even as he boarded the plane in Los Angeles earlier that evening. He had finally relented to the pressures and encouragement of his wife and children to return to London. There was never any thought of sleep as the night became darker and the engines roared. His thoughts went back to his childhood in London. He wasn't thinking of Siberia, Yokohama, or Canada. London was on his mind.

How would his old friend Willie look? What were Flora's children like? Would his sister and father recognize him? What do you say to someone after forty years? He somehow didn't want to talk about Siberia. Somehow it felt as if he had never left London but he knew that was impossible and he was frightened.

The thoughts of his days at Senrab Street School came into his mind, his outings to Victoria Park with his childhood friend Willie Weinberg, his short-lived boxing career at the Judean Club and the Ring at Blackfriars, and most of all his adventures with Willie to the West End. His thoughts naturally progressed to the Army and Salisbury Plain. His mind suddenly shut that out, along with everything that came later.

The stewardess came by and began lifting the shades of the windows. Morrie could see the autumn dawn breaking in the distance. He looked below and could see only green and brown squares of farmland through the broken white clouds. The voice of the captain came over the loudspeaker, announcing that they were over Scotland and would be landing in Heathrow in about an hour.

Breakfast was cleared away and Morrie could feel the engines begin to slow. He looked out the window, and suddenly he could see the brick row houses with their chimney pots. London! He felt himself flush as he realized that he would be seeing his family in a few minutes. It was a crisp October morning, and the plane began to slowly circle as it approached the glide path. Morrie looked down through the clouds at London. His heart raced as he picked out the familiar landmarks. The woman next to him chuckled as he called out the names: "Windsor Castle." "Hyde Park."

The plane's wings dipped to the left, and he saw the Thames twisting through the city and glistening in the morning sun. Morrie caught himself drawing out his A's and his youthful accent came back as he called out the sights for the woman. The plane circled lower and there was Tower Bridge. He quickly tried to locate St. Dunstan's church and his old neighborhood, but the wings suddenly rose and blocked his view.

The plane straightened, and in the distance Morrie could see the legacy of World War II. Shells of buildings remained all along the dock area in the East End.

Morrie handed his passport to the immigration officer, and for a few seconds fear went through him. He knew that it was stupid, but fear was an involuntary feeling he carried all of his life.

"Morrie," he heard someone shout as he came into the terminal. There stood Flora and her husband, Harry, forty-one years older than when he had last seen them. He turned away as tears came to his eyes. Flora threw her arms around him and Harry shook his hand.

As the taxi headed for London, they exchanged questions about family and friends. Flora and Morrie spontaneously began harmonizing "Take Me Back to Dear Old Blighty," and everyone had a good laugh.

The taxi entered the West End along Kensington Road, and then into Knightsbridge along the southern end of Hyde Park. Harry told the driver to go down Piccadilly as Morrie remarked how small everything looked. The streets looked so narrow after a lifetime in Los Angeles. The driver wheeled the cab into the Strand and then into Fleet Street.

They were in the heart of the city when Morrie began to see the damage of the bombings. "There's St. Pauls," said Morrie, as he proudly took over directing the cabby. "Go down Cannon Street and over to Fenchurch Street." It was all coming back. "Is the Aldgate Pump still there?" "Gaw Blimey," said Flora, "the Germans didn't hit everything." "They didn't get the Holborn Empire, did they?" "Gone" said Harry. "What about the Ring at Blackfriars?" "Gone."

The taxi rounded the corner past the Pump and entered Whitechapel Road. Bombsites were everywhere. Flora called off one site after another, places that Morrie knew so well as a young man. The London Hospital came into sight, and Morrie spotted Johnny Isaac's fish shop. "Still a hap'ny bit and a hapeth?" "Blimey, would you believe six bloody shillings and safety caps on the vinegar?"

The cab made a right turn into Stepney Green, and all at once there were the Dwellings, untouched by bombs. Morrie could see all the way to St. Dunstans three blocks away. Every building in between was gone.

"Zeida is waiting upstairs," said Flora. Ever since her children had been born she referred to their father by the Yiddish word for grandfather. They walked up the stairs and there in striped trousers, black coat and bowler hat stood Morrie's father. The once powerful figure had shrunk and the face was wrinkled. Morrie at once looked at his father's hands. They were the same ones that had held the goose press fourteen hours a day, six days a week.

The old man could only bring himself to say "my son Morrie." After forty-one years there was everything to say and nothing to say. Flora broke the silence. "How about a cup of tea?"

The tea was relaxing. Morrie still couldn't believe he was in London. He looked around the small room. Nothing had changed, even his favorite chair was still there. He wondered how his mother could have shared these tiny quarters with anyone other than her family. He remembered having to sleep on the floor of the parlor to make room for the "Peruvians" coming off the ships from Eastern Europe. Nobody could explain why they were called Peruvians.

"We called Willie. He lives with his wife in Stamford Hill. They've invited you to dinner day after tomorrow."

Morrie met Flora's children, Sam, Sadie, and Cecil. They asked him about Siberia and America. Somehow he avoided Siberia, but did go on for hours about America. He observed to himself that in all the years he had been away, mandatory education in England had only increased one year, to fifteen years of age. Not one child among his family or friends had been to a university, and only one or two had gone to a school beyond the required time. The children of his friends were taxi drivers, tailors, bookmakers, or petty merchants, while his own children had attended university and become prosperous.

Morrie spent the next day walking through the East End with Harry. They went down Commercial Road to Senrab Street School. It had survived the bombings, and he saw the "1907" carved in stone above the entrance. Morrie had been the second boy on the registration list that year, actually the second boy registered in the school. The two of them continued down Commercial Road. The Old Premierland arena was gone, as was the Judean Club where Morrie had boxed. Harry told Morrie the Ring at Blackfriars was so heavily damaged during the Battle of Britain that it had to be torn down.

"What about The Leicester Lounge?" "Bombed and gone," replied Harry. They passed the London Hospital to the corner of Sidney Street. "I stood on this corner watching Churchill in his top hat leading the Constabulary against the anarchists during the famous Siege of Sidney Street," said Morrie.

They had begun to walk back along Whitechapel Road, when Morrie suddenly winced. "Harry, this is the very spot where I was picked up by Scotland Yard. It seems like yesterday."

Morrie held the large box of dried fruit he had brought from California as they entered the stairway of Willie Weinberg's flat. Flora's son Sam had driven him to Willie's in his 1936 Jaguar. Morrie was nervous as he climbed the stairs. His thoughts went back to Pentonville Prison, the last time he had seen Willie.

The door to the flat opened and there stood a tall man with thinning gray hair. He was slightly heavier then Morrie remembered, but it was Willie for sure. He introduced his wife and they all sat down. "Morrie, before we say anything, would you like a Teachers whiskey and a Bass's Ale to follow like old times?" Willie's wife went into the kitchen to prepare dinner while the two men recalled their youth.

"Morrie, I never thought I would see you again when I said goodbye at Pentonville. Anyway, enough of that. You look great and I'll bet you can still go a couple of rounds." The two men swapped stories about family. Morrie at last described his ordeal through Siberia and the Russian Civil War. Willie sat transfixed and kept shaking his head in disbelief.

Dinner was served and Morrie began telling them how he had never gotten London out of his soul. "My son asks me why I've never learned to understand American football or baseball. I take him to the English style football matches. There are never more than twenty or thirty people there. My wife hates fish and chips and is very kind to go with me, as she knows how much I love it. I guess I've overdone it with my children about England. I'm sure they don't believe half of what I tell them."

The old friends stayed up until three in the morning trading stories. Finally Willie called a cab and they said their last goodbye.

Morrie spent the remaining few days in London searching out places from his youth, then it was time to return home. He had gotten it out of his system at last. He was finally going home to California after all the years of dreaming and thinking about England.

Chapter One

Morrie Kotler, until ten days ago, had never heard of Murmansk. They told him it was the northernmost city in the world, or tied for that honor with another place, Kirkenes, in Norway.

The BRADFORD, a decrepit tub of a freighter, was tied up alongside a Murmansk wharf on the morning of November 21, 1917. The sky was gray and heavy, and a light snow was falling through the gloom. Morrie could make out what appeared to be buildings made out of logs, a few shacks, and men who wore such heavy fur clothing that they might have been mistaken for bears.

"Lovely place, what?" said one of the British Marines who had been escorting the cargo, whatever it was, to the Russian forces still fighting the Bolsheviks, or the Germans, or who knows? The Marines didn't know, and they didn't particularly care. They were just making sure the cargo was unloaded at Murmansk, and what happened to it after that was none of their bloody business, as they frequently said.

"It looks like someplace the Eskimos would abandon," said Morrie.

That was an accurate assessment of Murmansk, as it was in the winter of 1917. It had only been established as a port three years before. It had one value, even though it was some four hundred miles north of the old port city, Archangel. Because of the warming effect of the Gulf stream the waters around Murmansk remained ice-free during the winter, while the approaches to Archangel were frozen solid from November through March.

The Bradford's throbbing engines were suddenly silent, and Morrie could hear the Russians on the wharf talking. It was a babble of unintelligible syllables. He couldn't understand a word of what they were saying.

"You're Russian," said the Marine. "What are them blokes talking about?"

"I haven't the foggiest," said Morrie.

"But you're Russian."

"Born there, like I told you a dozen times already. My mum and dad came to England when I was a baby, and I'm as English as you are." This was the lie that Morrie had, by now, told so often that he almost believed it.

"I'll never understand why you're coming back here," said the Marine, and walked away.

Morrie went down to the cabin he shared with three others.

These were real Russians, and he simply nodded to them as he gathered up his few belongings, stuffed them in a knapsack, and walked out. Back on deck, he went to where the gangplank had been slung and asked the deck officer when he could get off.

"Any time now, Kotler, any time at all," the officer said.

"Won't there be some immigration formalities, somebody I have to check with?"

The officer laughed.

"Not bloody likely. They don't need to have any immigration formalities, as you call them, here. Nobody in their right mind would want to go to Murmansk. It's a dead end. You see that?"

He stuck his arm out and swept it in an arc, pointing at the huts, the piled up snow, the few mules and horses and the bear-like humans. A forbidding backdrop, grim, white mountains in a semi-circular arc surrounded the town.

"Yes, I see it," said Morrie.

"What you see is what you got, my boy. That's all there is. That's your future home, and you're bloody well welcome to it."

Morrie started to walk down the gangplank. The officer grabbed him, and, almost like a mother, had him turn up his collar and pull the edges of his wool cap down over his ears.

"When it's this cold, young fellow, don't leave a bit of your flesh exposed. Two minutes outside, and you could lose an ear."

Morrie mumbled his thanks, then headed down the gangplank. As soon as he left the shelter of the ship, the wind tore at him, the cold was a living thing. He thought he had dressed warmly, but in an instant the wind and the cold had penetrated through every layer of his clothing. At the foot of the gangplank, as he took his first step onto Russian soil, he hit a patch of glazed ice and fell.

A hand roughly helped him to his feet. One of the human bears grinned at him with toothless gums, and he could make out a beard, a long nose, and hard blue eyes. The rest was all fur and heavy cloth. The man said a few words, but Morrie had no idea what he meant.

"Thanks for the hand, mate," he said, knowing the man wouldn't understand him either. So he said it louder. He knew that wouldn't help, but it seemed like the only thing to do.

The man pointed off to the left and waved his hand, indicating that Morrie should go in that direction. Morrie nodded, and the man moved away.

Morrie stood there, hunched against the cold and the wind and the snow, and seriously considered crying. He was eight months beyond his nineteenth birthday, and he had hardly ever been away from his London home before, except for those few weeks when he had been in the British army. Here he was in what appeared to be the most awful place in the world, knowing no one, not knowing a word that was spoken, practically broke, and without being able to tell anyone of his plight.

He had looked at the map aboard the ship. He knew that what the officer at the head of the gangplank had told him was true there was no place to go.

North? North was into the Arctic Ocean.

West? The ocean was there, too, and beyond the ocean lay England. He couldn't go back there. Impossible.

South? There was a war going on in that direction, and anyhow, there was no way of getting through the mountains and the snow. Murmansk was pretty well isolated.

East? That was Siberia. The very word, Siberia, was enough to scare anybody away. His Russian parents had used "Siberia" like his English friends' parents used "the bogey man," as a dire, dreadful threat. So no, he wasn't about to go to Siberia and get thrown into a salt mine, or be chained to a long line of poor, hapless souls and made to chop wood all day and all night.

He lashed his knapsack around his shoulder, thrust his gloved hands inside his pockets, and moved off in the direction the helpful man had indicated. He would probably freeze to death within an hour if he didn't move fast.

He never looked back at the ship, which had taken him away from everything he had ever known and loved.

#   #   #

Morrie Kotler grew up in three worlds. There was, of course, the primary world- the one in which he found himself, the one he was born into in London's East End. There were no walls around it, but it was a ghetto. It was where the refugees from the pogroms in Russia, the ones who couldn't go to America, congregated in London, mostly in the 1800s and 1890s.

That was the world Morrie knew well, as any child knows his environment. Narrow streets, teeming buildings, crowded flats, the smell of cooking, indoors and out. People speaking Yiddish, primarily, but the children speaking English as good as any Cockney. Morrie grew up there. He knew the streets and the alleys, the bobbies and the whores, the shopkeepers and the landlords. He also knew how to take care of himself.

There were two other worlds that he was familiar with, although on less intimate terms.

His parents, Berko and Elka, or Barnett and Alice as they called themselves, when they got to England, told him stories about the world they had fled. Russia, Poland, and the Cossacks, the shtetl and the pogroms, the cows and the horses and the rich, black land. There was a mixture of nostalgia and relief in their stories. Sometimes Morrie sensed their longing to return,but at other times he realized how grateful they were to be away from the fear of the midnight raids of the dreaded Cossacks. Here in

England the anti-Semites might call you names and pull your beard, but they didn't carry sabers.

There was another world for Morrie. It was the world of the English. As he grew older and more adventurous, he would edge out of the East End and look around. There was always a barrier between him and that world of luxury and gentility. He knew he was actually two giant steps away from that world. One step was class, the second religion. His non-Jewish English friends, schoolmates and boys from the streets near his home, were only one step away, but it was a monster of a step, one that very few ever bridged. England, then, was a society of rigid classes. The poor could rarely aspire to a better life. Morrie was not only poor, but he was also Jewish, and that was the second giant step.

The combination, he came to realize, made any ambition virtually impossible.

Still, he could look. As a small boy, he found that when he walked a few blocks west or north, he was in a different and better world. He would look at the lovely homes and the elegantly dressed men and women and wonder what sort of lives they lived.

He was too young to think of comparing their lives with his. Besides, his life was, to him, the normal life. He began to appreciate that his life was lacking in some material things, but still, he was not yet at an age when he could comprehend what it all meant.

He knew, primarily, from the constant repetition of his parents, that he should be grateful that he was born in England.

"You will never have to worry about going to Russia and being put in the Czar's army," his father would often say.

"When I was a boy, that was the big worry, I'll tell you. When a boy went into the Czar's army it was for twenty-five years."

Berko Kotler was a burly man, short and stocky and as strong as one of the Russian oxen that he often spoke about. Morrie was more slender, but strong for his size. He also had inherited his father's tendency to go into a rage at almost any provocation.

"Let me tell you what a temper like yours can lead to, Morrie," his father had said one evening, after Morrie had gotten into some curbside scrape. Berko told the story of his battle with the Cossacks again. Morrie never tired of hearing it.

It was back in Jasinowka. That was the little village where Berko had grown up, not far from Bialistok. On one sunny day, he was talking to a friend when they heard the familiar, horrifying warning call, "Pogrom! Pogrom!"

They looked up. Down the dusty road came four Cossacks on horseback, riding abreast, sabers drawn, screaming for blood. The people tried to get inside, but the Cossacks were too fast, too brutal. A lunge and a slash, and a Jew would be writhing on the ground, slit from chest to waist, blood and life pouring out of him.

"Leka, go back," cried Berko. He had seen his cousin, a pretty young woman, trying to run across the road. She was carrying her baby.

"Leka, no! Go back!"

She looked up and saw Berko, but she was confused. She hesitated, and one of the Cossacks was on her. Deftly, he flicked his saber down and plucked the baby out of its mother's arms. He gave a slight toss of the saber and the baby, screaming in terror, flopped into the air, then the Cossack skewered it as it came down.

"Swalich," yelled Berko. Leka was too shocked to say or do anything, but Berko leaped across the street, grabbed the Cossack by his belt, and yanked him off his horse.

There was a stream running beside the road, and Berko's momentum carried him and his enemy into the water. Berko held the squirming Cossack under until he drowned.

Fortunately for Berko, the Cossack's three companions had not witnessed the incident. They had ridden ahead. If they had seen it, they would have exacted quick and terrible revenge. Now Berko had a chance to run.

He escaped with no plan, nothing guiding his feet except terror. He simply ran, and as luck would have it, his flight brought him to a nearby village. He was panting and exhausted, but he was beginning to reason. In that village, he knew, was a blacksmith who was a distant relation. His father had often come to the village to see this blacksmith when a horse needed to be shod. Berko went to the blacksmith's forge.

"Ah, Berko! Where's your pappa? Where's your horse?"

"My father asked me to come here and ask you a very important favor," Berko said.

"And what is this important favor your father wants his old cousin to do for him?"

"He wants to borrow a few rubles from you. He needs to buy a new wagon. He told me to say that he would pay you back part of the money in a month's time, and, as for the rest in two month's time."

The request was strange, because Berko's father was known to be a proud man who had never borrowed money. The proper thing would have been to come and ask for it himself, not to send a son who stood there, all covered with sweat and fear. The blacksmith was suspicious, and yet tradition called for honoring, if possible, the favor that was asked of you by a relative.

"All right, Berko," said the blacksmith. He took a heavy stone out of the chimney and brought out a large leather purse. He gave Berko the money. "Tell your father I am honored to be of help to him, and I hope his new wagon brings him joy and prosperity forever."

Berko thanked him. He felt ashamed of his lie, but there was no other way. He could not go back to Jasinowka, because there was a dead Cossack lying in the stream by the road. No, he must flee the country and to do that he had to have money. He would repay the blacksmith someday, but, for the moment, he had to think only of himself.

"So you see, Morrie, what trouble a temper can bring you," he said. "With me, it meant I had to leave my home and my family, and it meant a dead man, a rascal he was but still he was a human, one of God's creations, and to kill is never a good thing."

"Well, I traveled north," said Berko, "from the blacksmith's village. I traveled at night, so nobody could see me, and I slept in the daytime, in barns or just by the road. I had a difficult time, let me tell you, but I was young, young like you, so I could do it. I got to Germany and couldn't speak the language, but there are some words that are the same in Yiddish and German, so I could understand them and they could understand me."

Berko continued his odyssey in Germany, but it took him several weeks to make his way to his goal, Hamburg, a port from which, he knew, ships traveled across the sea to London and to America. He had a sister who had made the trip some years before, and was now in someplace called St. Louis.

The money he had borrowed from the blacksmith was quickly running out. He went to the docks and asked how much it would cost to go to St. Louis. The men there laughed and told him that St. Louis was nowhere near any ocean, that he would have to sail to New York and then take the train across the prairie to get to St. Louis.

"It will take you four days on the train," one of the dock workers said.

"How much to sail to New York?" Berko asked.

When they told him, he realized he didn't have enough. He shrugged and said thank you. Then they told him he could go to London for a lot less, so he bought a ticket and sailed to London on the next passage.

It was only a four-day sail across the North Sea, but it was a rough trip and Berko was sick most of the way. When the ship finally docked, not far from the Tower of London, he staggered down the gangplank weak from being sick aboard ship and from the weeks of running and eating very little.

As an immigrant, he had to stand in a long line, but the examination was perfunctory. At that time, the English were admitting virtually anyone who wanted to enter. They asked a few routine questions, satisfied themselves that, at least on the surface, the immigrant was healthy, and then handed him a document to sign.

Many of the Jews didn't know how to sign their names. They would try to explain, in Yiddish, that they couldn't sign. The examiners would then tell them to make a mark.

"Make an X, like this," the examiner would tell them.

But the X was the sign of the cross, and to them, that was something they could not do.

They would hesitate and, in the spirit of commerce, offer to make a compromise. Instead of an X, how about a circle?

"X *nicht*," they would say. "*Kikel?*"

"*Kikel*" was the Yiddish word for circle, and they would say "*Kikel*" and make a circle in the air with their forefinger. There, "Another kikel," the examiner would say. "All right, then, make your bloody kikel." Eventually, the whole stream of immigrants from Eastern Europe became known, to the English immigration inspectors and eventually to the English as a whole, as "kikels," and finally just "kikes."

Berko could sign his name, however, and entered England without any problem. He followed the river of previous Jewish immigrants to East London, a few short blocks from where the ship had docked. He quickly made friends, found a room, and got a job as a presser in a sweatshop, making gents' suits. It was hard work, but Berko was used to hard work. Besides, he soon had a family to support and a debt to repay. He sent a little money to the blacksmith when he could. It took him almost ten years, but eventually he repaid every ruble.

Berko met Alice at a neighborhood gathering. He was taken by her lively brown eyes, her quick laugh, her robust figure. She was equally captivated by his strength, his attitude of self-confidence, his kind smile. He soon asked her to be his wife.

Her piety went beyond merely attending services or going to the synagogue alone to pray. She felt it was her duty, as a good Jew, to help the new immigrants as they arrived from Poland or Russia. She didn't actually go the docks and greet them as they came down the gangplank, but she did the next best thing. She would arrange to have them told that she was there, waiting to help them, and for many, their first stop in England was the Kotler flat on Stepney Green.

Alice's reputation spread back to the old country, and new arrivals in London frequently stepped off the ship with a piece of paper pinned to their coat with the name and address of Elka Kotler.

Morrie and his sister Flora could not understand how their own mother could give these total strangers something to eat while they, her own children, had so little. Alice tried to make up for the lack of food with hugs and kisses, but while they may nourish the spirit, they leave the body weak.

Morrie once—he may have been five or six at the time—threatened suicide to get some candy. He had asked for a farthing, which probably was the equivalent of a quarter of a cent, to buy a sweet. All of his friends were able to do that, but his mother said no, every farthing was needed to do God's work and buy food for the newcomers. Morrie stood on the stair railing and said he would jump if he didn't get the farthing. Berko grabbed him. Instead of a farthing he got a whipping, with the heavy leather belt that Berko kept hanging on the closet door for that purpose.

"You should be grateful for life," said Berko, his teeth clenched as he lashed Morrie across his bottom. He then took his son and looked him in the eyes, saying "you should be grateful for life. Life is a very precious thing, Morrie. Do not forget that, ever. Now, here is a farthing, the last time mind you."

One Sabbath afternoon Morrie was walking with his father near Charrington's Brewery. Morrie was eight and he loved to be with his big, strong father. It didn't happen often, as Berko was either working or out looking for work, but occasionally, on the Sabbath, Berko would relax enough to walk with his son.

They enjoyed looking in the store windows along Mile End Road. Morrie would say something silly and Berko would laugh, pick his son up, and give him a hug. "A hug like a Siberian black bear," he would say.

This day, as they strolled together, a *Yok*, the East End Jewish slang term for a gentile boy, dashed up, yanked Morrie's hat off his head, and ran away.

Berko roared. Morrie immediately knew that this was the sound his father had made when he yanked the Cossack off his horse back in Jasinowka. Berko caught up with the *Yok* in a few swift strides, picked him up, and slammed him to the sidewalk. He picked up Morrie's hat from where the other boy had flung it, carefully dusting it off and placing in back on Morrie's head.

"Poppa, you hurt him," Morrie said.

"Good. I should hurt him, rotten *Yok*."

"But he didn't kill the baby."

Berko stopped, looking at his son in wonder. He realized, of course, that he was still killing the Cossack every time he lost his temper. He went to where the gentile boy was lying on the sidewalk, crying.

"Sorry, young fellow," he said, in his hesitant English. "I should not mean to throw you, I should not mean hurting you. You all right? You go home now."

The *Yok* scampered away, as Berko and Morrie walked home. It was an incident that remained in Morrie's memory as long as he lived.

Morrie went back home to his bed in the alcove off the kitchen, to the grayed rug in the living room. Berko had found it in a trash bin soon after he and Alice had married. It was old then, and that was a dozen years ago.

Morrie realized that day, for the first time consciously, that he was poor. There was no statement to that effect, merely an understanding in his own mind that there were at least two classes of people, and now he knew where he stood. He was a have-not, and he didn't like it.

One afternoon after school, Morrie's aimless explorations took him to a building he had not noticed before. The sign said it was the Brady Street Club. He had heard some of the boys in school talk about a club that was open to all East End boys. It had a gymnasium, and inside were men who helped the boys learn boxing as a sport.

Tentatively, Morrie edged inside. There was a table with a pile of cards on it. They were applications for membership. He filled one out, and then went into the gym and watched the other boys working out in the boxing ring.

That was a fateful day in Morrie's life for two reasons. First, watching the boxers in action, listening to the instructions of the trainers, and enjoying the artistry of their graceful movements was a new sensation. Not all of them were graceful, there were some that moved like dray horses, and Morrie could spot them quickly. As he stood and watched, he found himself mimicking their movements. He threw a right when they threw a right. He ducked when they ducked. He was up on his toes, shuffling his feet in a pale imitation of a good fighter's dancing steps. He was lost in a world he never knew existed.

That led him to the second major event of that day. He collided with another young man.

"Sorry," Morrie said. "I didn't see you."

The other boy, taller than Morrie, had sandy-reddish hair.

"I've never seen boxers before. They move smooth, don't they?"

"Some do. That lad in the blue trunks, I rather fancy him, don't you?" Willie Weinberg introduced himself. They would become best friends.

A new world opened up for Morrie, and he began frequenting that gym and others in the East End. He kept his new passion secret from his family. His father might have understood, but not his mother.

Willie Weinberg and Morrie learned to swim together at the People's Palace in Mile End Road, and they learned discipline together when they joined the Jewish Lad's Brigade, which was a sort of Boy Scout organization founded by a retired Army colonel named Goldsmit. They marched and they sang, and their company, Deal Street Company A, Captain Ben Berger commanding, had uniforms.

Life for Morrie and Willie was one adventure after another in those blissful days. One day in 1911, when Morrie was thirteen, their wanderings took them to Sidney Street, just off Whitechapel Road. They were witnesses to a historic event.

They thought it was just another commotion when it started. A husband beating his wife or, just as common, a wife beating her husband. They soon realized that this was a commotion out of the ordinary, something well worth their attention.

A stout man in a high silk hat, smoking a large cigar, was evidently in command. It was Winston Churchill, The Home Secretary. There were five or six Scots Guards from the Tower of London and several London Bobbies. The Bobbies had no firearms but the Guards did, and they were pointing their rifles at an upstairs window.

Morrie and Willie joined the crowd of gawkers being held in check by other Bobbies. Then they spotted their friend, Constable Wensley. He had been the Constable on the beat that included their homes and they had grown up with him as a friend and companion.

"Constable Wensley," called Morrie, and the red-faced policeman turned. He quickly hurried over to where they were standing and shooed them away.

"Get back," he said. "There'll be shots fired, I promise you lads."

They listened to Constable Frederick Porter Wensley because, besides being a very nice person who often helped them out of scrapes, he was the neighborhood hero, who walked the beat on Stepney Green. He had been part of the team that investigated the Jack the Ripper case. Many years later, Morrie learned that Wensley had become Scotland Yard's chief Constable and was the man responsible for originating the Yard's noted Flying Squad.

The Sidney Street Siege dragged on for several hours.

Eventually the villains inside fired first, so the Scots Guards had no choice but to return fire. Churchill gave the command and a barrage of rifle bullets crashed into the offending flat. Somehow a fire started. The London Fire Department clanged into action, and firemen, Bobbies, and Scots Guards charged up the stairs, with Constable Wensley among them. The fire weakened a wall, which crashed into the street, killing a fireman. He was not the only casualty of that memorable afternoon. The bodies of the two men who had started the siege were found in the charred wreckage.

Mr. Churchill lit a fresh cigar, dusted off his silk hat, got in his carriage, and was driven away.

The Siege of Sidney Street became a signal achievement for Churchill. His biographers almost always mention it, and he himself talked about it at some length in his autobiography.

It was the high spot of that year for the two boys. It seemed to be a turning point for them, as well. While they were hardly innocents, until then the times in which they lived had sheltered them from major violence. There was no war and no major insurrection. They had grown up seeing street fights and domestic disturbances, but nothing really drastic. This was different. This was blood-letting.

Forces were at work, however, which were also violent in nature: the international machinations of bankers and industrialists and diplomats who gathered around polished tables and talked peace but meant war.

Morrie graduated from Senrab Street School on March 7, 1912. The end of the school year was in June, but poverty was so great in the East End that the Board of Education allowed the boys to graduate on their birthdays. This allowed them an extra few months to work.

Chapter Two

Morrie went to work for a firm in Islington, near Angel Station, that made women's dresses. He learned to cut cloth, to operate a sewing machine, and to do other fine tailoring work. He was the newcomer and he mostly ran errands, which suited him because he was outside and on the go, and that satisfied his restlessness.

He and Willie, both working now, both making money, were enjoying some small independence. They still lived at home, which meant that by far the lion's share of their income was turned over to their mothers. Still, there was some left for frivolities.

They had a few hours for fun, not much, but some. They worked long days, six days a week. They had Saturday the Sabbath, off. Many of their friends spent most of the Sabbath in the synagogue, but Willie and Morrie didn't dwell on religion. Saturday would find them playing football in Victoria Park or going to the Brady Street gym and sparring a little in the ring. They were both physically fit.

Sunday was a short day. It started at eight in the morning, as usual, but instead of working until seven at night, they were off at two in the afternoon. On Sunday's the young ladies of the East End gathered in their best clothing at Gardener's corner and paraded up and down Whitechapel Road and Commercial Road. Morrie and Willie were spectators.

The Sunday afternoon schedule was ordinarily crowned by a visit to John Isaac's where Morrie and Willie would pour large splashes of vinegar over their orders of fish and chips. It was a treat and, as the cost of an order was one penny, it was an inexpensive one. It was, however, messy to eat, as Isaac's served their greasy delicacies in a cone of newspaper, and when the vinegar was added, the whole thing got to be a slippery affair. The ink from the newspaper often ran, so the boys' fingers would be black from the ink and amber from the vinegar.

Afterwards they would stand in front of the Three Nuns Hotel where they watched the local prostitutes and their customers.

Morrie, laboring over the cutting machine at Islington, faced reality. He accepted his future—one of hard work and few rewards, with the sorrows and occasional pleasures of the average man.

Morrie was essentially a happy and optimistic youth, and to him, as to most young men, the future was simply an endless parade of uncommitted tomorrows. He was much more concerned with today. Morrie and Willie looked forward to their few hours off work. Often they would spend that precious time off hanging around the various boxing rings in the East End.

They soon discovered the Judean Boxing Club, on Prince's Square East, where Cable Street met Welclose Square. Somebody had converted an old warehouse into a gymnasium, mostly taken up by a ring in the center and some five hundred seats around it.

One day Morrie was at ringside, while a few fighters worked out. He remarked to a friend, Jack Hart, that he would like to do the same, but didn't have the proper shoes.

"Use mine, if they'll fit you, Morrie," Hart said. "Do you have the shorts and shirt?"

"Everything but the shoes."

"Go ahead." They had been watching Ted "Kid" Lewis sparring—one day, he would become the welterweight champion of the world. He was a hero in the East End, because he was one of them. His real name was Gershon Mendeloff, but nobody used his real name in the ring. Everyone was Kid this or Young that. Ted "Kid" Lewis was one of Morrie's heroes, and Morrie watched him, enthralled. Lewis moved like a panther, fast, sneaky, graceful. He was seldom hit squarely, and he had never been seriously hurt in the ring. He had a deadly punch with either hand.

Everybody knew Morrie, because by now he and his buddy, Willie, were regulars at the gym. Jack Hart and Louis and Georgie Ruddick and the Cohen brothers were part of the in crowd.

When Ted Kid Lewis finished, Georgie Ruddick bounced into the ring.

"Hey, Morrie, m'lad," he said. "You've got shoes, how about putting on some gloves."

"Done, Georgie." Morrie became "Kid Jackson."

Georgie had been going around with Morrie's sister, Flora, for some time, so they were friends. He and Morrie were about the same size and age, so they should have been fairly equal in the ring, although Georgie had some fighting experience.

Jack Hart, who later became one of England's most famous prize fight referees(he worked the Sugar Ray Robinson and Randy Turpin fight in 1951), helped Morrie put on the gloves.

"We'll go a couple of three-minute rounds," said Georgie. "I'll take it easy on you. I wouldn't want you to be telling Flora that I'm a bully, now, would I?"

Willie was the timekeeper. When he hit the gong, Morrie charged recklessly across the ring, ran right into a Ruddick uppercut and promptly hit the canvas. He staggered to his feet and another blow sent him back down again. He hung on to the ropes and vaguely heard both Jack and Willie yelling, "Box him, Morrie, keep your left up. Left! Left! That's the way!"

"You really looked good in there in that second round." "You were moving very well, I must say."

The months went by, and Morrie sparred with various opponents at the gyms he came to frequent. His skills developed. He was fast and hard to hit, but he never did have a really powerful punch. Morrie was more of a counter-puncher, a fighter who could pile up points but knew he would seldom, if ever, knock anybody out.

Morrie was now sixteen. He had grown into a solid, although lanky, 126-pounder. That made him, officially, a featherweight. Morrie became a professional prize fighter, with Willie encouraging him and promising to keep his secret from his mother.

He called himself Kid Jackson. Morrie Kotler was not a particularly threatening name.

"In this corner, weighing nine stone "KID JACKSON!"

Now that had a ring to it!

Kid Jackson and his handler, Willie, hung around with the boxing crowd in the East End boxing haunts, after work during the week and as long as they could on Saturdays and Sundays. There was the Leicester Lounge, on the corner of Wardour Street and Coventry Street, facing out on Leicester Square. All the boys were there, legends such as Freddie Welsh and Jimmie Wilde and even some of the touring American Negro fighters such as Joe Jeanette, Sam McVey, and Sam Langford. Morrie had never seen a Negro except for Carlisle and Welman, who entertained upstairs at the Lounge.

He found himself talking to the men in the Leicester Lounge, and he was a good conversationalist, so he had no trouble holding his own. He realized, too, that many of the fellows with whom he was becoming friendly were not Jewish, not even lower class. Some talked the King's English. His mother and father had suffered so much at the hands of gentiles that they were afraid of them, and that fear had translated, naturally, into hatred. Wilfull or not, some of that hatred had been passed along to Morrie. It took him a while to realize that not all Christians speared babies with sabers.

They treated him as an equal, at least in the Lounge. He was enough of a realist to know that, at some other place under some other circumstances, this would probably not be the case. He was also enough of a hedonist to enjoy what the fates had tossed his way. He laughed at their jokes and beamed when they laughed at his stories.

The love of boxing drew all of the Leicester Lounge crowd together. They listened to Morrie's views because, after all, he was a professional boxer. Morrie had stature, and he blossomed in the warm sunshine of the camaraderie of these new friends.

There was an occasional twinge of regret, however, during these encounters. The English youths, with their marvelous speech, all sounded so brilliant and well educated. The Oxford English accent had a way of imputing magnificent cultural achievements to all who used it, whether or not they actually had them. Morrie leaped to the conclusion that all these young men were brilliant. He therefore felt himself terribly inferior by comparison and wished now that he had devoted more time to his studies.

This had all happened so suddenly. Morrie and Willie had been watching the bouts at the Judaean Club one evening when Morrie whispered to his friend, "I think I can box professionally, Willie. I think I'd like to try it."

"You're nothing but a lunatic," Willie said. "Your poor ma will have a stroke or worse. She'll throw you out of the house."

"I can make seven shillings and sixpence and a cup of tea for a six-rounder here. I've been sparring with most of these blokes already, and for nothing."

Willie shook his head and kept raising objections. He reminded Morrie of the time, during a sparring match, when a wild left had broken Morrie's nose. He had had a terrible time making up a story to explain that scrambled nose at home. He told the family that he fell at the factory and broke his nose on one of the sewing machines.

Willie shrugged and told him, well, if he was determined to be a fighter, at least he should have the best manager London had to offer, namely, himself.

Morrie trained hard for his first professional fight, with Willie pushing him to his limit. The promoter at the Judaean Club matched Kid Jackson against Young Fresco. They knew Morrie, of course. Everyone in that rather small circle of London boxing fans knew everybody else. Young Fresco worked on the East India docks, lifting crates all day long.

The two featherweights fought for six anxious rounds on Sunday, April 11, 1914. Kid Jackson kept circling, trying to pick Young Fresco's defense apart. Young Fresco kept boring in, swinging wildly, hoping for the one time he'd connect solidly. He never did, but he connected obliquely often enough to win the verdict. *The Boxing News* reported the next morning: "Young Fresco beat Kid Jackson on points after a hard bout."

Still, Morrie was heartened. He had his seven-and-six,and he had his pride, because he wasn't even knocked down by that bruiser. He was a professional boxer. Not bad, for sixteen years old.

The fight was so popular that the promoter rematched the two battlers. This time, the result was a draw.

"Young Jackson and Young Fresco," wrote the reporter for *The Boxing News*, "gave an imitation of a couple of wild cats for six rounds, after which a draw was declared."

The fans clamored for another one and the promoter once again rematched the two.

"The warm weather proved too powerful for a few of the contestants on Sunday afternoon, but Kid Jackson and Young Fresco fought a good contest, and Jackson was flattered by the decision which went in his favor."

Morrie learned a little something each time he fought Fresco. He used his wit to come from a loss to a draw, and finally winning.

#   #   #

The cold was unbearable. Morrie staggered through the snow in the direction that the Russian had indicated. He thought back to that fight, that Sunday afternoon in May, when he had been so hot he nearly fainted. The wind was in his face, making every step a struggle. The snow crept into his boots, and his feet were

freezing. He knew he had to get inside soon, or he would die on his first day on Russian soil.

He squinted into the wind and the whipping snow that pelted him, trying to see if he was nearing any structure. He hunched his shoulders and took a few more steps. Maybe it was just a mirage, but there seemed to be something a few hundred yards ahead. Nothing definite, but there looked to be some large lumps in the snow. Could they be buildings?

As he drew closer he could see that they were, in fact, structures of some kind, blanketed with snow. There were thin black chimneys sticking out of each one, emitting gray smoke. Smoke meant a fire, and fire meant warmth.

He tried to run the last few yards to the nearest lump, but his legs simply wouldn't function at any speed beyond slow. As he drew closer and made out the door, he reached out his arms. Morrie realized that these were railroad boxcars, drawn up in a row along some railroad tracks. He climbed up the rickety, slippery steps and knocked on the door with all the force his freezing arms could muster.

The door slid open and a rush of welcome warm air embraced him as he staggered inside.

"Would you close the bloody door?" said a voice in English!

Morrie tried to oblige, but his body wouldn't function right. He just turned around and pointed to the white wasteland.

"You came from there, did you, now?" asked the voice. Morrie looked at the man. He was English, no doubt about it. He reminded Morrie of the proper British gentry he would meet on weekends in Surrey. He was the kind of man who would have been more at home wearing flannel knickers and smoking a briar pipe rather than sitting here wrapped in a fur parka.

"Have a cup of tea, young fellow. Do you understand English, by any chance?"

Morrie nodded vigorously.

"That's a surprise. Here's some tea."

Morrie sank to the floor, grasped the heavy cup of tea with both his gloved hands and sipped. The warm liquid carved a path of delicious heat down his throat.

"Oh, my, that's good," he said.

"Well now," said the man. "You speak English, too. A double surprise."

Morrie looked around. The boxcar had a few chairs and one wall of bunks, but of most interest to Morrie was the stove in the center. There were a couple of other men there, too, but it was the stove that attracted him. He struggled to his feet and went over and stood next to it, extending his hands and feet to bask in its warmth.

"Oh, my, that's good," he said, for a second time.

"Well, you're just not dressed for a Murmansk afternoon."

My name is Cooper, what's yours?" said the man.

Morrie introduced himself. Mr. Cooper further identified himself as one of a growing number of English refugees, forced out of their homes by the Bolsheviks. He had been living in St. Petersburg for ten years, where he had been England's Commercial Attache as well as the representative for the Lea and Perrins company in Russia.

As he thawed, Morrie could take some interest in his surroundings. There were six other men, who like Mr. Cooper, were obvious refugees. He quickly learned from their talk that they were waiting for a ship to take them back to England. They questioned Morrie eagerly about the vessel he had arrived on, the *BRADFORD*, and one of them plunged out into the snow to learn when that ship would be returning to England and if it had room for any more passengers. There were also three or four English Marines, assigned by the British Consulate in St.Petersburg to guard the refugees.

"Hey, guy," one of the Marines called to Morrie, "how about a wee dram?"

The Marine held out a small can of vodka and Morrie nodded, so the marine tossed it over. Morrie had watched how the Marines dealt with the cans. They would rap them on the bottom with their fists and apparently that blow, plus the fact that the can was full of 150 proof vodka, propelled the top of the can to the ceiling. Morrie tried it, nonchalantly, and was gratified when it worked.

The men, led by Mr. Cooper, were curious about who he was and, in particular, why any young Englishman in his right mind would choose to come to Murmansk at this particular time in history and at this time of the calendar year. Morrie had invented a story to explain this seemingly irrational behavior. He explained that his parents were Russian-born, as was he, but they brought him to England when he was six months old, so he had no memory of Russia at all.

As he told it, it was a convincing story, and a sad one. With everybody popping cans of vodka, there was a general feeling of sadness that pervaded the boxcar. They all started telling him their stories, as if to reassure him that, although his tale was undeniably tragic, he could have been in worse shape. The refugees spoke with each other, painting grim pictures of the horrors they had been through.

"The Bolsheviks in Petrograd were nothing but wild animals," said one of the men.

"Absolutely right," another agreed.

"They came running in the front of our house, and we dashed out the back. We hid in the root cellar for six hours until they'd finished their dirty work. There wasn't anything left that wasn't smashed to bits. I sent the wife on to Vologda. Most of the British were there, but I came here."

"We want to see the Admiral and find out what is going to become of us."

They explained that HMS Glory, Admiral Wyton Kemp commanding, was in Murmansk harbor. He had agreed to see them the next morning.

"Perhaps, young fellow," said Cooper, "you'd care to come with us? It's possible the Admiral could figure something for you too."

Morrie thanked him for the suggestion, but said that he would prefer to make his own way. He couldn't tell them that if he put himself in the hands of British authorities, he might be shot.

"Well, suit yourself. What will you do? This is a perfectly dreadful place, you know. Absolutely nothing here but snow and ice, and when it thaws, it will be a mud bath. Awful country, and this is the bottom of it."

"Morrie tossed the empty vodka can into the barrel, wondering if it was all over for him. Would there ever be any more dancing or singing or laughing, any more young ladies, any more good friends? What had become of Willie? What had become of all the old crowd.

#   #   #

His speed had helped him through many a tough round, and Kid Jackson became a well-known fighter in London. He was fighting almost every week, at the most popular boxing clubs, Premierland and Wonderland. The purses were never large, but he was making as much money fighting as he made at the tailor shop. He always had money in his pocket, and not too many East Enders could make that statement.

The promoter kept booking him. The bout with Kid British was next.

"He's a rough, tough *Yok* from Bermondsey," said Willie. "And he's not above breaking the rules, so I've been told. In fact, some tell me he's the dirtiest fighter in London."

"I think you're a comer, young fellow," said Feeney. "You can have a good career in the ring and can make some money. If it's all right with you and your manager, we'll put you in 'The Ring' on June 20th."

They always referred to the Blackfriars ring as The 'Ring', and they said the words with reverence, almost as though it was a holy place.

Morrie's opponent at Blackfriars was a veteran named Kid Zimmer, a real boxer like Morrie, not one of the street brawlers he had fought so often before. In the years to come, he would remember this as the best fight he ever had, because he and Zimmer were well matched. They were both good, clean boxers who relied on their speed and their skill. Morrie remembered it as a good experience for another reason too, he won. He was younger and apparently in better shape, and in the last two rounds the older man slowed appreciably, and so Morrie won going away.

His next fight, a week later, was against another veteran, a man named Blink Murphy. Morrie had seen Blink fight a few times, in the days before he had become a fighter himself.

"If you do well in this one," Feeney told him as he dressed for the bout, "it won't be long before I'll put you in a ten rounder."

Morrie climbed into the ring. Blink Murphy came down the aisle with the crowd cheering. He was a Blackfriars favorite, and the crowd was cheering.

Morrie looked across at his opponent. Murphy's nose was scattered all over his face. There were scars under and over both his eyes. His ears were ugly, cauliflowered lumps, both of them. The man grinned over at Morrie, and there were huge gaps where his teeth had once been.

"What's wrong, Morrie?" asked Willie, seeing Morrie shudder.

"Look over at that poor bloke. If I keep fighting, I'll look like that in a few years."

"No, you're too fast to get hit that often."

"Willie, I'm not going to take that chance."

Without a backward glance, Morrie climbed between the ropes and walked out of the ring.

Later, as the two walked home, Morrie said that he just didn't want to take a chance on becoming punchy. He had seen too many old, washed-up fighters, jumping at shadows and hearing bells that weren't ringing.

"I'll keep working out at the gym," he told Willie, "but I've had my last fight."

He longed to shake up his life.

Although he didn't know it at the time, that chance would come eight days after he walked out of the ring and left Blink Murphy standing in punch-drunk puzzlement. Archduke Ferdinand was shot to death on June 28, 1914, on the streets of a city in Bosnia, in central Yugoslavia, called Sarajevo. The political and economic forces that had been assembling behind the scenes of the various European capitals took this crime as the starter's whistle and World War I soon erupted.

The British Expeditionary Force sailed across the Channel and landed in France. The English Army asked for a half-million more volunteers, and, as the conflict quickly turned into a bloody, hopeless, weary fight in the muddy trenches, more and more volunteers were required to feed the fires of war.

Morrie Kotler was sixteen when the war broke out. At first it was something of a lark and an adventure to him, at first. He cheered when troops marched down the street. He put the Union Jack in his window and avidly read the newspaper accounts of the first action of the B.E.F. He felt elated at the early reports of victories and was stunned at later stories telling of defeats and enormous casualties.

His parents were more interested in the stories coming out of Russia. The Russian Army seemed to collapse in early 1917, their will to fight gone. The reason quickly became apparent. The flame of revolution had been kindled, and the Tsar was gone in March. Berko and Alice were thunderstruck by the news.

"No more Tsar? How could this be?"

"It says the Tsar is captured," the other said, "Can you believe it, the Tsar a prisoner? How could this be?"

It wasn't that Berko and Alice had any love for Nicholas and all the Romanovs. Russia without a Tsar was a concept they simply could not grasp. It would be like trying to conceive of a tree without any roots. Unthinkable.

Yet, apparently, it had happened. Morrie paid little attention to the events that were going on in Russia. He could pinpoint the Argonne Forest, Chateau Thierry and Ypres, and all the other major battlegrounds on a map. He had never heard of Kerensky, who headed up the first provisional government in Russia after the Tsar was overthrown. He certainly was not aware that a counter-revolution was brewing. During the winter, when ice choked off the major Russian harbors, the Gulf Stream's warm waters kept the harbor at Murmansk ice free. Allied vessels were continuing to stream into Murmansk with supplies for the White armies which were going to kick the Bolsheviks into the back pages of the history books and force Russia back into the war against the Kaiser.

Morrie experienced the war's first air raid. He witnessed the changes in England's way of life. Later, when air raids became more frequent, he witnessed more changes. The London authorities announced that, henceforth, there would be no more cab whistles, because a whistle was to be the signal for approaching enemy aircraft. Sirens would come later. Whistles were the original air raid alert sound.

There were anti-German riots in the East End. London bully boys were attacking anyone they thought was a "heinie" or a "kraut," and the Russian-born Jews whose Yiddish might possibly be mistaken for German, began painting crude signs on their homes and businesses:

WE ARE RUSSIAN! or HERE LIVE RUSSIANS!

Along with the taxi whistles the lovely old London buses also disappeared from the streets, along with the whistles. They were sent to France, used to bring fresh troops up to the trenches and wounded men back to safety.

Army, Navy, and other uniforms were the norm, and there were more and more events staged that were war-related. Money had to be raised, so there were shows and rallies on every other street corner.

A people at war has always demanded to be entertained, and the English in World War I were certainly not the exception. The West End theaters were full of shows, generally light-hearted and full of what the English consider comedy, music, dancing, and escapist fare.

Flora had become engaged to a neighborhood boy, Harry Pearl, who was in the navy. He was serving as the chief steward aboard HMS *Reliance*. Harry and Morrie liked each other immediately, and when Flora said, "You're finally getting the brother you always wanted," Morrie gave Harry a big, brotherly handshake.

When he was home on leave, Harry would generously include Morrie when he and Flora went out for the evening. They all particularly enjoyed the Holborn Empire music hall and the great music hall stars of that era, Marie Lloyd, Kate Carney, Charles Colburn, and in particular, Harry Champion. When he sang songs such as "Any ol" or "The Longer you Linger," Morrie, Flora and Harry would join in on the choruses and then jump up and scream and whistle and applaud. It was the war songs that the people in the pubs and on the street corners were singing: "It's a Long Way to Tipperary" and "Take Me Back To Dear Old Blighty." There were hundreds of recruiting booths throughout the city, and, usually there were small bands and groups of singers outside each of them. The idea was to kindle patriotic fervor in the manly bosoms of the young men passing by, so they would rush in and sign up.

Although he fantasied about being a soldier, Morrie was still too young. He was torn between wishing the war would end and hoping it would last long enough so that he could enlist and do his duty as an Englishman.

The belligerence that was encouraged for the benefit of the soldiers spilled over into the non combatants, as well.

"Hey, Morrie," said Georgie Ruddick one day "We've got us a new game. It's a lot of fun. Want to come along?"

Ruddick and his brother, Louis, were part of the old boxing crowd. Those two, plus the Cohen brothers, urged Morrie to accompany them on their *"Yok*-busting" expedition.

"Here's what we do," said Georgie. "We go over to Mile End Brewery and wait until we see one of them Hassids."

The Hassidic Jews were the most orthodox of the orthodox, with long beards, side curls, and long black coats, generally walking along the street with hands clasped as if in prayer. The five boys found a Hassid walking along past the Brewery with his eyes on the ground, his lips mumbling some portion of the Torah. They followed him.

"What are you doing?" asked Morrie.

"Ssh. You'll see. The first *Yok* who makes a remark to our Hassidic friend here gets his."

"Let's not look for trouble," said Morrie, and made as if to go. They grabbed him by the sleeve.

Morrie was about to leave when a teamster, driving a wagon loaded with wooden kegs of beer, approached the brewery. Without any provocation, the driver took his whip and flicked it at the old Jew, lashing him across the back of the head and, in the process, knocking his hat on the ground.

Louis Ruddick grabbed the teamster's whip, yanked on it, and hauled the driver out of his seat.

"You picked the wrong man, you *Yok* bastard," said Georgie, and punching the teamster in his large belly. The man gave a satisfactory "Ooof" and began to sag. Louis clipped him on the jaw as he fell.

"That's the last time you whip a harmless old man, you bully bastard," said Georgie, and his brother and the two Cohens contributed further insults and warnings. Morrie had not participated, but neither had he tried to stop the beating.

Every day, the war became a larger and more personal part of the lives of the Londoners, and Morrie as well. One evening as he read in his room, Morrie heard screams. They came from Flora, who had been out and had just reached the flat when it happened.

"Zeppelins," she was yelling. "They're dropping bombs on us!"

It was the first attack of the German airships, which came slipping through the night sky, unleashing powerful bombs. The long yellow tongues of the searchlights sought them out, and guns from the ground went "ack-ack." A few fires were started where the bombs had detonated, and ambulances and fire engines and police were rushing to the scenes of carnage.

"Oh my God, what will we do?" asked Alice. She buried her head in Berko's broad and receptive shoulder.

They all grew accustomed to the routine within a few weeks after a dozen or so air raids. The whistles of the Bobbies sounded to alert the public that enemy aircraft were approaching. Then came the throbbing engines of the zeppelins, the whine of the bombs, and the thud of their explosions. Morrie and Willie, almost every day, debated the wisdom versus the folly of enlisting. They kept physically fit while they waited and debated, with workouts in the gym, football on Saturdays in Victoria Park, and long walks around Hyde Park.

They began going to a café in Piccadily called the Popular Café. It was a melting pot, a haunt for East Enders such as themselves as well as for young men from the upper classes, refugees from Oxford and Cambridge. These young men laughed at the English language as it was practiced by

Morrie and Willie and others of their class. Morrie continued to marvel at the beautiful language that oozed out of those upper class lips.

The men would exchange confidences after everyone was mellow on ale and whiskey. The Oxfordians told of their home life, and even though their stories were true, they were so incredible to Morrie that they seemed fictitious. Perhaps the bluebloods could not believe some of the stories that Morrie told them of the way he and his family, and the other East End families, lived.

The evenings in the Popular Café were full of laughter, and clinking glasses, and song. Every week, however, the group was
reduced, as more and more of the collegians enlisted.

That was one more way in which the war touched their lives. The music hall shows now were all war related, and some of the great stars, even Sir Harry Lauder himself, had lost a son in action. The music stars sang patriotic songs and exhorted the audience to more and nobler sacrifices.

Parliament enacted the Military Service Act in January, 1916, designed to encourage recruitment. It didn't produce the necessary results, so in May a second Military Service Act was passed. This one called for all able-bodied men between eighteen and forty-one years of age to be called up to serve. Morrie had turned eighteen in March.

He came home from work in August to find that he had a letter. He seldom received mail, but from the look of this particular letter, he knew immediately what it was. There was a crown embossed on the envelope, and his address was printed in black bold type, so official and so forceful that he had no doubt about the contents.

"You have been called to serve your King and country," read the notice. "Please report for physical examination at Peoples Palace, Mile End Road, at 8:30 A.M. on August 31, 1916."

Morrie ran out to tell Willie the news. Willie was a few months younger that Morrie, so he figured that he would get his summons momentarily. They went and had a pint to celebrate Morrie's forthcoming adventure.

Morrie took his physical and was pronounced fit and able to serve. He was told to report to Waterloo Station at 6:30 in the morning of September 15, to begin his service as a soldier in His Majesty's Army.

Chapter Three

It had been a glorious dream. Morrie was going to fight heroically for his beloved Great Britain, maybe even die heroically. He and Willie had often fantasized about triumphantly snapping off salutes, quick-stepping into battle, and modestly accepting their medals. It was a boy's dream of a soldier's life. The reality was basically ugly.

The first rude awakening came on the first day of Morrie's career as a member of the British Army. Typically, he had arrived at Waterloo Station fifteen minutes early, though his last night as a civilian had been a long one. He and Willie and some other friends went to a few of their favorite spots, and Morrie, beginning to feel a little apprehensive now, took pleasure in his last night of revelry. He drank more than he usually did. He didn't care if his collar was buttoned or not. He shouted and laughed and sang at the top of his lungs.

It was after three when he fell into bed. The next morning, after a tear-stained farewell breakfast with his parents and Flora, he was at Waterloo Station fifteen minutes before the 6:30 a.m. call. The sergeant-major, who talked with a thick Irish brogue and had a large red mustache that curled up and over and about, had his new charges line up, a maneuver they accomplished only with great difficulty.

"Fall in, you miserable excuses for human beings." Morrie smiled. A decent sergeant-major should talk like that. "Single file now. That means one after the other, for the benefit of you blighters." "Right aboard the train there." They filed aboard the train and took the seats the non-coms directed them to.

"Men," said the sergeant-major, as the train chugged off, "you are all Squarebashers now, but before we get through with you, you'll all be proper soldiers. We,re going to have a spot of training at Salisbury Plain. A few months from now, if you don't cause too much trouble, you,ll probably be taking a nice sea voyage to France. You'll have a week's leave before that, so best get ready for that now."

He then passed through to the next car where he gave the same speech. The men relaxed and surveyed each other. Morrie could tell, from the way they talked, that they were mostly Scots and Irishmen.

They stopped and looked at him with tough expressions as soon as he tried to join in their conversations. "Well, now," said a scrawny youngster, "it looks like we've got us a Kike from Jewtown here."

Morrie had to restrain himself. Yesterday, if anyone had spoken to him like that, he would have thrown himself on the offender with a vengeance, but he was in a new world now, and he was a soldier. He had to control himself.

He tried psychology. Morrie just smiled and looked out the window at the green countryside.

His tactics worked. The others ignored him for the rest of the trip, which fortunately was not too long. When they reached Salisbury they marched off the train and into a fleet of trucks. After they arrived at the camp the group was marched into a warehouse to be issued uniforms.

"This jacket has a hole in it," Morrie complained to the soldier who had handed it to him.

"Probably a bullet hole in it, my boy," said the soldier.

"Consider it a sacred garment. I fancy it's a lucky one. A bullet never lands in the same jacket twice, they tell me. Keep it and live a long happy life."

Morrie took it and found that, considering the weather, it was not a particularly fortuitous jacket. It was late September and the winds and rain frequently blew vigorously

across Salisbury Plain, into that sacred bullet hole in the jacket. He took to pinning a handkerchief behind it, but that didn't help.

His jacket, however, was the least of Morrie's concerns in the British Army Training Camp on Salisbury Plain. He had a more immediate social situation to deal with the rampant anti-Semitism of his fellow recruits. He was, unfortunately, the only Jew in his brigade, and he was taunted continually.

It began as soon as he was assigned to a barracks. As Morrie inspected his uniform, somebody across the aisle said, "ain't you a tailor, guy? You people are all tailors so you can sew up that hole nice and tidy."

Again, he ignored the remark.

The next morning, Morrie and the others reported outside. They found that the non-coms had marked the drill field in fifty yard squares, with chalk lines separating each square. The recruits were all assigned to squads, and each squad was assigned to one of those squares. They were to do all their drilling and exercises, for the next three months, inside their own assigned square.

Since they were exhorted to "bash" hard as they marched, hit the ground solidly with their feet, they were known as "squarebashers." It was a long-standing and honorable nickname for an army recruit.

That first morning, as they were assembled, ready to begin training, the sergeant-major told them something of their future.

"You men," he said, "are going to be replacements for a very distinguished outfit, one of the most distinguished outfits in the entire British Army. As you know—at least you should know—this is a Godawful bloody war, and men are dying in France by the thousands. Most of the outfits have had so many casualties they need replacements, and they need them now, and they need good ones."

"It's going to be my job to make sure you are good ones, and it's also going to be my job to get you ready as soon as possible. So, now, let me tell you about your outfit. Corporal, pass out those shoulder patches."

The Corporal walked down the ranks, handing each of the new soldiers a small green - and - black shoulder emblem.

"That patch," the sergeant-major continued, "signifies that you are now members of the P.O.R.S, that's the Post Office Rifle Brigade, Second Battalion. You should be damn well proud to be a P.O.R. It's an outfit with a fine tradition. If it weren't for the fact that they had so many killed and wounded, they wouldn't be taking the likes of you blighters."

The Post Office Rifle Brigade, as Morrie was required to learn in the weeks to come, stemmed from a volunteer organization that was formed in 1867. In that year when the Fenians were rioting they attacked the Clerkenwell Prison in London, and then tried to attack several post offices. The London police swore in a thousand Post Office workers as volunteers to defend those buildings, and they fought so well that they became a permanent Army unit. Later, they fought in Egypt and then went to Sudan as part of the expedition to relieve General Chinese Gordon. The P.O.R. fought gallantly in South Africa during the Boer War, and in 1914, when World War I erupted, they were mobilized at full strength. They had been involved in the battles at Aubers Ridge, Festubert, Loos and Hohenzollern Redoubt, suffering enormous casualties. A year later they would achieve lasting fame at Vimy Ridge and the Battle of the Somme.

Training was speeded up because of the need to send replacements to France quickly. Morrie and the others marched in their assigned square, from sun-up until dark, pausing only to grab a quick lunch out of their rations.

Morrie was always there, always doing his share or more. His great physical conditioning saw him through weeks of tough training that caused many others in his unit to collapse. That angered the men even more. They couldn't stand it that when this Jew proved to be a better man then they were.

They harassed him, but he went about his business, although he was smoldering inside. He had one friend, a young and naive Welshman named Fred Jones, who came from Aberdare, a coal mining town in Glarmorgan Country, not very far from Cardiff. Morrie had always liked the few Welshmen he had met, finding them honest and seemingly devoid of prejudice. He began, at Fred Jones,s urging, to use an old Welsh expression,

"*Yach y dar*," whenever the two had a drink. It was somewhat like the old English "bottom's up," Jones said.

"Morrie," Fred said one night, as the two stretched their weary bodies out on their bunks, "can you tell me something? Why do the other fellows go on about your being a Jew? For the life of me, I can't understand it. We're all God's children, so I've been taught."

"If you figure that one out, let me know," said Morrie.

"They were on you all day long today. How do you stand it?"

"One of these days I'm going to hit somebody, and hit him hard."

"For God's sake, don't do that," Fred said. "You'll only get yourself in a pint of trouble."

Morrie said he knew that, but it was hard restraining himself. He added, then, that he had been a professional boxer, and had had enough fighting to last him a lifetime.

Fred was a good friend. Morrie thought about Willie, but somehow he understood that that friendship was over. They would always think good thoughts about each other, but Morrie had a feeling that they would never again be as close as they were. Their paths were certain to continue to diverge, even in the Army they were heading in opposite directions. Willie,s last letter to Morrie said that Willie had been assigned to an outfit that trained and recruited Romanian aliens. Willie had been born in Romania and spoke Romanian fluently. His duty kept him in London, he said, and he could live at home. It was a lovely way to spend a war. He would never know the hardships that Morrie was enduring.

Morrie knew that after the war, he could never go back to working in a tailoring shop. There had to be something else. He had no idea what that something might be or where it might be, but he knew he had to give himself a chance at a better life. Willie, on the other hand, was content where he was. This was the main reason why he was convinced that Willie, good friend though he was, was someone in his past, not his future.

Fred was not a friend of the future either, but certainly he was developing into a staunch friend of the present. He was loyal, and Morrie could confide in him. That was important, because otherwise Morrie's present condition was unbearable.

All of the men in his unit were going through rough times, in some measure, although they didn't have the added burden that Morrie's religion thrust on him. They all shared one horror in common, though: Captain Wesley Wood.

None of the men could ever understand how this runt of a man got to be an officer. He stood barely five feet tall, and, like many small men, he made up in bombast what he lacked in height. He made speeches at every occasion, delivered in a voice that must have been made for another body—large, deep, resonant.

The men snickered at his oratory, and when he gave a command somebody in the back row would always say, "And a little child shall lead them." The men would try desperately to swallow their laughter. Captain Wood never deigned to notice those remarks, nor the snickers and dirty looks the soldiers gave him.

One rainy morning the men were routed out of their barracks long before daylight. They were told to be outside in five minutes, dressed and carrying full field packs. The packs contained roughly fifty-five pounds of gear, so it was no minor task to get them packed, stowed, and hurled over onto to one's back. The rain was teeming down, and the men stood in the mud in Salisbury Plain for a half-hour, until the captain strolled over.

"Attention!" called the sergeant.

"Men," said Captain Wood, "this is the morning for our little twenty-mile hike across the Plain. I thought the mud would add a nice little touch."

He turned, as if to go, but then remembered something and turned back. "And bye the bye, I think you should know this. A little child shall lead you but on a damn fine horse."

This time, it was Caption Wood who snickered. No one ever mentioned his size again.

It was a few days later that Captain Wood sent for Morrie. He said he had heard that Morrie had been a boxer in civilian life.

"I had a few fights, sir," said Morrie. "I won a few and I lost a few. I wasn't the greatest."

"Kotler, I've decided the men need a little entertainment. I think a boxing match would be the best thing. Don't you think the men would enjoy that?"

"I guess so, sir."

"And I have decided that you should be one of the participants in that match."

"I don't think I want to fight, sir."

Caption Wood used his sternest tone. "Soldier, what you want and what you don't want is of small concern to me. I am not asking you to fight. I am ordering you to fight. You people from the East End are just too brash for my taste. You are saying to your commanding officer that "you don't think you want to fight, as if you have some choice in the matter. Suppose we're in France and I said I wanted you to go into the trenches. Would you say, "I don't think I want to?"

"No, sir."

"Damn right you wouldn't. You'd get shot if you did. Well, consider the boxing ring I'm going to have built as your private trench, Kotler. You are going to climb into that ring when I tell you to climb in, and you are going to fight. Is that clearly understood?"

"Yes, sir."

"And I want no more Yid backtalk from you. Understood?"

Morrie bit his lip hard, but managed to say, "Yes, sir."

He saluted smartly, turned and walked out. Wood never bothered to return his salute.

The bout was hastily arranged. Morrie's opponent was to be a fighter named Tom Flyer, champion of the British Empire in his weight division. Flyer was also in the same outfit but in a different squad, and Morrie had never met him. Both men met, however, as they trained, because they were given time off to do some sparring, road work, and shadow boxing. Flyer smiled in a friendly way. He looked tough, but not tougher than some of the fighters that Morrie had met in his brief pro career.

Morrie didn't want to fight. Not that he was frightened, or that the prospect of getting knocked out worried him. It was just that fighting, for him, was a thing of the past. Moreover, he knew that the fight with Flyer was simply an elaborate hoax, another means of picking on him because he was a Jew. They expected Tom Flyer to beat the daylights out of him, and they were all, from Captain Wood down, eagerly looking forward to witnessing that spectacle.

Freddie Jones told him that he had to get out of it somehow. He told Morrie what Morrie already knew—that this was a set-up, that Flyer was the Empire champion, that Morrie was overmatched, that all the men were waiting to see "the Jew-boy get 'is 'ead 'anded to 'im."

The boxing ring was erected on the Salisbury Plain drill field and the fight was held on the afternoon of September 25, 1916. It wasn't anything you'll find mentioned in any history of boxing, but to the men of the Post Office Rifles, it was a fight they talked about for a long time.

The fight was set for ten rounds. Morrie had never gone past six, but he was in the best condition of his life, so the distance didn't worry him. What really worried him were two things: first the fact that the crowd and the officials and, presumably, the referee were against him: and second, Flyer's famous right hand.

"Flyer's right," Jones had told him, ominously, "can take down a horse."

As Morrie climbed into the ring, attended only by Fred Jones, the mood of the crowd was quickly apparent.

"Watch out for your nose, Morris," came one voice.

"That was pork in the stew at the noon meal," said another. "You'll be sick."

"He'll be sicker after Tom gets through with him."

"Hey Morris, turn around. I want to see that yellow streak down your back."

Flyer's arrival was greeted with cheers. He was a couple of inches taller than Morrie and probably five pounds heavier {although nobody had bothered with the niceties of a weigh in} and his long arms gave him a much longer reach.

The bell sounded and Flyer charged across the ring. Morrie stuck to his plan, circling to his right, away from flyer's right hand even though the crowd called him a "runaway" and urged him to "get off your bicycle and fight like a man," he kept moving away.

It was, he felt, his only chance. He didn't have much hope of victory, but he did nourish a faint hope of getting out of the ring that afternoon alive.

Morrie had always been a pretty good counter-puncher, and when Flyer landed a right to his body, he quickly flashed back with a one-two to the champion's head. Morrie had never been a knock-out puncher, and he knew that he probably couldn't knock

Flyer out. But he was counting on the fact that Flyer didn't know that. Perhaps, if he tagged him a few, the champion might have a little respect and be a little more wary.

The rounds wore on and Flyer kept boring in, swinging away. Morrie would keep away as best he could, but when he was hit, he would hit back. Both fighters sustained cuts and began bleeding. Fred Jones and Flyer's second put damp cloths over the wounds, but that wasn't much help.

Suddenly in the middle of the fifth round, with both fighters flailing away, blood spattering the ring and the spectators at ringside, Captain Wood jumped into the ring.

"This fight is over," he said. "No decision."

He offered no explanation, but Morrie didn't care. Fred threw a towel over his shoulder and they ran back to their barracks.

"What happened, Fred?" Morrie asked.

Jones shrugged. He was too busy trying to tend to Morrie's cuts to care about what happened.

"Why did Wood stop it?" Morrie persisted. "I'm damn glad he did. That Flyer would have killed me in another round, but I can't for the life of me figure out why he stopped it."

"It doesn't make a difference, does it?"

"Not really, I suppose, but I'm curious. It wasn't like him. Go find out what they're saying."

Freddie ran out. He came back in a few minutes with the information that Captain Wood stopped the fight because he was simply afraid.

"The whole thing was against regs," said Fred. "Wood figured it would be over in less than a round, that Flyer would put you away with his first punch, so he risked it. But then, when you stayed up, and what with the noise of the cheering and all, he got scared that the brass would find out and it would be a court-martial for him."

Jones was laughing as he told the story, laughing out of relief that it was all over, laughing at the predicament that Captain Wood had squeezed himself into, and laughing over the way Morrie had surprised them all. Fred, as he worked on Morrie's assorted bruises, said he was surprised, too. He had thought Flyer would cut him to ribbons.

Morrie hoped that the fight would make the others change their opinion of him, but Fred said he doubted there would be any change at all. They might respect him a bit more, but, if anything, they hated him a bit more, too. Fred said he didn't understand that hatred.

Fred Jones was right. The harassment continued. The day after the big fight, the men were on maneuvers. Trenches had been dug, the size and shape of the ones at the front lines in France. As live ammo was fired above them, Morrie and his squad stayed low to the ground, inching their way along and then diving into the trenches. Morrie had just landed and was flat on his stomach when another soldier plunged in, crashing on top of him. The new arrival was carrying his canteen ahead of him, and he deliberately jammed it into Morrie's back and then let his own full weight slam on top of that. So the metal canteen was shoved roughly into Morrie's right kidney, which produced excruciating pain that persisted all the rest of that day, through the night, and into the next morning.

Morrie limped to the medical tent as soon as he could and explained what had happened. After a half-hearted examination, he was sent back to his duties.

That injury, never diagnosed, plagued Morrie for the rest of his life. Often, in the middle of the night in the years to come, he would wake up when the pain returned. It was sometimes severe enough to cause him to call out in agony.

There was nothing he could do at the time but go back to his barracks, to his unit, and keep on with his training. The training was speeded up, as the British Army was taking a severe battering in France and replacements were needed at once. Morrie's unit was told that they would be going to France in October. It was already late September.

They were told they would have their leave before shipping across the Channel and into the front lines. On Saturday, September 28, 1916, the men lined up in their square, looking crisp and soldierly, a far cry from the ragged group that had started barely a month before.

"Men, your passes are ready for you at the mess tent," the corporal said, and everybody cheered. "Private Kotler, you will report to headquarters office. That's it. Dismissed."

Morrie ran to the headquarters office. He wanted to get whatever it was over with, so he could pick up his pass and head for London. Sergeant Smith was waiting for him. "Well, you did it this time, Kotler. You failed the inspection. Your area of the barracks was not proper. So it's no pass for you for the rest of this week. You are confined to your barracks, and you will be working on the kitchen police squad."

Morrie was stunned. He had been extraordinarily careful to have his area clean. The inspection was held with the men out of the barracks, and when he left to go outside, he knew his area was spotless. Even a white glove could not have picked up a speck of dust.

"What was wrong with my area, sergeant?"

"Papers under your bunk."

"There were no papers under my bunk."

"No more arguments, Jew boy. That's it."

Angrily, Morrie were back to the barracks, where Fred was waiting for him. Morrie told him what happened. Fred said that the sergeant was right, there were papers under his bunk. The truth was, however, Smith had put them there himself. Fred had been at the other end of the barracks, and he had seen the sergeant crumple some papers and throw them under the bunk and then laugh and say to his cronies, "Well, so much for the Kike's pass."

Morrie was infuriated. He ran out of the barracks and back to the headquarters office. He slammed the door, and Smith looked up from his desk. Morrie told him there was something he had to show him, outside.

"What is it?"

"I can't tell you. I have to show you, but believe me, it will interest you very much."

"You haven't got anything that interests me, Kotler."

"Please, sergeant, this is important."

Smith hesitated, then shrugged and followed Morrie out of the building. Morrie led him around in the back where it was empty and quiet. Without another word he hauled off and belted Smith on the jaw, and the non-com slowly collapsed to the ground. Morrie hit him twice more, a left and another right.

Smith covered his face with his arms. Morrie leaned down and spoke right into his ear, holding his clenched fist right in front of the cowering man's eyes.

"You listen to me, you son of a bitch, you go and tell the captain that you put the papers under my bunk, and you get me my pass, or by God, I'll kill you. Understand?"

The sergeant didn't seem to have heard. Morrie grabbed him by the collar, hoisted him halfway up, and repeated his demand, throwing him back down to the ground. Smith nodded that he understood. He got up and stumbled back into his office with Morrie following close behind. They went into Captain Wood's office, and Smith blurted out the truth. He had put the papers under Private Kotler's bunk and he was sorry. Captain Wood should now give Private Kotler his pass.

Wood ordered Smith to wait in his office. "I'll talk to you about this later, Smith." He angrily wrote out Morrie's pass and signed it. He told Morrie not to tell anybody about what had happened and Morrie said he wouldn't. He was happy to agree to that stipulation. He picked up the pass, saluted smartly, and ran back to his barracks. He grabbed his things and raced off the post. He was on his way to London.

It was a grand homecoming for the family hero. Nothing was too good for him while he stayed with his parents. Alice had spent a whole week's food budget on one glorious welcome home dinner, with everything Morrie particularly loved: a brisket of beef, boiled potatoes, snap beans and a cherry trifle for dessert.

"A meal fit for one of the King's finest soldier boys," said Alice, and Berko lifted a glass of wine in a toast.

L'chayim, "" he said.

"*L'chayim,*", Morrie replied, and the rest of the family echoed the age-old toast. Morrie added in a whisper, "*Yach y dar,*" the Welsh toast that Freddie Jones had taught him.

As the family ate and toasted and laughed, there was a knock at the door. Berko went to the door and then came back to the dining room, telling Morrie there was a soldier there who wanted to see him. Morrie was afraid, thinking it might be the Criminal Investigation Division to arrest him for striking a non-commissioned officer. For a split second, he thought of making a run for it. Yet, on second thought, he doubted that Smith would press charges, not after the way Morrie had threatened him. Perhaps, in time to come, the sergeant might regain his bravado, but not just yet.

Morrie was right. It wasn't the authorities, it was Freddie Jones. Morrie was stunned to see him, figuring his friend would be halfway to Wales by now. But Freddie said he couldn't go home until he told Morrie what had happened in the barracks after Morrie had left for London.

Smith had come back. His face was badly bruised, and he was boiling mad. He told the men what had happened and then swore them to a murderous pact, saying that he had to have revenge. They had all agreed to his plan: when they were on the ship, going across the channel to fight in France, they were going to kill Morrie and throw his body overboard.

"I tried to talk some sense into them," Freddie said,

"but they just called me a Jew-lover and said if I wasn't careful, it could happen to me, too."

Freddie said that Smith was red in the face with his hatred and anger. All the other soldiers clasped hands and made the pact to kill Morrie before the ship docked on the French side of the channel.

Smith had told his friends that they all might die in France anyhow, so why not first get the satisfaction of killing "that Kike bastard who did this to my face."

Morrie didn't feel much like eating any more, not after that news. Would it be a bayonet in the ribs? Or would they just hit him over the head with the butt end of a rifle, and then toss him over the side?

He invited Freddie to stay for dinner, and the young Welshman ate with gusto. Morrie just played with his food, eating enough so his mother wouldn't get suspicious. Freddie had never tasted anything like Alice Kotler's cooking. Welsh food was a far cry from the Russian-English cooking that had evolved in the East End of London among the Russian immigrant Jews.

Morrie thanked Freddie and offered to accompany him to Paddington Station, but Freddie said he could find his way. Later that night Morrie and Willie had their long-awaited reunion. As they sat at a table in the familiar Leceister Lounge Willie told Morrie about his own soldiering and working with the Romanian recruits. He said, "They are the slowest people I have ever met in my life. It takes them a week to do what you or I would do in a day. Their hearts are in the right place and they want to help, so they try damned hard, I'll give them that.

Then he said, "All right, old son. Tell me what it's like to be a real squarebasher."

Morrie told him the whole story, ending up with the fearful news that Freddie Jones had just told him.

"I can't believe they actually mean to murder me, Willie," he said.

"I can believe it. I've heard stories of soldiers killing their own officers and their own non-coms if they didn't like them. It's rather common in wartime, you know. When death is all around, one more killing hardly makes a ripple."

"So what do I do?"

Willie made circles on the table with his glass, thinking about his answer for a long time.

"I'll tell you what I'd do if it were me," he said, finally. "Now, you won't like this, I know you Morrie, and I know you're not going to like what I'm about to tell you. But I think it's the only way to come out of this alive."

"All right, then, tell me."

"French Leave." That was the slang term for desertion.

Morrie was thunderstruck. Desertion! Why, that was the most heinous crime for a soldier, an offense against the Crown. He would be shot if he were caught. It was also something that went against his personal code. He had dreamed of being a good soldier since the war began. Maybe that was no longer possible, maybe the events on Sailsbury Plain would force him to be just an ordinary soldier, but surely he was not going to be a bad solider, a deserter.

"Absolutely not," he said. "I would never, ever desert, not under any circumstances."

"I thought that was what you would say," Willie said, still not looking Morrie in the eye, still making circles on the table. "Okay, then, what other avenues are open to you?"

"I'll just go back, next week, and....? His voice trailed off.

"And they'll stab you on the ship going across the Channel and throw your body overboard."

"I can stay away from them, Willie. Maybe I can get sick on the day of transport, and hold over for the next shipment.

"From what you told me about the doctor and about your commanding officer, I don't think that'll work either."

Morrie was silent. He knew that Captain Wood and the doctor would never let him off for a make-believe sickness. He thought of several other ideas and rejected them immediately. They finally decided to keep thinking about it over the remaining six days of Morrie's leave.

Morrie went home to Stepney Green and tried to be happy, although the problem was gnawing at him inside. His parents felt that he was simply, and understandably, worried about the prospect of going into battle, so they didn't press him. He did tell Flora, and she advised him to desert. She said she would work with Willie on some way out of his dilemma, but the first thing, she said, was for him to protect his life.

"We can always find a way for you to survive," she said, "but you've got to be alive for us to do it. So under no circumstances will you go back next week. I don't want my little brother getting killed by some anti-Semitic *Yoks*! You'd be just another victim of a pogrom, so why would Mom and Dad have left Russia?"

He was being asked to desert from the Army to validate his parent's immigration.

On the day he was supposed to go back to camp, he said goodbye to his parents. He put on his uniform with the green and black patch on the shoulder, waved cheerily, and was gone.

Around the corner he met Willie, who spirited him to a tiny flat he and Flora had rented for Morrie in Plumber's Row. It wasn't an entire flat, just a room occupied by some refugees, Jews from Poland, who spoke no English. All they cared about was that the rent money that Morrie would pay would allow them to live for another few days.

Willie had found Morrie a job working in a ladies' tailoring shop in Dunk Street. Good workers were hard to find because of the war, so he was paid considerably more than he had gotten in his last job.

Morrie had to be very careful where he went, who he saw, and what he did. He and Willie found new hangouts, and Morrie even took to walking with a slight limp, so nobody would ask questions about why he wasn't in uniform. Still, whenever he saw any C.I.D.s on the street, he carefully made himself scarce.

Flora said that a few days afer he failed to report back to camp, some C.I.D. investigators had shown up at the Stepney Green flat. They asked Berko and Alice about the whereabouts of their son, but since they knew nothing, they could tell them nothing. Morrie's parents were worried and asked Flora why the *polizei,* as they called them, had come looking for their son.

"He is back with the Army," they had told the investigators, and they believed it. The men told them that he had never gone back.

So they worried. Most parents were worrying in those awful years, but Berko and Alice had more mysterious worries. They worried that the *polizei* lied when they said he had not gone back to camp; or even worse, was their son lying dead somewhere?

Flora finally told them that Morrie was alive and well, but she couldn't or wouldn't say more. She did add that he was no longer in the Army, which just mystified them even more.

Willie was a true friend during those few months of danger. The two friends went out two or three nights a week, visiting music halls, where there was safety in the huge crowds. They sang along with the people as Sir Harry Lauder sang his beloved "I belong to Glasgow" and "When I've had a couple of drinks on a Saturday, Glasgow belongs to me" and wound up with "Roamin in the Gloamin." By then everybody in the audience was up and cheering.

The people of London dodged the bombs as German airships raided the city on many nights. One night the sky suddenly burst into flame. An R.A.F. pilot, for the first time, had succeeded in hitting an airship, the LZ31, amidship, and it exploded in the blue- black London night. The midair fire, north of London, was seen for miles around. The sight of that burning airship with its flaming bodies and its black ribs silhouetted against the fire, remained in Morrie's mind for the rest of his life.

On New Year's Eve, as 1916 faded into 1917, Morrie and Willie had a private celebration in Morrie's room. They had a bottle of wine and a tin of sardines, and gave toasts to a better year for both, especially for Morrie.

The months passed, and spring had come and gone. One warm July evening Flora came to Morrie's room in Plumbers' Row. She held a copy of the *East London Observer.*

"Morrie," she said, "look at this. I think it's good news for you."

She pointed to an article about the passage of the Conventions with the Allies Act by Parliament. It explained that some thirty thousand to forty thousand young men of draft age, who had been born in Russia but presently lived in England, were now eligible to join the British Army or return to Russia and join the Russian Army, since both armies were fighting a common enemy, Germany.

Morrie shrugged. He didn't see how that new act was good news.

"Keep reading," Flora said. Morrie then came to the part which stated that "the usual exemptions for physical disabilities would apply."

"Don't you see?" she asked. "It's your way out. If I can get some papers, stating that you have a physical disability, a bad knee or some such thing, then you would be exempt from serving in any Army."

Morrie suddenly grasped it. He started laughing.

"So all we have to do," Flora said, "is get you papers that prove you are Russian-born. It's simple, really."

It was easier than any of them actually imagined. Flora, who once boasted that she could find anything illegal through the people working with her at the cigarette factory, found a source who could produce false Russian papers. It took all of her savings, plus what little Morrie had amassed, but she got them within a week. They were very official looking, adorned with the seal of the Russian Embassy.

"Look at your new name," Flora said. "You are now Alexander Chernofsky. You were born in Vasilkov,—that's near Kiev—and you have a bad shoulder. Dislocated. You can't lift your arm over your head. That's why you're not in the Army."

Morrie was now equipped with documents bearing a fictitious Russian name and his picture, proving that he had been born in Russia and was, therefore, not subject to being called up into the British Army. He had, it seemed, acquired an exemption! Morrie carried the papers everywhere, and so he was not quite as furtive in his movements as he had been. He even toyed with the idea of going home, telling everything to his parents. He knew that Berko, at least, would sympathize with him for hitting Sergeant Smith. Berko would only have wondered why he had waited so long before hitting him.

Morrie kept to his routine work, spending evenings with Willie—not much fun, but at least he was alive. He often wondered where Freddie Jones was, how the unit was doing in France, and what happened to Captain Wood, Sergeant Smith and the rest of them. Particularly, he hoped that Private Frederick Jones would make it.

Once in a while, when Morrie would meet somebody new, he would explain that he was Russian-born. He was, actually rehearsing a story that he would often tell in the future, although he had no way of knowing it then.

He came to the reluctant conclusion that, somehow, some time, he would have to get out of England. Maybe he could go to America. There were some Kotler cousins there, in St Louis and New York. He began thinking of ways and means of escaping. He would ask Flora. If the people at the cigarette factory could get false Russian identity papers, surely they could just as easily get him a false passport. He began saving his money for that document and for a steamship ticket to somewhere.

He wondered if he should confide his plans to Flora. Yes, she would have to know. Willie? Certainly, his advice would be useful.

In the month United States entered the war, and soon American soldiers were everywhere in London. Morrie met some of them and he grew to like the Yanks. He found them so relaxed, so informal, so friendly. He had to learn a whole new language to converse with them.

A Yank in a pub, one evening, asked him "where is the can"? Morrie pointed to the bar, where cans of various sorts were stacked up. The Yank laughed, then explained in more detail what he wanted.

"Oh, you mean the toilet," said Morrie, and directed him to the men's room.

He and the Yank had both learned a new word.

Another year went by, somehow. This New Year's Eve, which saw 1918 arrive, was far different from the last one. Back then, it had just been Willie and Morrie and a meager celebration. This time he splurged and went to the Trocadero Club, on Shaftsbury Avenue, and had a marvelous dinner and even a bottle of champagne with some of the Yanks.

"Here's to a great New Year to us," said Morrie, and they all clinked their glasses as the last second of 1917 ticked away and 1918 was born.

As soon as the holiday was over, Morrie started the wheels in motion for his plan. He talked to Flora, who said she would see what could be done about getting the false passport he needed. He went to the Cunard office to inquire about passage across the Atlantic. There was nothing direct from London to New York, not since the U-boats were sinking so many ships, but they did still have routes that went south to Dakar in French West Africa. They poured on the coal and dashed across the Atlantic at its narrowest point, from Dakar to Recife, in Brazil. Then the Cunards sailed north, hugging the coastline as closely as possible, and eventually reached New Orleans. It was a longer trip and, therefore, more expensive, but it was possible. Morrie found out how much a ticket would cost, and he seriously began saving up to buy one.

He was walking with Willie on a windy February day, his mind wrestling with his problems, when suddenly two big men, wearing heavy black overcoats, stepped out of a doorway and blocked their path.

"I'm sure you boys have some identification," one of the men said, very politely. He pulled out a wallet and showed them his own identification. He was with the C.I.D.

Morrie's heart turned ice cold.

"I'm in the Army," said Willie, and showed the men his pass.

"Very good," said the C.I.D. "And what about you, young fellow?"

Morrie pulled out his papers, the ones that identified him as Russian-born.

"You're a Russian, then?"

"Yes, sir. Alexander Chernofsky."

"You don't sound very Russian."

"I came here when I was six months old."

"Where are your parents, then?"

"They live up in Leeds."

The two men studied Morrie's papers a few moments longer and then said, still politely, that it was surely a routine matter, and they would have to ask Morrie to come with them.

Willie asked them where they were taking Morrie. They said they would be going to the police station on Old Street, and they were sure it would be resolved within the hour, two at the most.

"Tell Flora, will you?" asked Morrie, and Willie promised he would.

When Morrie never showed up, and when he didn't return again the next day, Willie knew the worst had happened. He told Flora that he was sure that Morrie, still guilty about being a deserter, had blurted out the truth.

Willie went to Pentonville Prison the next day. He had gone to the Old Street police station, where they told him that the prisoner, Alexander Chernofsky, was at Pentonville.

There was a visitors' room, and Willie sat on a bench and waited. He was facing heavy wire mesh screen, and Morrie came through a door on the other side and sat down on a bench. The guard told Willie that he would have five minutes.

Morrie was pale. He managed a small smile for his friend. "Blimey, Willie, what do you make of this?" he said.

"You haven't said anything rash, have you?" Willie asked.

"Oh, no, nothing. Willie, they say they are sending me to Russia."

He explained that the authorities had worked out a deal with the Russians. The English would ship Russian-born men of soldiering age back to Russia, and the Russians would do the same with any Englishmen they found. It would help both sides.

The two men talked a few minutes, and then Willie's time was up and he had to leave the prison. He didn't see Morrie again for almost a half-century.

While he waited in Pentonville prison, Morrie was assigned to a unit making rope. Soon his hands were covered with little cuts from the stiff bristles on the rope, but it kept him busy.

A guard told him that he was going to be sent back to Russia on the first available ship.

"You can go wherever you want, once you get there," the guard said. "You'll land in Murmansk. That's the only seaport that isn't frozen at this time of year."

Morrie thought, briefly, of mounting some sort of protest. Perhaps he could explain the situation and say he wanted nothing more than to serve His Majesty, to fight for his country, to bear arms for the United Kingdom. There was no getting around it. No matter how he would paint his situation, or how sympathetic his audience might be, the technical truth was that he was a deserter in the unforgiving eyes of the military law.

He considered how fate and his temper had gotten him to this point. He could still go to the C.I.D., tell them the truth, and avoid being deported to Russia. But that course was unthinkable, because he would be shot as a deserter. Maybe could try to escape but then he would be on the run for the rest of his life, even if he succeeded, and Morrie didn't fancy the life of a fugitive.

His only course was to go to Russia, to Murmansk, and then try to make his way to safety from there. Maybe he could figure out a way to bribe the ship's crew to let him stay aboard. After it left Murmansk, the ship might be coming back to England, or at least going on to some more hospitable port.

So he would go to Murmansk. There was no way to avoid it. In Russia he knew, he would be what the East Enders used to call newcomers to

London, a "Peruvian." He would be the Peruvian to end all Peruvians, because he would know nobody and know not a word of the language.

When he left the prison, he saw some of London from the C.I.D. van window for what he thought might be the last time. The sky was leaden gray, appropriately matching Morrie's mood. The guard in the van offered him a cigarette, but he shook his head. He still hadn't smoked.

There were four others in the van, other deportees. These men spoke Russian fluently. They tried to open a conversation with Morrie, but he just shrugged and smiled, indicating he didn't speak the language. They ignored him after that, and continued to ignore him throughout the rest of their mutual voyage.

The rest of the trip to Newcastle was a blur. Morrie later recalled going to the Kings Cross Station and remembering that he had used that station in happier times. The train ride itself to Newcastle was equally a blur in his memory. He didn't see anything out of the window too clearly because there were a few tears in his eyes. The train station in Newcastle was close enough to the dock area for Morrie and the others to walk. They were marched by the guards to a dock, and then right up the gangplank aboard the *BRADFORD*. There the guard turned them over to the Marines who would guard them until they disembarked at Murmansk.

The *BRADFORD* was a tub. The sailors who sailed aboard the ship called her a rustbucket. Actually, she had been doing yeomen service for the nation during the war, one of the merchant ships that ferried supplies back and forth across the channel, with an occasional voyage to some other port, such as this one to Murmansk.

The Marine in charge of the five deportees led them down some narrow stairs to their room, which had six bunks, three high on each side. He pointed out the bathroom and he lectured them on what was expected of them while at sea.

"If one of you bastards so much as lights a match on deck at night," he said, "overboard you go. The German U-boats are still sniffing about, and they would like nothing more than to send us to the bottom."

"The mess is aft. Hours are posted, so be on time. You don't eat if you are late. Have a nice trip, you Russian bastards."

The Marine could have saved his breath. The other four deportees didn't understand a word of what he had said. They looked puzzled, and Morrie would have liked to have enlightened them, but he was not equipped to translate. He did try to act out a charade, to let them know not to strike a match on deck. They nodded to indicate they understood.

Morrie went up on deck to watch the ship being nosed out of its berth by the tugs and head out to the open sea. He started talking to a burly, red-bearded sailor, asking him about Murmansk. The sailor told him it was just a settlement, really, just used in the winter when the major port, Archangel, was iced over.

"Are there really subs still around?" Morrie asked.

"Well, that's subject to dispute, the sailor answered. "We have warnings all the time. You'll go through a lot of them, I'm sure, but I've only spotted one and I've been sailing a couple of years now. That was up off the Norwegian coast, and we had a proper escort. A couple of destroyers. They made a run for the U-boat before it could fire anything at us."

Morrie pressed him some more, and the sailor, who enjoyed having an audience, told stories of his adventures. Morrie enjoyed listening. It took his mind off of who he was and where he was going. He was more curious, however, about Murmansk.

"Let me tell you about your precious Murmansk," said the sailor. "I've never seen a dirtier place or been in a place that smelled as bad. That's because the people there haven't any sanitation, and they just dump everything outside. Murmansk at this time of the year is covered with snow, so it won't be so bad. Wait until spring if you want to get a jolt."

"As for Murmansk itself, it's about thirty miles from the sea, up an inlet. There are about two dozen or so log huts. There'll be a lot of shipping in the harbor. Always is. There's one old Russian warship that ran aground and will probably always be there. When you see the way the Russians take care of their ships or don't take care of them, you'll understand how the

Germans kicked the crap out of them so fast. You'll see one proper vessel in Murmansk harbor. The *Glory* is there now. They moved her up from Archangel so she wouldn't be iced-in all winter."

The sailor told Morrie that if he wanted to know more about Murmansk, the first mate had some books about the place, and he was sure he would let him look at them. Morrie took advantage of that source of information. He learned virtually all there was to learn, which wasn't much, about the place where he was going to disembark.

As soon as the *BRADFORD* left the shelter of the Tyne river, and headed out into the North Sea, the ship hit heavy waves. Morrie and virtually everyone else aboard, including the experienced seamen, became seasick. He stayed that way for three days, until he got his sea legs.

Morrie read that the port in Murmansk never froze over and the ground never thawed. That, Morrie realized, explained why there were no sewers or garbage dumps. A railroad to Petrograd was also constructed at the same time the port was built.

Early one morning, a few days after they had left the English coast far behind, Morrie's sleep was rudely interrupted by cries from the deck:

"Ware submarine! Ware submarine!"

They had been told ,in the event of such an alert, that they were to get dressed, lace on their life jackets, and get up on deck as fast as possible.

Morrie was excited as well as cautious. He looked out to sea, in the direction the crew was looking. It was still dark outside, although the sun, rising in the East, was just about to show itself. He could make out the silhouettes of a few of the other ships in the convoy, as well as some sparks from the smokestacks of the destroyers as they dashed in and out among their charges, sniffing out the offending submarine. The destroyers dropped a few depth charges. Morrie could clearly hear their muffled thud from underwater and see the luminous spray over the site of the explosion. There seemed to be no pattern or method in their search, yet it apparently did the trick, for within fifteen minutes he heard the cry from the bridge, "All clear!"

The voyage lasted ten days. Morrie was relaxed for the last half of it because he had made friends among the sailors and Marines who were the ship's armed guard. They all wanted to hear his story, because they simply couldn't understand how a bloke, an obviously English bloke, could be deported to Russia. Morrie told his story so often that he virtually had it memorized. It seldom deviated from the approved text.

The sailors pointed out the sights. The most exciting to Morrie were the icebergs, silent, white, immense.

He was staring off at those frightening bergs one afternoon when the ship shook and he heard an ominous thud below his feet. He knew enough about icebergs to know that you only saw a bit of them, that they extended far below the ocean surface. The ship seemed well away from the nearest one, and yet he was certain that they had hit an iceberg. His imagination conjured up a vision of a slash in the hull, with the frigid water pouring into the ship, and he thought he sensed a list to port.

Morrie ran to where his red-bearded sailor friend, whose name was Charles McKinnon, was lounging against a deck post.

"Did we hit something, Charlie?" he asked.

"Not to worry, Alex. Just the cargo shifting a mite."

Morrie went down to his cabin, where he found his four Russian cabin-mates on their hands and knees, retrieving their belongings. The shift of the cargo was like an earthquake at sea, and everything in the cabin had spilled onto the floor. Morrie joined the others, picking up his scattered belongings.

Charlie had been right. The shifting cargo had caused the ship to list some, which in turn meant she could no longer steam at full speed.

As it turned out the *BRADFORD*, was now too slow to keep up with the rest of the convoy. The others steamed ahead, destroyers and the other merchantmen, leaving the *BRADFORD* on her own. Charles said that they would probably not run into any U-boats this far north. They stayed mostly in the more southerly reaches of the North Sea, seldom braving the iceberg-strewn waters of the Barents Sea.

Charlie and some of the other sailors had been to Russia before, and they talked to Morrie about the character of the Russian people. They had not been favorably impressed.

"They are a bunch of lazy bastards," Charlie said. "The *Moujiks* don't want to work, and the rich ones don't have to."

"What's a *Moujik?*" Morrie asked.

"I guess the closest thing in English is peasant," said the sailor. "They're everybody but the rich people. They work the land and chop down the trees and work the mines. It's all frozen over eight months out of the year. What a bloody awful country. No wonder they all have bad tempers."

"I never heard one song out of any of them," said Charlie. "They're smelly and dirty, they can't read or write and they all have bad teeth."

"Sounds a lovely lot," said Morrie.

"Well, Alex, old boy, they're your people, after all, and you're jolly well welcome to them."

The *BRADFORD* turned east, following the shoreline of the northern coast of Norway. It was cold and there was a constant fog blanketing the area. One morning it broke, and Morrie and the others could see the outline of a large ship anchored in a small bay.

The sailors told him that was H.M.S. *Cochrane*, a British ship that had discharged 150 Marines at a place called Petchanga. The sailors couldn't figure what the government would want with 150 Marines up there where there were no enemies and, in fact, no friends either. There was literally nothing there, except now there were 150 British Marines.

A few hours after Petchanga, the *BRADFORD* suddenly turned sharply to starboard and entered a narrow inlet. Going at only five or six knots, it took the old ship five careful hours to make the last thirty miles from the sea to Murmansk.

And there it was. There were many ships were in the harbor, as the sailors had predicted. Quite a few, of course, had been part of the *BRAD-FORD'S* convoy, which had arrived a day or so earlier. There was also H.M.S. *Glory* and several Russian naval vessels. It was easy to tell them apart, because the *Glory* gleamed, even in the gloom, while the Russian ships, even at a distance, were obviously unkempt.

Morrie left the safety of the BRADFORD and walked down the gangplank to face his unknown future.

Chapter Four

Morrie joined the other men in the boxcar for breakfast tea, which was everywhere, and the staple black bread with a spread of congealed condensed milk.

He listened while the Englishmen talked about the war. The situation was chaotic. "The Bolsheviks are in control in Moscow and Petrograd, but anarchy seems to be the rule. There are minor generals with private armies who have seized control of various areas." Britain and their allies were still hoping the Russians could be maneuvered back into the war against Germany, because a Western front was, they felt, essential to the winning of the war.

Morrie listened and heard names he had never heard before. There was Alexander Kerensky, who had been head of the provisional government. There were the major figures of the Bolshevik movement, Lenin and Trotsky. There was Kolchak, the Russian admiral, who was still trying to fight the war, without men or ships or guns.

"What's the latest with the Czech Legion?" one of the Englishman asked.

Morrie learned, from listening, that the Czech Legion had been recruited from Czechs and other Slovaks who had been living in Russia. They had fought with the Russian Army. When the Russian Army collapsed, the Czech Legion didn't. It was still intact, still armed, still disciplined and, according to the rumors the Englishmen in the boxcar had heard, they were spoiling for a fight.

"They're ready to fight anybody, I hear."

"Where are they now?"

"In Siberia somewhere, according to the reports. Nobody knows for sure if they are going east, toward Vladivostok, or trying to go west."

The Allies, apparently, had recognized the Czech Legion as part of the Allied army after the Russian collapse. Now the Allies wanted the Czechs evacuated from Russia, but that was considerably easier said than done.

While the conversation swirled about him, much of it involving people he had never heard of, and concepts he didn't understand, and problems he didn't care about, Morrie once again began to consider his own plight.

He was, momentarily, warm and fed. Obviously this was only a temporary state. He couldn't stay in this boxcar forever, even if they permitted it. The same old problem, so far an insoluble, one remained.

Where could he go?

Morrie left the comfort of the circle around the stove and went to where one of the Marines was seated, looking out a slit in the boxcar door. He struck up a conversation with a Marine and eventually asked what he should do.

The Marine pondered the question. There was no easy answer, he said, but he suggested that Morrie speak to his commanding officer and pointed out into the snow where that officer had his office. Morrie didn't say so, but he immediately decided that conversations with a British officer were not desirable.

Neal Cooper and another of the English businessmen, who identified himself as Henry Pike, had come over to where Morrie and the Marine were talking. They joined in, trying to give Morrie some constructive advice.

"Ordinarily," said Pike, I would urge my young friend here to go to Petrograd, primarily because the only train service out of Murmansk is the line to Petrograd. That is not a good idea, presently, because the Bolsheviks are in control." He added "they were a nasty lot."

Cooper and Pike fell silent and pondered the problem. When they spoke again, however, it was not to offer a solution, but merely to comment on how grave the problem was. They said that Murmansk and all of Russia was a madhouse at the moment.

"Confusion reigns," Cooper said.

"Total chaos," Pike agreed.

There were English refugees and Russian refugees, French, Italian, even a few Americans, as well as the Chinese who had been brought in to build the railroads. They were all now marooned in the Murmansk area. They said that inevitably this human logjam would have to move, and Morrie could move with them. But it would probably be several months before that would happen.

"I want to go now," Morrie said.

"I have it," said Pike. "I wager the Red Cross people will have an answer for you. They're mostly Yanks, and they're good people. There is a Red Cross car just down the tracks, about two hundred meters up to your left. I'm sure they'll have some good advice for you. At least, they'll know the situation a great deal better than we do."

Morrie headed left, as he had been directed, plowing through the snow. Cooper and Pike told him that the Red Cross car was entirely different from the other cars. It had red and gold stripes on the side and, they said, looked like it might have been from the Czar's private fleet of railroad cars. With that decription, it was easy for Morrie to spot it.

It wasn't one of the boxcars, but a passenger car. There was a door and Morrie stood there, hesitating. He had nothing much to lose. He banged his gloved hand on the door, and it quickly slid open.

"Can I help you?" The man who opened the door was tall, thin, and was wearing rimless glasses.

"I hope so. May I come in?"

"Step right in, young fellow," Morrie could tell that the tall man was an American. There was no mistaking that nasal, flat speech. He had heard American entertainers on the music hall stages and had met enough Yank soldiers in the pubs to be able to recognize that speech pattern. They all sounded like cowboys.

"I'm Wardwell, Major Wardwell. American Red Cross and who might you be?"

"I'm Alex Chernofsky, from London."

"What's a kid from London doing in this God-forsaken spot?"

Morrie told his story. While he related that now - familiar tale his eyes were roaming around the interior of the coach. It was incredibly opulent. The walls were covered in light green satin, not paint or wallpaper, but actual material, and there was gold brocade molding. The chairs were upholstered in rich, dark green velvet, again trimmed in gold. The tables were of a wood that had been polished so highly that it seemed like it had a covering of glass, but when Morrie idly rubbed his hand across the top of the nearest table, he realized that it wasn't glass but simply the intense polish on the wood. The lamps had shades of silk, with fringes of gold.

"Here, let me take your coat and gloves," said Major Wardwell. "Then we can talk a little more comfortably. Tea?"

There was a samovar on a large table at one side of the car, and it appeared to be solid gold.

"It's only brass, not gold," said Wardwell. He could tell from the way Morrie was staring at everything, that he was in awe. "This is quite a palace, isn't it? We don't know for certain, but we believe it belonged to the Czar, or at least to somebody in the royal family. Now it's our little home away from home."

Wardwell poured the tea. The cups had obviously not come with the car. They were plain official-looking white china. He gestured for Morrie to sit down.

"What can I do for you, young fellow?"

"I need help, Major. I have to get out of Murmansk, but I don't know where I should go, or how to go about getting there."

"I think maybe we ought to get the rest of the gang in on this," the Major said. He got up and knocked at a partition at the end of the car, and asked his colleagues to come in.

"There's a problem here that needs our help," he said. Four men followed him back into the main part of the car, and Morrie saw quickly that one was a Russian soldier.

"Your name was Chernofsky, right?" the American asked. Morrie nodded. Then Wardwell pointed around the room. "I'd like to introduce you to Hugh

Martin, he's the American passport control officer here in Murmansk. This is Jesse Halsey, Reverend Jesse Halsey of the American Y.M.C.A. This fellow is Major Thomas Thatcher, like me he's with the Red Cross and this is Captain Ilovaiski. He works with us as our Russian interpreter."

Morrie shook hands with the four men. They all went to the samovar and poured themselves a cup of tea. Morrie would soon learn that no business or conversation was conducted in Russia until the ritual cup of tea was poured.

Morrie relaxed in his luxurious green velvet chair. He had never sat in such comfort or opulence before, even in his London days, and certainly it had been a long time since he had felt the joy of just leaning back in a chair. Morrie felt very comfortable with the car warm as toast from its several kerosene heaters, with the tea flowing in his stomach, and sitting in that magnificent chair.

"Why don't you tell these men your problem, Morrie, and we can figure out what to do. You've stumbled into the den of the greatest brains now operating on Russian soil."

They all chuckled politely, and then Morrie told his story again. When Hugh Martin, the passport officer, asked him some questions, Morrie felt he needed a translator. Martin, he learned, was from some place called Mississippi, and while theoretically he was speaking English, Morrie had a very difficult time understanding him.

"Gentlemen, I need help badly. I don't know where to go. Should I go to Petrograd? What will I do when I get there?"

Wardwell said that he was going to Petrograd in ten days, and Morrie could come with him if he could stand Murmansk until then.

"There's nothing for you there, I'm afraid," he added. "The Bolsheviks are all over, and if they get a hold of you, which they probably would, they'd put you in their Army, the Red Guards, before you knew what hit you. Even if you got lucky and avoided the Bolsheviks, how would you survive there? Everybody who speaks English is getting the hell out now."

Wardwell asked Captain Ilovaiski if he didn't agree.

"Yes, Major, I agree with you with completeness," the Russian said. He turned to Morrie. "Mr. Chernofsky, you must understand that Russia is, in the present instance, full of chaos and upset. There is here today a full-type Civil War. There is no place that abounds in safety."

"There must be some place for me to go," said Morrie, making the statement into a question.

"If I were you, young fellow," said Hugh Martin, "the first thing I'd do would be to get to Archangel. At least there are trains to other places. It's a much bigger place than here, so there are more opportunities. There are a lot of ships there, and when the thaw comes maybe you'll be able to find a ship that will take you out of here."

Morrie didn't catch all of Martin's Mississippi-flavored words, but he understood the gist of what he said. At last Morrie had heard something positive.

Martin told the story of his own perilous trip to Murmansk a few months before. He had been the passport control officer in Archangel, but when winter came and the port froze there was no need for his service there for the time being. He was reassigned to Murmansk, but the Bolsheviks would not issue him a permit to travel from Petrograd, where he had gone to await reassignment.

"So I figured I'd give them a taste of Yankee ingenuity," he said. "I took the train from Petrograd back to Archangel, where I knew everybody. I hired peasants and their sleighs to take me from village to village until I reached a small city called Soroka, on the Petrograd-Murmansk rail line. I then hopped a freight from Soroka to Murmansk."

"And here I am. I only went about twelve hundred miles out of my way, and I did it without one of their precious travel permits. But I made it. I think you should do the same thing, only the other way around. Get down to Archangel on sleighs, with the Moujiks. It's really a great way to see the country."

"What will I use for money to hire the sleighs?" asked Morrie. "I have a few British pounds, but no Russian money."

"I tell you what, Alex," said Hugh Martin, and Morrie continued to marvel at the way the informal Americans used first names so easily. "I'll make you a small loan. When you get down to Meridian, Mississippi, after this stupid war is over, you can repay me. Have we got a deal?"

"Mr. Martin, I'll do anything to get out of here. I give you my word, I'll pay you back. It's a deal."

The others laughed, because it did seem the height of bravado for a kid from London, in what may have been the Czar's private car in the middle of a Murmansk blizzard, to promise to go to Meridian, Mississippi to repay a loan of what probably amounted to five dollars.

"Don't worry about repaying him, Alex," said Wardwell. "If I know my buddy, Hugh Martin, that's not his money he's about to lend you, but Uncle Sam's. Am I right, Hugh?"

"We don't ask questions, do we, Morrie? We just take the money and go about our business."

Martin pulled out a battered wallet and took out a hefty wad of money, peeling off some bills and handing them to Morrie. He looked at them, but they didn't make much sense to him.

"You'll have to explain this money to me, sir," he said. "And tell me how to go about hiring sleighs and what I say and all that. I don't speak a word of Russian."

They broke out the vodka, and they all sat back in overstuffed elegance while Martin described how it was, from Murmansk and Archangel via Soroka.

"First of all, Alex, there is nothing but snow all the way. Actually it's very beautiful when you think about it. In a practical sense it can be a damned nuisance, practically, however. Don't look for anything except snow."

"You'll find the people, the *Moujiks*, are very accommodating. Not very sophisticated, of course, but very pleased to be able to help for money, you understand? Nobody here does anything out of love or loyalty or for any reason other than financial gain."

"Slip them a few kopecks and they'll help you. A few rubles and they'll give you their wife, daughters, and the fur off their backs. Give them a few kopecks and they'll give you some food and a warm place by the fire to sleep in their little cabins. It's not the Savoy, but it'll keep you safe from the wolves."

"You'll be okay. The *Moujiks* have good sleighs and good horses, and there is a tradition of helping strangers."

Martin said that he would give Morrie some names of friends who would help him once he got to Archangel.

"You can either stay there until May or June, when the port thaws and you can take a ship out," he said, "or you can get a train there for Vologda. Our Embassy has just moved down to Vologda, and I can give you the names of some our people at the Embassy who will help you there."

Morrie listened. He also ate. It was his first real meal in a long time.

The cook in sparkling whites, topped by a chef's hat, brought in a huge bowl of something the Russian captain identified as *salianka*. It was a soup, hearty with meat and tomatoes and full of spices, like Morrie's mother had made at home in London.

"These are just like the pickles we used to get in the East End back home in London," Morrie said. He realized that, obviously, his parents and the other refugees from Russia had brought their own pickling ability with them.

That remark of Morrie's piqued the curiosity of the men sitting around the table. They began asking Morrie about the life he had lived in London. He talked of his past, although carefully skirting around his army experience. They wanted to know what the average Englishman thought about the Russians and the war.

"Frankly," said Morrie, "it wasn't a major topic back home when I left. Our people were primarily concerned with the war in France, with the trenches and the airships dropping bombs right on London, things like that. The Eastern Front, well, that's not important to the average Englishman."

The cook came back in with the next course. He was a squat Russian with high, Mongol-like cheekbones. He carried the food in on a large, elegant silver tray.

"*Zoarkoi,*" he said, and plopped the tray in the center of the table.

It was a large chunk of roast beef, surrounded by boiled potatoes. Morrie salivated as Hugh Martin carved the meat and passed the filled plates around the table. Morrie thought back to the other boxcar. The Englishmen, obviously highclass types, were undoubtedly dining on black bread with condensed milk spread.

The men talked about politics and the war again, as they ate their main course. None of them seemed able to understand what the Bolsheviks were about. Trotsky first appeared to want to stay in the war against the Germans, they said, but then did an about face and screamed that Russia would never lose another man in defense of the British throne.

The Americans also told the story, for Morrie's benefit, of Admiral Kyetlinski. He had been the Czar's officer in charge of Murmansk, the *Glavny Nachalnik,* or senior naval officer in the port. The Bolsheviks let him stay on, because they had no one with his qualifications to run the port. He was solidly pro-Allies. Some sailors aboard the Russian ship *Askold,* anchored in Murmansk harbor, felt the revolution should be going faster, so they tried to blow up the ship. Kyetlinski had those sailors shot. The Bolsheviks, in Petrograd, as they were beginning to call it, then sent an order to arrest Kyetlinski, but there was nobody to carry out the order. The local Bolshevik leader ordered the sailors to arrest the admiral, but they wouldn't do it; they just put a loose sort of guard around his house. The Bolsheviks then took the guard away. Kyetlinski went for a walk and a couple of sailors shot him dead.

"So Murmansk," they told Morrie," is today a political mess." Three organizations were running the port; the Murmansk Soviet, representing the Bolsheviks and some labor organizations; the *Sovzheldor,* which was the powerful union of railroad workers that also represented the sailors; and the *Tsentromur,* which was the Central Soviet of the Murmansk Squadron.

"Nobody can get anything done around this place," said Wardell, "because if you get one of those organizations to agree, the other two are bound to say no."

They lingered over a dessert and cigars. As Morrie was wondering where he could sleep, they told him that he could curl up in a small extra bed they had in the room off the galley. Morrie was asleep in two minutes.

The Russian cook woke him up happily clanging an iron spoon against an iron frying pan. He laughed when Morrie jumped up so quickly that he almost bumped his head on the low ceiling.

The same group breakfasted on tea, black bread, cold cuts, and a couple of tins of sardines. They talked about Morrie's situation, and Hugh Martin had apparently thought about it for a long time after Morrie went to sleep. He had polished the plan he had first advanced the previous day.

He had Captain Ilovaiski write a note in Russian for Morrie. The plan was for Morrie to take the Petrograd train as far as Soroka. There, he would have to show the note to some likely looking peasant, and hope that the peasant could read. If not, he should shop around until he found someone who could read, and then hope that the person had a sleigh for hire.

Martin took out a map and showed Morrie the various towns he would have to pass between Soroka and Archangel. The *moujiks* wouldn't go too far, even for money. He could probably get one to take him to Suma from Soroka, some thirty miles away. The next stop, Onega, follows the shore of the Gulf of Onega. "The note will get you a place to sleep in Onega." Then along the Litny Peninsula, following the Gulf of Archangel, to a village called Rikasikla. He'd spend the night there, and the next day, across the Dvina River, he'd go on to Archangel.

"Don't lose that note. It could be the difference between getting there and freezing to death in the snow. The Russians are good people but they don't understand English, so without that note they won't know what you are trying to do."

Morrie put the note in his wallet, along with two of Martin's business cards with other names written on the back. One name was Jim Anderson, who was Martin's good friend, the passport control officer in Archangel. Morrie was to look him up as soon as he arrived. The other was the name of a friend of Martin's in Vologda, should Morrie's travels take him there.

Martin said that they should go to the station now, to see when the next train for Petrograd would be leaving. He would have to buy a ticket for Soroka. Martin told him to show that note, which apparently had everything on it, to anybody on the train, and they would let him know when they reached Soroka. The train made quite a few stops, and it would be disastrous to get off anywhere else.

There were last- minute instructions: "Don't drink any water unless it's boiled; better stick to drinking tea," and the cook handed him a canvas sack full of food. He could smell the chocolate bars even through the tightly closed canvas.

Morrie shook hands with the men, thanked them, and walked a few hundred yards, past the line of boxcars. He tried to pick out the one where he had spent his first night.

A crowd of people milled about the tiny station. A stove was roaring in the center of the room, and a man was methodically stoking it with tree limbs. The crowd consisted of a wide assortment of people, some Russian, some English, some Oriental. Many languages were being spoken. In one corner there was a short, stout Russian lady with a babushka around her head. She was tending the samovar, selling tea and hot water. Morrie would see her, and other women looking remarkably like her, throughout his journey. One of the Russians approached the tea lady, carrying a pot. He reached in one of the pockets of his heavy coat and pulled out a handful of tea, put it in his pot, and held the pot under the spigot of the samovar. She filled it with water and he gave her a coin. The transaction was routine, done without a word.

Martin asked a few people if they spoke English, and eventually they found a man who did. He was a Frenchman, but he had been a sales representative for the Singer Sewing Machine Company, and spoke many languages. He, too, was now on the run, having been forced from his

Russian post by the revolution. Martin asked him when the next train was due to leave for Petrograd.

"We must say Petrograd now, monsieur," the Frenchman said, looking about him nervously. "It is due to leave in just two hours, so they say. You never know, do you?"

Martin gave the Frenchman some money, and asked him to buy Morrie a ticket to Soroka. The Frenchman said he would be happy to do so. Martin explained to Morrie that for political reasons it would not be a good idea for him to be seen buying a ticket.

The Frenchman returned shaking his head sadly. "The money, it is mixed up here now," he said. "I gave the ticket person the rubles you gave me, Imperial rubles from the Czar's time, and look at the change he gave me. Kerensky money. Kerensky is gone now, so what is this money worth today? I think nothing."

"This gentlemen speaks the truth," said Martin to Morrie. "Be sure to check the change you get when you buy anything from now on. There are different kinds of money, and some are no longer worth the paper they're printed on."

Martin gave Morrie a bunch of Kerensky rubles. "They might not be good here," he said, "and yet they might be good somewhere in some other part of Russia. At least it was better than having no money at all."

"Don't forget," he said, with a smile, "you owe me those too, when you get down to Meridian Mississippi after the war."

Martin left and Morrie was once again totally on his own. The Frenchman who had bought his ticket disappeared in the crowded station. Morrie bought himself a cup of tea and something to eat. It was some kind of meat that he was almost glad he could not identify, wrapped in a flaky pastry. The waiting room was hot and stuffy, with the fire blazing and the crush of bodies, but when he went outside it was so frigid that he quickly returned to the station.

Finally a big, burly, uniformed Russian stepped up on an overturned box and clapped his hands loudly. The crowd, which was babbling wildly, fell silent. The conductor carried a green flag and waved it over his head. He yelled a few sentences. Everybody trooped outside into the sub-Arctic twilight. Morrie followed. The people formed themselves into a line, and Morrie elbowed his way into the line. They filed up to the conductor, who had stuck his green flag into a niche in a post, and gave him their tickets. The train chugged slowly into the station while this was going on.

The train had stopped by the time Morrie had gotten to the conductor. He looked around to see what car he would board, but he was distressed to see that the train seemed to be made up of boxcars, not passenger cars. The other people appeared to be unfazed by that, as though that was the norm. They scrambled up into the boxcars. Morrie raced ahead to a box-car that appeared to be less jammed, and crawled up into it. People were clapping their hands to get rid of the snow. That appeared to be the first thing that Russians did often when they came inside, almost a ritual of hand-clapping that always made Morrie think they were applauding the fact that they had survived another bout with the winter.

So he clapped his gloved hands, then found himself a spot to sit, a wall to lean against, and finally surveyed the people with whom he would share the ride. He was wondering if there was a literate person in the car, someone to whom he could show his precious note and thus be sure to disembark at Soroka, rather than at some unknown snow bank.

He had just about picked his target, a thin man who had about him an air of intelligence, when, as the train started to move, two British Marines jumped aboard.

Morrie's first impulse was to hide. It was always possible they were looking for him. He quickly realized that fear was absurd. They could have picked him up before if they knew he was in Murmansk.

"Sure was a near thing, catching this train," said one of the Marines, clapping his hands in the approved fashion and taking a deep breath.

"Five more minutes and we'd have been stuck here for another bloomin' day," said the other.

They found a spot across from where Morrie was sitting. The two Marines had evidently run to catch the train, and it took them a few minutes to recover. Morrie wondered whether he should identify himself as an Englishman, or wait. The decision was taken out of his hands.

"Good evening, all," said one of the Marines, a husky, sandy-haired young man with a cheerful smile.

"Save your breath, Jack," said the other, who was equally husky, but with brown hair and more of a scowl than a smile. "None of these blighters can understand you."

Morrie smiled over at them.

"Gor blimey!" he said, and the one called Jack laughed out loud.

"Well, Lawrence, here's one bloke who understands me." Jack got up and walked over and stuck out his hand. "Good to see you, laddie. I'm Jack Phipps, and my dubious friend here is Lawrence Wedder."

"Alex Chernofsky here. Nice to have you on my private car here for this scenic journey."

They all laughed and sat together, telling their stories. The Marines were part of the contingent that had been aboard the *Cochrane* at Pechanga, and were now supposed to go to Archangel. Morrie said he was headed for Archangel, too.

"How are you getting there?" Morrie asked them.

"Not much choice," said Jack, the more talkative of the two. "We'll get off somewhere between here and Petrograd and get us a sleigh. Not sure where to get off, that's the thing."

"The Red Cross blokes in Murmansk told me that Soroka was the best bet," said Morrie.

"Soroka, eh?"

"That's what they told me. Problem is to tell when we get there. I've got a note in Russian, and if I can find one of these blokes who knows how to read, we'll be all right."

"Never fear, laddie. Lawrence will take over. Lawrence has a few words of Russian."

Lawrence got up and went over to a fat Russian lady who was slurping tea from a glass. He said, "*Pashalsta, zhenshchina, Soroka stantsiya.* Okay?"

The woman laughed, showing the usual Russian rotted teeth, and pointed a finger at Lawrence. She obviously understood him even though just as obviously she thought that the way he had mangled the Russian language was very amusing.

"Okay Soroka," she said. She held up five fingers, and Morrie and the others interpreted the gesture as either meaning five hours or that Soroka would be the fifth station. They would find out.

The ride was a lurching, clanging, banging affair. The boxcar bounced and swerved so violently that Morrie had to anchor himself with both his arms. Jack and Lawrence quickly fell asleep, curled up on their coats on the floor, despite the noise and the motion. Morrie couldn't sleep.

Where was he going? All right, he reassured himself, you are going to Soroka and then you are going to take a very nice sleigh-ride. How often as a boy had he longed for those Russian sleigh-rides that his mother and father had told him about. Now won't that be fun? A lovely ride on a nice comfortable sleigh, with a thick fur blanket tucked under his chin and maybe a mug of hot chocolate. He laughed at his own fantasy, then figured that if he was fantasizing, he might as well go all the way, so he added a dollop of whipped cream to that mug of hot chocolate.

That brought him back to reality again. It wasn't fun any more. Suddenly he was just a scared little kid from the East End, riding on a cold, bumpy, noisy boxcar in the middle of the Russian winter, going from a place he had never heard of before yesterday to another place he hade never heard of.

He must have dozed then, because suddenly he was jarred awake when the train's brakes squealed and there was a shuffling in the car. It was night now and there were no lights. He saw a burly figure approach them. The figure lit a candle, and he could see it was the woman to whom Lawrence had talked.

"Kem," she said, gesturing outside. The three Englishmen realized that she was telling them that the name of the town at which they had stopped was Kem. "*Soroka adin.*" She held up one pudgy, gloved finger. She was saying that Soroka was one more station, the next station.

The railroad between Kem and Soroka seemed even bumpier than before. They had to hold on to the walls or the ceiling to keep upright. There were fewer people now, as many had gotten off with the fat lady, at Kem, but the train was still far from empty.

The car suddenly screeched to a stop. The engineer must have applied the brakes full force without warning. The car screeched to a stop. One man, who had the misfortune of being erect at the time, lost his balance and went careening into the stove, screaming in pain as his face collided with the red-hot metal. A large, ugly yellow blister erupted on his cheek while Morrie watched. One of the Russians yanked the door open, leaped out, and grabbed two fistfuls of snow. He came back and applied the snow to the man's wounded face. The man shrieked and then fainted.

The Russian who had jumped out motioned that he could use more snow, so Morrie, Jack, and Lawrence obliged. They jumped into the snow bank at the side of the track, filled their caps with snow and clambered back aboard the car. The Russian nodded his gratitude and kept putting the snow on the injured man's face. The man regained consciousness, moaning and crying, but gradually the snow apparently helped ease the pain. He asked for "*chai,*" and when the Russians brought him a glass of tea, Morrie had learned his second Russian word.

Lawrence had a first-aid kit among his possessions, and he took out a large gauze square and carefully bandaged the man's burned face. Jack gave the man a cigarette as Morrie wiped his brow, which was covered with perspiration. The injured man was recovering nicely after being aided by the two Englishmen, Morrie, and the Russian who had initiated the help. The train then chugged into motion again.

Jack dug into his baggage and produced some chocolate bars. Everyone drank chai and ate the chocolate. Soon they were all laughing and chattering away, even though it was almost impossible to understand each other.

When the train next stopped, the three assumed that they were in Soroka.

"Soroka?" Morrie asked the Russians still in the car, with a question mark in his voice.

"*Da*, Soroka," they answered, in a chorus.

The Marines slid the door open, and the three men climbed out of the boxcar. They were near a tiny station. It was night and there was only one pale bulb shining in the building. They crunched through the heavy snow to the station, where the station master slept soundly on a bench, covered by the ubiquitous green flag that all Russian railroad functionaries seemed to carry.

Also asleep on benches were two other British Marines.

Jack and Larry recognized them as part of their contingent. They told Morrie that there were other Marines heading for Archangel, so it was no real surprise to find them in the Soroka station. Jack and Larry shook them awake.

There was a grand reunion between Jack, Lawrence, and the two Marines in the station, whose names were Griffin and Fedders. Morrie never did learn their first names.

"We're arranging for your transport to Archangel," Griffin said. "The Captain has us spotted anywhere we can catch the blokes as they come into town. There's a sleigh for you in the morning."

Then they caught sight of Morrie.

"Who's this chap?"

Jack explained that "Alex" was a friend, another Englishman headed for Archangel. In the dimly lit, ice-cold Soroka station, Morrie told his fictitious story of who he was and what he was doing in Russia one more time.

"Will there be room for me on the sleigh?" he asked.

"Plenty of room, plenty of room."

Jack asked them where they should spend the night, and where they would find the sleigh in the morning. Griffin said he would show them, while Fedders would stay in the station watching out for more stragglers.

They crunched through knee-high snow, led by Griffin with a lantern, for about two hundred yards.

"Here we are, gents," said Griffin.

They had reached a simple log hut. There was obviously a fire burning inside, and that meant warmth, and maybe even a place to sit or even lie down. There were three shallow steps up to the hut's door, but to Morrie it seemed like climbing a mountain. Someone opened the door, and Morrie could feel the glow of the fire in the stove at the center of the room. There was a Marine sergeant inside, who greeted Jack and Lawrence.

They introduced "Alex," and the sergeant asked him, with a little suspicion, Morrie thought, what a young and healthy Englishman was doing in the middle of the Russian wilds. Once more Morrie told his rehearsed story. The sergeant produced some hot chocolate from a pot on the stove and asked Jack and Larry about the train ride down. Morrie took off his heavy clothing and sank wearily onto one of the cots as the heat from the stove and the hot chocolate warmed him. He listened to the talk between the sergeant and his two friends, and heard them discuss the plans for the next morning.

There would be two sleighs. Morrie could ride in one, and Jack and Lawrence would ride together in the other.

"All right with you, Alex?" Jack called, and Morrie just waved his agreement. He was much too tired to talk about it.

They would have to be up early, because the Russians liked to start before the sun was up. They talked about how the driver would take them all the way to Archangel, and that made Morrie smile, for the idea of having to hire new sleighs and drivers along the way had always seemed perilous to him. There would be one flat fee. "What will be the cost?" asked Morrie. Three hundred rubles. Is that satisfactory, Alex?" Jack called again, and once more Morrie waved an arm to indicate approval.

Morrie didn't really know if he had three hundred rubles, but he would give them what he had and hope they took it. Right now he wasn't going to worry about it. Now there was only this lovely warmth and his exquisite cot.

The sergeant was talking some more. He had some supplies and would give them food to take along. They would be stopping twice for overnight stays, and at both places they would get hot meals. The sergeant cautioned them again about drinking any water except boiled water. He said it would be allright to drink soup, because that was boiled, and the famous Russian black bread was fine. Nothing wrong with the vodka, of course. They would have plenty of food with them.

Jack come over to where Morrie was dozing off and offered him a can of vodka. He took a drink, and that finished him off for the day. He fell into a sound sleep. It seemed like only a moment later the sergeant was shaking his shoulder.

"All right, young fellow, the time has come. The sleigh is outside already, so better rise and shine."

Morrie got up. He had fallen asleep with even his boots on, so he didn't have to dress. He splashed some water from a bucket onto his face, had some black bread and hot chocolate, and quickly gathered up his gear and went outside.

The moon, almost full, gave a silver sparkle to the snow outside the cabin. There was a gray haze in the East signaling the future arrival of the sun, and the shadows of the trees against the snow made beautiful patterns. Morrie looked around and saw the two sleighs, red and green, with two hulks that were evidently the drivers, and two horses standing quietly, their breath showing as sprays of steam. The Russians came over. They were both heavily bearded and smiled the same toothless smiles. Both had the high cheekbones that indicate a Mongol heritage.

The sergeant gave them money, including three hundred rubles that Morrie had given him. There was some argument, but the drivers accepted the money.

"He took it," the sergeant said, "but he said that's the last time he takes any Kerensky money."

Morrie walked to the sleigh that was going to be his. The driver helped him up into the seat and showed him how to fix the rough blanket around his legs. Then he climbed up next to him.

"This is going to be a long, cold, lonely ride," Morrie thought. "Nobody to talk to, nothing to read; just sit and hope the time goes as quickly as possible."

"*Dvigat!*" called both drivers, almost in chorus, and the horses reluctantly plunged into the heavy snow. Within a minute, the two sleighs were out of sight of any civilization. There must have been people there before to chop down enough trees to make the road on which they were traveling, but otherwise, Morrie could have been the first person in the history of the world to come this way.

Nothing but white birches, as far as he could see. From their sturdiest limbs hung icicles, making it all look like the interior of a cave, festooned with stalactites. The sky was invisible because of the trees. The darkness above gave way as the sun gradually came up.

The road meandered through slight hills and valleys, but there were no major inclines. There would be another sleigh, once in a great while, going in the opposite direction. The drivers would give each other bear hugs, briefly stopping to chat, and some delicately maneuvering to fit the sleighs past each other on the narrow road.

For a short while, the driver attempted to engage Morrie in conversation, but from Morrie's shrugs and embarrassed smiles, he quickly learned that this was an ignorant foreigner who couldn't speak the language. He therefore ignored Morrie for the balance of the trip.

It began to snow lightly and Morrie marveled at the silence that surrounded him. There was, of course, the steady squish-squish of the horse's hoofs in the deep snow, and the sound, almost like a hum, of the sleighs runners gliding along. All around were the trees and the snowflakes, and an occasional frozen lake, generally with one small hut next to it and a comforting plume of smoke coming from the hut's chimney.

Morrie occasionally risked taking off his gloves a few seconds to rummage in his bag for the chocolate bars. He would share them with the driver, who smiled one of those toothless smiles, mumbled "*spasibo*," and proceeded to mangle the chocolate with his gums.

Morrie dozed off a few times, because the ride was so smooth and so quiet that it was almost hypnotic. The cold, however, would soon awake him. He had to hold the blanket around his shoulders or it would slip off.

It was mid-afternoon when the driver nudged him and pointed ahead.

"Suma," he said. Morrie could see several plumes of smoke against the sky. They rounded a curve and there were six or seven log huts. The two sleighs stopped in front of one of them. The two horses were sweating but within five minutes after they stopped the sweat had frozen and the poor animals were covered in a thick sheet of ice. The foam from their mouths also froze, forming a series of icicles that dripped down. They tried to shake them off but were unable to dislodge them. Eventually the drivers went over to the horses and broke the icicles off.

It was difficult for Morrie and the two Marines to get down from the sleigh. Sitting in virtually the same position for so many hours, cramped and unable to move in the bitter cold, they had just about frozen in that position. Morrie forced himself to get up, but he was bent over at the waist and only gradually was able to straighten up. Jack and Lawrence were in the same physical state, and the three laughed at each other's awkwardness.

They walked around a few minutes, until they were able to loosen their joints, and then the drivers led them up a few steps and pounded on the door.

A tall man with a beard and unkempt hair opened the door but said nothing, merely beckoning them inside. Once inside, the bearded man said a few words to the drivers, who turned to the three Englishmen and held up seven fingers. Morrie found a ten ruble note in his hand and gave it to the bearded man. He put it in his wallet and gave Morrie three bills in change, of a kind Morrie had never seen before. It could have been old money {Imperial Czarist money}, or middle-aged money {Kerensky provisional money}, or new money {Bolshevik money}. Morrie didn't know, and at that point he didn't particularly care. The others also paid their seven rubles, apparently the going rate.

They all sat down on rough wooden chairs, dragging them close to the fire to enjoy the delicious process of thawing out.

The host, or who ever he was, put a big kettle on the shelf over the fireplace, which obviously also served as a stove. He added more birch branches to the fire and soon ladled out mugs of a thick, welcome soup.

"*Sup*," he said.

"This isn't going to be such a hard language to learn," Morrie said. "If 'soup' is '*sup*' it should be a pipe."

"That's the easy word," said Lawrence, who had been in Russia, off and on, for four years now, and had been trying very hard to learn to speak the language. "The rest is uphill all the way."

The road from Suma to Rikskla, their next stop, was basically the same as between Soroka and Suma. At one point the driver looked around. Everything seemed to be the same as it had been for hours, but he could apparently detect a difference.

"Litney," he said.

"What's that mean?" asked Morrie.

"It means we've reached the Litney peninsula," said Lawrence. He explained that the peninsula jutted out into the White Sea. Archangel was at the extreme eastern end of it.

Now the terrain gradually changed. There were more open fields between the stands of birches, and you could look up and see the sky. There were fewer hills, and the road was now virtually flat and straight. The sleighs were moving faster.

They came to an area where there was a large tin-roofed building, with heavy smoke coming from a tin chimney. The two Englishmen concluded that it was probably a saw mill, since there were piles of trees at one side. As they saw no workers, there didn't appear to be any activity.

Rikaskal was Suma all over again, except that this time the host was a woman, one of those typical Russian ladies, short, stout, and with a babushka permanently affixed to her iron- gray hair. This time, too, the cabin was larger and it even had an upstairs, a dormitory-like room where Morrie and the two Marines slept.

The woman had two little daughters, who were very curious about the visitors.

"*Americanski?*" they asked. "*Nyet,*" one of the drivers said. "*Anglaterri.*"

The little girls seemed disappointed. Apparently they had wanted to see an American, while an Englishman was not that much of a novelty. Their faces fell and they went about their duties. They served the cabbage soup and roast chicken dutifully but unenthusiastically.

"Alex," said Jack. The voice snapped him out of his dreary reverie. "You look like you're a million miles away."

"A thousand is more like it," said Morrie. "I was thinking of my folks back in England."

"I thought you said they were over here somewhere."

Morrie realized his mistake, and tried to cover it up. He said that, yes, they were here now, but he meant he had been thinking about the way it used to be when they had all lived back in London. Jack seemed to accept the correction.

The Russian lady sat down with them to eat, along with the two sleigh drivers. They carried on a conversation in Russian at one end of the table, while the three Englishmen chatted at the other end.

The only cross-conversation was tactical, such as "*Khleb pashalsta,*" which Morrie quickly understood, from the pointing finger, to mean, "bread, please."

Morrie asked his two new friends about Archangel, where they had both been stationed for some time. Jack, the more articulate of the two, said that the first glimpse of that city, when one reaches it via the sea, is fantastic.

"The water in the White Sea," he said, "is the bluest I've ever seen. I'd have to call it crystal blue, and clear. Why, you can see almost to the very bottom. Then you come into the river, the Dvina River, and it's like a fairyland. A narrow channel through a beautiful forest. We'll be approaching it this time from the land side, so we'll miss all that."

"We'll still see the cathedral." said Lawrence.

"Ah, yes, the cathedral. What a magnificent sight that is! It has those domes shaped like onions, four of them, and all in different colors, gold, green, white, and brownish. It's like something out of the Arabian nights. Now, though, I imagine it will all be covered with snow, but it'll still be spectacular."

The two Marines told Morrie that Archangel was immense, when compared to Murmansk. More than one hundred thousand people lived there. It was loaded with supplies and stores, shipped by the Allies to Russia when the country was still in the war. Now those supplies were just sitting there, and all the warring factions in Russia had their eyes on them.

"Last we heard," said Lawrence, "the Bols were in charge and they were shipping the supplies south, as fast as they could."

It was mid-morning, and they were encountering something new, traffic. They were obviously getting close to Archangel, and there were many sleighs, more and more huts, another saw mill, and people who always dropped whatever it was they were doing to wave at the passing sleighs. Morrie waved back.

They crossed a wooden bridge over a frozen river. This, Morrie realized, must be the Dvina which Jack had spoken about.

The sound of the horses' hoofs clip-clopping over the wood of the bridge was new. This was the first solid material they had encountered since Murmansk. They rounded a bend, and then Morrie caught his first glimpse of Archangel, lying in a bowl with the ocean at its back. He clearly could make out the dominant structure with its four domes, which must be the Archangel Cathedral.

As they drew closer, Morrie could see hundreds of barges tied up along the shore, with their cargoes covered with tarpaulins. Perhaps the Bolsheviks had already shipped a lot of supplies south, as the Marines had talked of last night, but there were plenty of supplies still there.

The sleighs deposited the three men at the British Consulate on the Trotsky Prospekt, which had been renamed since the revolution. The Russian drivers, as Morrie would learn, were very emotional. They gave their three passengers huge hugs and kissed them on both cheeks and on the lips, which the proper Englishmen found embarrassing. Somehow it struck a responsive chord in Morrie. His parents did that with their friends, and they hugged and kissed them back.

Morrie had his note from Hugh Martin, the American in Murmansk, addressed to Jim Anderson at the American Consulate. He had learned that the British and American Consulates were next door to each other. He told Jack and Lawrence that he would see if he could locate Anderson, but if he wasn't successful, he would come back and bunk with them until he found out what his next step would be.

The consulates were not prestigious buildings. Like most of Archangel's structures they were made of wood, and the American Consulate resembled nothing more than a Midwestern farm house, even having a large porch that circled the building. Morrie climbed up the few steps to the porch, scraped the snow off his boots on the iron snowscraper that was there for that purpose, and knocked on the door. There was an eagle painted on the door, and Morrie knocked right on the eagle's beak.

A Marine guard opened the door.

"Can I help you?" he asked. He repeated the same question in Russian before Morrie could reply.

"I'm looking for Jim Anderson, the passport control officer," said Morrie, and the Marine looked relieved. He wouldn't have to try to speak to this fellow in Russian.

"Upstairs. Second door on your left. Are you looking for a passport? You sound like a limey."

"No, at least not now. I just came in from Murmansk, and a friend of Mr. Anderson's there asked me to say hello for him."

"Come on in, it's open," said a hearty voice.

Morrie found himself facing a short, happy-faced man who looked hearty, just like his voice sounded. He was seated behind a desk covered with papers, stacks of passports, and folders.

"James Anderson," he said. "My friends call me Jim."

"I'm Alex Chernofsky. I have a message for you from Mr. Hugh Martin in Murmansk."

"Old Hugh? Well! How is the old goat?"

"He was fine when I saw him three days ago. He gave me this note to give to you."

"Sit down, sit down." Anderson cleared a pile of papers from the only other chair in the room and pulled it over in front of his desk. He put on a pair of glasses to read the note.

"Well, Alex, it seems like you're in a spot of a jam, as you English blokes say."

"Yes, sir, Mr. Anderson." "Jim, call me Jim." "Okay, Jim. I sure am in a spot of a jam. I'm hoping you can give me some advice."

Anderson asked for the particulars of Morrie's difficulties, and Morrie trotted out his usual story. He toyed with the idea of telling Jim Anderson the truth, but he was still too frightened. After all, he didn't know this man that well, and despite his hearty exterior, he could have the interior of a typical minor functionary. He could then turn Morrie over to the British authorities as a fugitive from British justice, or simply be so outraged at the bald fact of his desertion that he would refuse to help. Morrie, believing in discretion, told his familiar old yarn about his parents.

"I'll have to give your problem some damned serious thought, Alex," he said. "Sleep on it, as matter of fact. Meanwhile, you can stay here, at least tonight. We have plenty of rooms in this barn. Why don't you go upstairs now, have a nice hot bath, and be back down for dinner at seven in the dining room."

Bath! That prospect filled Morrie with joy. The idea of being able to take all his clothing off at the same time seemed like something out of paradise.

"Sounds wonderful," he said. "I haven't had a proper bath since I left England."

He began to think that perhaps this whole experience might turn out to be positive, an adventure, a lark. Reality then set in. He realized that he couldn't spend the rest of his life soaking in a tub. At some point, he would have to get up, dry off, and face the fact that he was still a man without a country, without a destination, without funds.

Yet there was a funny side to it. Back in London there had been no bathtub in the Stepney Green flat, just a big iron pot that you had to stand up and sponge yourself off in, one leg at a time. Here he was, an exile, luxuriating in the world's greatest bathtub. He lay back and enjoyed it a few more minutes, then got out feeling like a very new man.

He shaved, washed, and dressed in the best clothes his meager wardrobe provided actually- his only clothes- and went downstairs. Anderson was waiting, decanter at the ready, and introduced Morrie to American bourbon whiskey. Morrie said how much he liked it, but in truth he found it raw compared to the Scotch Whiskey he knew from home.

There was another man there. Anderson introduced him as Felix Cole, stressing the fact that he was "a Harvard man." Morrie didn't know what that meant, but gathered from the way Anderson said it that it was a good thing. "Cole has been in several U.S. Consulates around Russia for five years." He knows the situation here better than anybody else. I asked him to join us for dinner, figuring that maybe he could give you some sound advice."

"Thanks. I need all the advice I can get."

During dinner they talked about the general situation. They were curious about Morrie's trip from Murmansk and wanted to know everything he could tell them about the political conditions there. They also asked about Hugh Martin and the others. But the subject of Morrie's plight was never opened.

The three men moved into the library, where Anderson and Cole lit up big, black cigars. Morrie declined when they offered him one, then finally Anderson asked Felix Cole if he had any suggestions for Morrie.

"I gather you can't go back to England," Cole said. Morrie nodded. "That would be the best and fastest thing, but if you can't, you can't. So we'll skip that."

"You could stay here until June, when the thaw comes, but that's about three months away. There's no work to be found here, and besides, the Reds might get the idea you should be in their Army. After all, being a Russian-born person and all, if they get you, they've got you."

Cole digressed and started talking about how the Reds were plundering the stores that the Allies had sent to Archangel. He had a remarkable memory, and rattling off facts and figures about how many guns, how many bullets, and how much barbedwire fencing and other supplies the Russians had filched.

"Let's stick to the subject, Felix," Anderson said, mildly, and Cole laughed and got back on track.

"You know, Alex, this city is full of odds and ends like yourself, no offense, people who are drifting around and have no place to go. I ran into a bunch of Lithuanians who had been working in Scotland in the coal mines. If you've never heard Russian spoken with a Scottish brogue, you just haven't lived. Some of these poor rascals had married Scottish girls. Just like you, they had to come back here because they were born here. They told me the only thing they could do was join the Army, the Lithuanian Army. However they couldn't find it. I think they couldn't find it because there certainly isn't a Lithuanian Army here, that's for sure."

Cole paused.

"Mr. Cole," Morrie said.

"Call me Felix."

"Okay Felix, what do you think I should do? What would you do if you were in my shoes?"

"Do you have any relatives in Russia, other than your parents?"

"No, our family wasn't very large. My father has a sister who is living in St. Louis, America."

"You should try to get to St. Louis, but you can't get there from here. I don't mean to be making jokes, but that's the God's honest truth."

"Where should I go?"

Cole got up and pulled out a big map. He pointed to a spot at one side. "This is where we are now, Archangel."

He unrolled the map to its fullest extension and pointed to another spot at the opposite side.

"You have no choice. You have to go there. Vladivostok."

Cole explained, and Anderson nodded his agreement, that European Russia was a mess and likely to get worse before it got better. He predicted that there would be a lot of bloodshed before the sticky problems of who was to run this vast country would be resolved.

"Go East, young man," he said. "Go to Siberia."

"Siberia! Salt mines and Russian prisons, that's all I know about Siberia."

"Actually, there's a lot more to Siberia than that," said Cole. "It's really a pretty nice place in the spring and summer. The political situation there is sort of tangled but it's spread out more. I believe you can make it to Vlad if you follow the railroad across Siberia.

"There's the Czech Legion somewhere out there." He pointed on the map to the mid-Siberian section. "There is talk that they are going to Vladivostok so they can get a ship and get back to the Western front and fight. They may be going to Vlad figuring it might be easier to get to the Western Front by going all the way around the world rather than trying to cross Russia these days. There are a bunch of autonomous armies like Semenov's, the Whites, the Reds and God knows what all."

"And you think I can get across there?"

"Sure we do," said Anderson. "After all, it's only five thousand miles of emptiness, a bunch of wolves, and a lot of nuts shooting at each other. A piece of cake."

Anderson got out another map. This, he explained, was a map showing, according to the latest intelligence, who controlled what in Russia and Siberia today. The territory controlled by the Reds was marked in red, a triumph of bureaucratic logic, and the territory controlled by the Whites was in white.

"It looks like a bed sheet with the measles," said Cole.

The map was basically white with many red splotches of varying sizes. Cole pointed out the thin black line that was the Trans-Siberian railroad. That, he said, was how Morrie should make his way across Siberia. "Some of it is controlled by the Reds, and some by the Whites."

"That's all very approximate," said Cole. "Besides, it changes from day to day. We really don't know who's running things along the railroad."

"How would I get through all that?"

"Use your wits, young fellow. They got you this far. Even if that story of yours is true- and I'm not saying it's not- it indicates a degree of self-reliance. I suggest you can use that same self-reliance to take you to Vladivostok."

Chapter Five

Morrie, Anderson, and Cole talked well into the night over cigars, brandy, and maps. All the names and figures and information buzzed around in Morrie's head like a swarm of summer flies. He wasn't sure if he should avoid Vologda or go to Vologda, whether he should try to hook up with the Czech Legion or run away when he saw them, or whether the Whites were the good guys or the bad guys.

He went to bed totally confused, but happy from the good food, good drink and good fellowship. He woke up the next morning and the confusion remained. Also remaining was Cole's intimation that Morrie's story was false.

He found the two men, Anderson and Cole, sitting around the dining room table again. The maps were out as they had been when he had retired.

"As I was saying, Alex," said Cole, as though he was picking up a thread of conversation from a moment before, "get yourself to Vologda and then go all the way across Siberia on the Trans-Siberian to Vladivostok. It's the only thing to do."

"I don't give a damn who you are or what you are doing here," said Cole. "None of my business, officially, since you aren't an American. All I know is you are a nice young fellow ,and I like you, but that story of yours is so transparent. Really, you'd better get yourself a new one."

Jim Anderson laughed. Morrie didn't know what to say, so he said nothing.

"There are thousands of people like you in Russia today," Cole went on. "Thousand of people without passports or papers of any kind, and thousands of stories to tell about why and how they got here. Yours is absolutely the worst but I really don't care one way or the other. The big problem, as I see it, is what you should do now, and I think what I've been suggesting is the only sensible answer."

So they sat down again, pouring over the maps. This time they drank tea and ate a typical American ham-and-eggs breakfast. Cole drew a thick, black line on the map. "This is Vologda, the western terminus of the Trans-Siberian railroad. It's technically not the Trans-Siberian at all. The actual official western terminus is Omsk. The line from Vologda to Omsk, via Viatka and Perm, is considered by most of us to be really part of the Trans-Siberian."

He told Morrie how to get to Vologda, and from there to make for Omsk and head east on the Trans-Siberian to Vladivostok.

"With your gift of gab and your personality, and a little bit of luck, it should be a cinch. The weather should turn better in a month or so."

Once in Vladivostok, what do I do then? Morrie asked himself that question, but then pushed it back into a far corner of his mind.

The waiters cleared the dishes from the table, and the map alone remained. The distance, five thousand miles, seemed too vast to grasp. Morrie remembered hearing somebody once say that a journey of a thousand miles begins with a single step. That was a charming philosophy, but this was a time for facing up to some hard, cold facts. Five thousand miles was a very long way.

"I thank you for what you say about my gift of gab and my personality, Mr. Cole," he said. "I have practically no money and I don't speak the language. There are people shooting at each other where I'm going and to be honest about it, I'm scared."

The red and white splotches on the map seemed to dance before his eyes, forming menacing shapes. One of them suddenly looked like a fist, and another took on the form of a rifle pointed at him.

"It's natural to be scared," said Jim Anderson, "but you can do it. Just take it one step at a time. Don't think that you are going from Archangel to Vladivostok all at once. Think about it as a trip from Archangel to

Vologda, then from Vologda to Ekaterinburg, Ekaterinburg to Omsk, and so on. Step by step by step."

"The first step," Cole chimed in, "is to get to Vologda. When you get there, check in at our Embassy. I gather you have no burning desire to check in with your own Embassy for reasons that are none of my business. We have some people there, friends of mine, who will help you and won't ask too many questions."

They asked him how much money he had. He emptied his wallet and his pockets, laying out a small pile of crumpled paper money of various colors, some Imperial, some Kerensky, and some Bolshevik-issued money. Cole rifled through the pile for a few seconds, and with his sharp mind he quickly calculated that Morrie was about four hundred rubbles short of what he would need to get to Vologda.

"What will we do about that, Jim?" Cole asked Anderson.

"Do you think we could spare one of the passes?"

"Why not? Look, Alex, here's the deal."

He explained that they had several passes for the railroad run between Archangel and Vologda. They could let Morrie use one to get to Vologda, providing he turned it into the American Embassy when he got there. Morrie quickly agreed.

Morrie spent the rest of the day wandering aimlessly around Archangel. It was one of those rare winter days when the sun was out and its rays sparkled on the brilliance of the white snow that covered the city. Children were out playing, building snowmen, and pelting each other with snowballs.

It was a pleasant day for him, and he had a pleasant thought to go with the day. He realized that not once since he had been in Russia, mingling primarily with Americans, had anyone asked him what his religion was or made any reference to his being Jewish. The word "Jew" had never been uttered in his presence. Perhaps all those things he had heard about America and its tolerance and equality were true.

He went back to the Consulate in the evening for dinner, bursting with this new found love for his fellow man. He was perhaps too emotional about it, too effusive, in telling Anderson and Cole about how much he appreciated their hospitality to a total stranger.

"Thanks, but don't make such a big deal out of it," said Anderson.

"Big deal?" Morrie hadn't heard that expression before. They explained what it meant, and he liked the sound of it. It was so typically American in its ring.

They told him that the train for Vologda would leave the day after tomorrow; that gave him another day in Archangel. Anderson said that things were slow at the Consulate with the port still frozen. There wasn't anything for a passport control officer to do, so he'd like to show Morrie the sights, such as they were. Morrie protested that he didn't want to take up his time, but Anderson said it would be fun for him.

"I don't want to make a big deal out of it, so thanks," said Morrie, and it sounded funny, even to him, because American slang never sounded exactly right with a British accent.

Before he left the next morning, Morrie had a chance to go to the British Consulate, where he found Jack and Lawrence, his traveling companions from Murmansk. He told them that he would be leaving. They were friends who had shared an adventure, and that automatically qualified people for old friendship status.

"If you ever get to Manchester, look me up," said Jack.

"That goes twice for me, in Leeds," said Lawrence.

"And you fellows look me up too," said Morrie.

"Where?"

"If I knew that, I'd be there now," said Morrie.

Jim Anderson had a sleigh with a Russian driver. Anderson, as they drove, gave Morrie some details about the city as though he were an official with the Chamber of Commerce. The population had climbed from thirty-five before the War to the current figure of approximately one hundred and twenty thousand. Everything for all those people to eat had to be shipped in and stored when the port was open, for there was no farming in the Archangel vicinity. There were some cows, for milk, and some hens, for eggs, but nothing was grown. The soil just never thawed to that extent.

The streets all had wood- plank strips down the middle. That was to give the pedestrian a bit of breathing space during the spring thaw, when the streets were ribbons of mud.

Now, in March, the streets were frozen solid, and so was the river. Anderson told the driver to take them to Solombola, an island in the middle of the Dvina. There was a summer bridge across the river to Solombola, but it was taken down in the winter because when the river was frozen it was simpler to just walk, ride, or drive across.

Morrie had developed a slight cold. "Welcome to the club," said Anderson, "you've got the Czar's revenge." It was too much work to dig through all the layers of heavy clothing he had on to reach his handkerchief, so he sniffed and dripped. He found that a small icicle had formed at the tip of his nose. Quickly, he knocked it off, but it took a bit of skin with it, and he inadvertently said, "Ouch!" Anderson realized what had happened and laughed.

"Don't give it a second thought," he said. Everyone in Russia during winter has raw skin at the end of their nose from knocking off icicles. That's how they can tell who the newcomers are, because the newcomers don't have a raw spot. So it looks like you've become an old-timer already."

The two drove all over Archangel, with Anderson acting like a tour guide for the curious young Englishman. The most beautiful sight in the city was its glorious cathedral. It had four domes, snow-covered now, but with slender icicles hanging down. It looked like one of these fancy birthday cakes that Morrie used to see in the bakery shop windows in the West End of London.

Anderson drove to a smaller city across the river, about two miles further upstream. This was Bakaritsa, which was actually where most of the cargo from overseas had been unloaded. There were rows and rows and piles and piles of crates and boxes sitting under tarpaulins, covered with snow. Obviously, even after the Bolsheviks had taken so much war material, a great deal remained. Anderson led Morrie through the immense store-yard of goods, and Morrie could see that the crates had come from all the Allied nations. They contained everything from rifles to gas masks to mess kits.

As they walked, three pony carts trotted up and the three drivers began loading boxes into them.

"God damn Bols," muttered Anderson.

Apparently there were no guards and nobody was sure to whom all the supplies belonged. The Bolsheviks took the goods without any fear. Maybe when all was said and done the goods belonged to them anyhow. Nobody knew. Nobody cared.

They didn't seem to know or care what it was they were taking either. They indiscriminately loaded a few boxes on each of the carts, then trotted off.

"God damn Bols," Anderson muttered again only louder. He muttered all the way back to the Consulate. He was, ordinarily a cheerful man, Morrie had learned in their brief acquaintanceship, but the Bolshevik thievery brought on a black mood. He glowered through dinner but then, magically, his good nature returned over the brandy and cigars portion of the meal.

"Your train leaves at nine tomorrow morning," said Felix Cole. "A couple of men from the Consulate staff will also be going to Vologda. You might as well all go together. You'll have a little company for the trip. "Okay with you?"

It was better then okay with Morrie, it was marvelous news. He was still a little afraid of the unknown, and surely there was nothing more unknown to him than traveling across Russia alone. Cole called the two men in to meet Morrie. Bob Newman was a very tall, very thin, very bald young man. Jerry White was shorter, chunkier, and had a big, bristling black mustache. They talked a while, then everybody went to bed, arranging to meet at breakfast the next morning.

Over the breakfast of eggs and ham, Anderson gave Morrie the pass and again impressed on him the need of returning it in Vologda. He could give it to either Bob or Jerry after he got off the train. Cole gave him his business card and suggested that in Vologda he look up a couple of his friends at the U.S. Embassy, writing their names on the back of the card. Morrie realized that he had been traveling on luck so far, that everyone he met had helped him move along and had always forwarded him on to someone else.

The first step was another sleigh ride, from the Consulate to the station with his new friends. Morrie said his good-byes to Jim Anderson and Felix Cole, thanking them for their help. The weather was bitter cold, with a north wind bringing snow flurries down from the Arctic. The sleigh driver was busily chipping icicles off his beard when Morrie, Bob, and Jerry climbed aboard and wrapped blankets around their legs.

The sleigh passed the British Consulate, and Morrie looked wistfully at the Union Jack flapping in the fierce north wind. Every day was taking him further and further from his homeland, and he wondered if he would ever see London again. Well, for the time being he couldn't think about that. All he could concentrate on was surviving, step by step. That would become his motto, the rallying cry of his spirit.

The Archangel railroad station was one of the few structures in the city built of stone. It was a busy place, with many people moving through, all wearing heavy fur coats and fur hats.

The Vologda train was in the station, its engine wheezing steam. The three men ran from the sleigh through the station and climbed aboard the train. The seats were wooden and without any upholstery at all. It would be a long trip. Morrie noticed that the Russians all sat on their fur hats, which gave them a small substitute for a cushion. He quickly did the same. They all kept on their heavy coats, as the car was unheated, so he did the same. Morrie was beginning to think like a Russian.

Bob said he had often made the trip from Archangel to Vologda and back, as he was the Embassy courier. He had memorized the names of all the stations between the two cities. He explained that the trip would take about one day, depending on whether they had to stop for the crew to shovel away snow from a landslide. It wasn't exactly a pleasure trip.

"No dining cars on Russian trains," he said. "You have to jump off when it stops. There are people out selling food. You have to jump off quickly, run over to one of these people, buy some food, and jump back on again. People have been left waiting for their change."

He told Morrie that the Russian measure of distance was a *verst*, which was almost exactly a mile and a half. The distance between Archangel and Vologda was 267 *verst*, or around four hundred miles. He suggested that they plan on their first meal at Yemtsa, about four hours away. It was a good lunch station, he said, both because the timing was right and because the stop there was a bit longer than usual. They wouldn't have to race so fast.

The windows were dirty and quickly fogged over, so Morrie could see very little of the passing scenery. Bob and Jerry wanted to know his story. It was, they said, unusual to find a young Englishman "bumming around" in Russia during wartime.

Morrie wondered what story to tell. Since Felix Cole had been so dubious, maybe the story he had been telling needed some work. He had thought about perhaps making up a totally new yarn, but he couldn't actually come up with anything that made better logic. So he told Bob and Jerry the old one and was gratified when they seemed to accept it. Perhaps, he thought to himself, Felix Cole was just one of those people who doubted everything. He would stick to his story. He had told it so many times he almost believed it himself.

Bob called out the stations as they passed them. He really didn't have to rub the frost off the window. He seemed to know them simply by the time.

Tsakogorka.

Tundra.

Kholmogorskaya.

Oboserskaya.

Bob said that Yemtsa would be the next stop after they pulled out of Oboserskaya. That was lunch, and Morrie was getting hungry. Bob briefed Morrie and Jerry on what their tactics should be at the station. It was apparently a very tricky bit of business getting lunch at a Russian railroad station.

"When we get close," Bob said, "we'll move to the door. You have to be off first or the line gets too long. I'll do the chicken. Jerry will be the soup. Alex, since this is your first time, you'll get the easiest job, you'll be the hard-boiled eggs. Whoever gets finished first gets the bread. We then run back to the train. Whoever gets back first gets the tea."

They waited a little while longer, then Bob said, "Now" They casually got up. "Do it slowly, we don't want to start a stampede." Bob moved nonchalantly toward the door. There were a few others waiting in front of them.

The train stopped. Bob led the way, glancing both ways and quickly sizing up the situation.

"Jerry, soup is the green babushka over there. Alex, the egg lady is the brown babushka by that pole. Bread is blue. See you guys back on the train."

Morrie spotted the brown babushka and raced off. He was third in line. He held up six fingers and she gave him six eggs in a little pail. Bob had told him the procedure. He took the pail, then transferred the eggs one by one to his pockets. The man behind him was grumbling, and a grumble in any language is the same. Morrie knew he was being chided for being too slow. He gave the lady back the pail and gave her the money that Bob had said would be enough to pay for six eggs. She turned up her nose at it.

"*Mnogo dyengi!*" she screamed.

The man behind him grumbled louder and started to poke Morrie in the back. The woman behind the man was also yelling. The whole line was obviously upset. Morrie dug into his pockets to find his wallet. He got another bill. He didn't know how much it represented but offered it to the egg lady.

She shrugged and took it. The shrug was eloquent. It spoke of insufficiency, but of discretion. Better to take it, she was saying, then spend precious time haggling when there were many more customers waiting in line, and not another train until tomorrow.

Morrie ran off to the blue babushka for bread, but Jerry was already there. He made a sharp right turn and headed back to the train. Morrie was the first one there, so he went up to the tea lady with three glasses and came back with the tea. Bob was there with four chickens. "We'll save one for a snack later on." Jerry had three pots of thick soup full of barley, and with the eggs and bread it was a good meal. They had barely resumed their seats when the train chugged off. Somehow all the passengers made it back onto the train, although several hadn't had time to buy any food and looked longingly at the feast Morrie and his friends were having. Morrie and the two others pretended not to notice.

Morrie hopped off at each station during the long afternoon's ride to get some air and stretch his legs. He was intrigued to watch the way the railroad personnel operated. Three or four workers on the platform hurriedly loaded birch logs onto the car immediately behind the engine, with the engineer loudly directing them in the manner he wanted them stacked. There was always an imperious looking official, with his green flag, directing all the operations and telling the engineer when he should depart. Each station had its complement of venders, usually selling chickens and bread and eggs, but occasionally more exotic foods.

An incredible assortment of ethnic types were aboard the train. Orientals of many sorts, from a few who were obviously Chinese to some who, Morrie believed, must be pure Mongol. The babble of various languages and various Russian dialects was loud and incessant. Morrie realized that the English he and his friends were speaking contributed greatly to that babble.

Shalakusha.

Shozhma.

Nyandoma.

Vadysh.

The afternoon wore on. Jerry, Bob, and Morrie wore out the usual subjects of conversation and inevitably started to discuss the war. This was increasingly fascinating to Morrie because he was now finding himself in the middle of a fermenting stew of national and international politics.

"I really don't understand all this business of Reds and Whites and all that," said Morrie. "I guess I've been like an ostrich with my head stuck in the ground, but I just don't know what's going on out there. Could you please explain it to me?"

Bob was delighted with the chance to expound. He hoped to be a university history professor back in the United States, and this was a marvelous opportunity to give his first lecture to the class he dreamed of teaching, History 11: Introduction to Modern European History.

"It's complicated," he said. "Remember that it all began with two events that happened in the long view of history almost simultaneously. Russia's disastrous participation in the Great War, and the Russian Revolution."

The Great War began in 1914, I know that, Morrie thought to himself, but this is a long ride so I'll just let him talk. Russia joined the Allies to fight the evil Kaiser, but, despite a few victories, in general they were soundly defeated by the German forces and lost, according to the most recent reports that Bob had read, one million men.

The Russian Revolution erupted in March of 1917, by which time the Russian Army was, to all intents and purposes, out of the war against Germany. Kerensky took over for a while, but then the Bolsheviks gained control. "I'm oversimplifying here," said Bob, "but it's too complicated to go into great detail. They negotiated the Treaty of Brest-Litovsk, which was just signed a few days ago. The news arrived last week. It has officially ended the Russian participation in the Great War."

"But it didn't end the fighting in Russia, or Russia's agony." Bob continued. "The Germans invaded the Ukraine, but they will probably withdraw now that the Brest-Litovsk treaty has been signed. There are Russian units still loyal to the Czar that are offering pockets of resistance to the Bolsheviks. They're called the White Russians. They are refusing to accept the Bolshevik's rule and they are being helped by the Allies, who still harbor the forlorn hope of getting Russia back into the Great War. They hope to keep an Eastern Front operating and thus relieve pressure on the Western Front."

Bob said he expected that the Allied help to the Whites would continue and grow more and more open in the months, and maybe years, to come.

"The situation is further complicated by the Czech Legion and the various bands of autonomous Russians like the ones led by Semenov, who is fast becoming a folk hero. They had never really been subjugated by the Czar and certainly would not pledge allegiance to the Bolsheviks."

"We are living on the pages of history," said Bob, and Jerry applauded. Bob realized he had gone from lecturing to outright pedantry, and he had the decency to blush and apologize.

"I'm sorry. I got carried away. The fact is that what I said is absolutely true. I don't know what's going to happen to this country. I don't know if the Bolsheviks will be able to unify it and turn it into a major power. I just know it will be fascinating to watch and see what happens."

He turned to Morrie. "I envy you, in a way," he said. "Where you're going, Siberia, is where it's going to happen. Oh, the center will be Moscow or Petrograd, but it is how the Siberian peasants react that will determine whether or not the Bols can survive and take charge of things. You'll be on the front line."

They would, from time to time, go up and refill their tea glasses. Jerry taught Morrie the Russian way of drinking tea, holding a lump of sugar between the teeth and straining the tea through the sugar. It was a tricky technique to learn. Morrie dropped a lot of sugar and swallowed a lot of unsweetened tea before he mastered it.

Bob continued to know exactly where they were with no more than a quick glance out of the window, after first rubbing away the accumulated frost.

Konosha.

Luktonga.

Vozhega.

Punduga.

The next stop, Kharovskaya, would be their last chance to get food, Bob said. There would then be three more stations, Semigorodil, Morzhenga, and Sukhona, before Vologda.

At Kharvoskaya they repeated their battle station technique of getting food, with the same productive results. This time, instead of chicken, there was stew. Bob had anticipated that possibility and had equipped himself with tea glasses with which to carry the stew back onto the train.

Morrie found himself speaking Russian, or at least enough Russian to purchase two loaves of bread. "*Dva khelp, pashalsta,*" that gave him a good feeling.

It was still dark when they reached Vologda. Bob and Jerry insisted that Morrie come with them to the Embassy, where he could at least stay a day or so. He gave them the precious pass. It had become something of a joke because Bob Anderson and Felix Cole had so often reminded him not to forget to return it, and they made a production out of accepting it.

As he got off the train, Morrie felt that there was a change in the weather. It was cold, but not the knife-edge cold that he had experienced in Murmansk and Archangel. He didn't even put on his gloves as he walked with Bob and Jerry along the train platform.

Two of the Embassy staff members were there with a large sleigh to meet Bob and Jerry. They introduced Morrie to Earl Johnston, he was the Ambassador's personal secretary, and Philip Jordan, who was identified as the Secretary of the Embassy. They both shook Morrie's hand heartily.

"What brings you here, Mr. Chernofsky?" asked Jordan. Should he go into his song-and-dance and tell The story? He was too tired for all those details and the inevitable questions.

"Just traveling around," he said, and let it got at that.

Jordan looked at him strangely but didn't say anything. He might ask later, but that would do for now.

Johnston told his friends that he had hoped to meet them in the Ambassador's new Ford, the first and only automobile in Vologda, but there was still too much snow on the streets for the car to navigate. He said he couldn't wait until the thaw.

"We'll make the Russkis eyes pop when they see that car," said Johnson.

For about a half-hour, they drove through the quiet of the early dawn, and Morrie had the impression of a fair-sized city, full of wooden houses and wooden sidewalks. The Embassy, when they reached it, was also wooden. It was something like the Consulate in Archangel, only on a larger scale. It, too, had a porch around it, which gave off an impression of informality.

Inside there was a brass samovar, and all of the men went immediately and poured themselves a glass of tea. Only then did they begin to talk.

"How was the trip?" Johnston asked.

"The best kind. Uneventful," said Bob.

The four old friends talked on, and Morrie tried to listen. The Yank slang and dry intonation, coupled with the fact that he was very tired, made it all seem like a not- too- intelligible buzz. He let it go past him while he pondered his next move.

Morrie realized that he had been lucky, very lucky, since he first set foot in Russia. He had met good and kind people who had helped him, passing him along from Murmansk to Archangel and now to Vologda. He had just passively gone along with the current. It was, in fact, almost as though he were a twig being carried along in a rapidly flowing stream. But now the twig was caught behind a rock and if it was to go any further it would have to generate its own power.

"Hey, Alex!"

He realized that they had been trying to get through to him while he was considering his plight.

"Sorry, I was daydreaming."

"Have something to eat."

They had brought in baskets of good Russian black bread and crocks of *masla*, the thick, creamy, and very yellow Russian-style butter. They told him that the *masla* was made locally, and they all said it was the best butter in the entire civilized world.

Jordan and Johnston were curious about the war situation in London, and asked questions of Morrie as though he were the Prime Minister. They wanted to know all about the war budget, the allocation of troops, and what effect the Zeppelin bombings were having on civilian morale. Morrie tried to answer, but they wanted details, and all he could give them were his personal impressions.

"Come on, give the kid a break," said Bob. "He's not part of His Majesty's government, you know, he's just a kid. Look at the poor guy, he's three-quarters asleep already."

They let him go to bed. There wasn't room in the Embassy itself, so Morrie, together with Bob and Jerry, were given rooms in Earl Johnston's house, a three-minute walk away. Johnston explained that it was one of several houses the American government had rented from the Bolsheviks, who had confiscated them from the wealthy men who had owned them before the revolution. Johnson's house had belonged to a big lumber merchant. The Embassy personnel used the houses for sleeping, but they all ate together at the Embassy mess.

When Morrie woke up he had the house to himself. He washed and dressed and there was a full-length mirror in the bedroom that had evidently once belonged to Mrs. Lumber Merchant. Morrie had the time and facilities to take a long look at himself for the first time since he had been imprisoned.

"My God, how I've changed," he said to himself. The young square-basher was gone. Instead there stood what looked to Morrie's prejudiced eyes like a dashing soldier of fortune. He had his long coat, given to him by the Pentonville Prison authorities, and the big heavy boots. His English cap was covered by the Russian fur hat he had acquired in Murmansk.

"I bet they bloody well wouldn't recognize me in London," he said to himself. He was pleased with his appearance, with his look of adventure and bravado.

He walked back to the Embassy. There had been a snow storm the previous night, and the cold front had sent temperatures falling. The snow crunched under his feet as he made his way along the clear, cold Vologda streets.

When Morrie walked in Bob was the only one in the mess. Morrie learned that his plight had apparently been the main topic of conversation at the Embassy all day. The idea of a young Englishman about to make his way across Siberia was, in itself, unusual enough to be captivating. Bob didn't say it in so many words, but the intimation was clear. They all suspected him of running from something, although they weren't sure from what. They sympathized with him because they all liked him.

"The problem with crossing Siberia right now," said Bob, "is that the political situation is in a state of flux. Both Earl and Phil say that there is absolutely no way of knowing if the trains are running all the way across. Maybe the Czech Legion has destroyed the tracks, nobody knows. The Whites may be in control, or maybe the Bols. You're just going to have to take a chance, that's all."

Bob went over to a map hanging lopsided on the wall. He pointed to Vologda.

"This is where we are now," he said. "This little black line is the railroad. See, it goes from here to Viatka, then Perm, Ekaterinburg, and then Omsk. That's where it joins the railroad from Moscow, and that's where the Trans-Siberian railroad officially commences."

It was about seventeen hundred miles from Vologda to Omsk and then thrty-nine hundred more across Siberia from Omsk to Vladivostok.

"Blimey," said Morrie. "How am I going to get there?"

Once again the whole thing seemed foolhardy, insurmountable. Step by step by step.

"It's all so confused out there," said Bob, pointing at the central and western extremities of the map, "that if you keep your wits about you, you'll make it."

"But it's just so...."

"Yeah, it is, isn't it? Look, Alex, all the others will be here for dinner, and afterwards we'll all figure out some ways to help you. We're on your side."

Morrie felt good again. His emotions were on a roller-coaster ride. Left alone, where he could brood about the future, he was depressed. But when people like Bob Newman were there to lift his spirits and encourage him, he felt like a soldier of fortune, the grand adventurer he had seen in the mirror.

It seemed to be fashionable among the English and Americans in Russia at the time to consider the Bolsheviks as objects of derision. The consensus of opinion was that they could not possibly stay in power very long. They had no experience in the art of governing people, and certainly the Russian people just now would be very difficult to control. They had just thrown over their oppressive rulers and expected immediate results. The Bolsheviks would be lucky to maintain power, let alone institute any real reforms, as they had to fight the Whites as well as all the other sovereign rebels.

The men talked about an absent colleague, a man named Raymond Robbins, who was the American Red Cross chief in Moscow. Morrie gathered from their conversation that Robbins was the one who was most willing to give the Bolsheviks a chance. He thought they might, just might, be able to consolidate their rule and wind up in control.

"Hey, that reminds me," said Jerry White, bringing Morrie into the conversation again. "Didn't you say that the Red Cross guys helped you up in Murmansk?"

"Yes. The Red Cross helped me, and also the Y.M.C.A. people. I'd probably be frozen stiff in a snowbank up there by now if it wasn't for them."

"Red Cross or Y.M.C.A. same difference. They're your ticket to Vladivostok. They're both working on the trains along the Trans-Siberian tracks, helping people, bringing them food and medical help. Chocolate, cigarettes, boots, that sort of thing. You should be able to hitch a ride with them because their cars are attached to the regular Trans-Siberian trains."

"How do I contact them?"

Jerry suggested they all adjourn to the lounge, with their tea and cigars, and hash over Morrie's predicament. Jerry, full of admiration for the Y.M.C.A., told Morrie something about the organization, and particularly about its place in Russian history.

"They've been in Russia since 1900, first as the American Young Men's Association before it changed to its present name. There were four hundred staffers in Russia at the height of the war. They were primarily helping prisoners of war, but when the U.S. entered the war, they began a more active role, assisting the Russian Army. The Russian government of Kerensky had given the Y a special charter, allowing them free access to any railroad in the country, and exempting them from having to pay import duty on material they brought into Russia."

Jerry said that he admired them tremendously and felt that Morrie would be in good hands if he could travel with them. The others joined in to echo that sentiment.

Inevitably, they brought out a map. It seemed to Morrie as though no conversation in Russia these days could be held without looking at a map, preferably one with all those red and white blotches.

Earl Johnston was the evening's expert. He said that they really didn't know what was going on out there. He gestured to the vast expanse east of Omsk, saying that from reports filtering back it was a genuine mess.

"The thing is," he said, "the Allies are trying to get the Russkis back into the war, but right now they are acting like they don't want any part of it. Can't say I blame them, but it sure would be a big help to us and to the Limeys. No offense, Alex."

The latest result of the Brest-Litovsk treaty, said Johnston, was that the Russians had just last week freed all the prisoners of war they were holding in Siberia. Now all of them were traveling west on the railroad, while the Czech Legion was going east. The Germans—most of the ex-prisoners were German and Austrian—hated the Czechs, and the favor was returned, so here and there skirmishes were being fought along the railroad."

"That's in addition to all the problems there were before," Johnston continued. "Another thing is that the Bolsheviks keep changing their minds. One day they issue orders allowing the poor Czechs to proceed east to Vlad, then the next day those orders are countermanded and the Czechs are not allowed to move. I guess the Bols keep appointing new people, starting up new bureaus. They are great ones for bureaucracy, so one day Comrade Lenin says the Czechs can go, but the next day Comrade Trotsky is in charge and he says no."

Bob Newman added that he had a hunch that before long there would be Allied soldiers in Siberia, and naturally they would be along the railroad somewhere. After all, virtually everything in Siberia was along the railroad—ninety percent of the people, the industry, and the natural resources.

"If the British and Americans and French land in Vladivostok," he said, "and start moving west along the railroad, and the Bolsheviks try to stop them, there's going to be a helluva battle somewhere out there. If you're lucky, Alex, you may be right in the middle of it."

Newman wasn't being sarcastic. He wished he could be part of a battle, and he particularly wanted to fight Bolsheviks and Germans. It looked to him as though Siberia would be the site for that classic confrontation. The good guys, the Allies, versus the bad guys, the Germans and Bolsheviks.

Morrie wasn't particularly keen on the notion that he might be heading into a major battle.

"It won't happen that soon," said Johnston. "We still need all the troops we have on the Western Front. If we begin to see some signs of German softening there, then we can spare some men and ship them to Vladivostok and on across the railway. All of that takes time. Alex should be in Vladivostok before that happens."

The talk in the lounge grew more confusing to Morrie. Other men drifted in, joining the conversation, and the room grew heavy with the smoke from large black cigars. The men talked about the supposed imminent arrival of Japanese troops in the port of Vladivostok. The Japanese were, the stories had it, supporting the independent rebels, Semenov and

Kalmykov, who were battling the Bolsheviks in the far Eastern reaches of Siberia, where the border between Russia and China was fuzzy and nobody knew or cared which country they were in.

There was an American ship, the cruiser *Brooklyn*, lying at anchor in Vladivostok's harbor. Nobody was quite sure what it was doing there.

The Whites were here and there, under generals whose names they all knew and recognized, but nobody had an inkling of how they were being supplied or what they hoped to accomplish.

It certainly was a mess, they all said, and Morrie agreed. He was about to jump, head first, into that mess. He tried to draw the conversation back to himself and his plight but had no success.

"But what should I do first?" asked Morrie several times.

"It's a mess out there. Do you know that when the Czechs go to Vladivostok and join the Japanese who are already there, and the British and Americans who are coming, why there will be more Allies than Russians in that damn city. Then there really will be a blow-out."

"Do you think I can make it all the way?"

"It's really a mess out there. The other day, according to what I heard, three Japanese clerks were murdered in Vladivostok. The next day the Japs came storming off their ships and, for a time anyhow, they controlled the city."

"How is the best way for me to proceed?"

"One day the Reds are running things in Siberia, the next day the Whites, then the Cossacks. I have a feeling that eventually it'll be the Czechs in charge, because at least they are organized and disciplined and have officers who know what they are doing."

Morrie gave up. He let the words and the smoke swirl around him, and let his own mind wander. He remembered something that his old friend Willie had said to him that day he visited him in Pentonville Prison.

"Wherever you go, Morrie, find some Jews. Remember, they are your brothers and your friends and they will help you."

Were there any Jews in Siberia? There were many in Russia, of course, but mostly in Western Russia, Poland and Lithuania. In Siberia? He would have to ask about that.

Eventually they all started giving Morrie practical advice. Yes, he would have to go first to Omsk, where he would connect with the Trans-Siberian itself. Trains from Vologda to Omsk ran three times a week. It was about a seventeen-hundred- mile trip. They told him the fare. He said he had a couple of English pounds left and they said that would convert into enough for a ticket to Omsk. They said they would take him to the bank tomorrow where he could exchange his pounds for rubles.

Bob and Jerry took Morrie back to the house. Jerry had been quiet during the earlier discussions at the Embassy, but now he voiced his doubts. All of the others, he said, had been very generous with their advice about what a "piece of cake," {another new expression to Morrie} it would be for him to cross Siberia.

"They aren't going to have to do it," said Jerry. "You are the one. I get a kick out of old Earl Johnston telling you what a breeze it will be. Even Bob, saying that if you're lucky, maybe you'll find yourself in the middle of a battle. That's a lot of crap and you know it. Nothing fun about a battle. I've been in one, and that was more than enough for the rest of my life."

"You know what I meant," Bob spoke up.. "I meant it might be fun to watch some of the action. I didn't mean you'd want to get too close to it, or get shot at, or anything like that."

"I know," said Morrie. "It's all right."

But that didn't placate Jerry. He said he thought it was the height of folly to go off to Siberia, like they wanted Morrie to do, when he really was totally unprepared for such an undertaking.

"The only thing," Jerry said, "is that don't think you have any choice. I've tried to come up with some alternative for you and there just doesn't seem to be any other option open."

They crunched through the snow to the house and then sat on the overstuffed chairs in the living room. Bob made some tea and they talked on into the night.

"I wish there was some other way, I really do," said Morrie. "I have to get to some place where I can make my way to the States or to Canada, and Vladivostok seems to be the only place. I feel like a real Peruvian here."

He had to explain to them that "Peruvian" was the East End London slang term for a newcomer. That got them all started on the relative merits of American versus English slang. Morrie gave them a few samples of Cockney rhyming slang, which was totally new to the Americans.

"That's not English, that's a total foreign language," said Bob. "What does it all mean?"

"Well, it goes like this. Rosie is from Rosie Lee, which means tea. Titfor is from tit for tat, or hat. Cherry, that's from cherry ripe, or pipe. Dickie is from Dickie Dirt, or shirt, and sky is from sky rocket, or pocket. A pretty girl is a boat race or pretty face."

They asked for more as they laughed. Morrie explained that going up the stairs was "apples and pears or stairs."

The men raided the kitchen, found some cake, and had more tea. Only now, in deference to Morrie and his Cockney rhyming slang, they called it "Rosie" instead of tea.

"You know," Jerry said, "I'm sure you'll be able to make it to Vlad, Alex. "I didn't mean to sound pessimistic before. I just want you to go into this thing with your eyes open, that's all. It's going to be a difficult trip."

"It won't be so bad," said Bob. "Don't let Jerry discourage you. He's a real Gloomy Gus."

"When I first landed here in Russia," said Morrie, "somebody told me to take it step by step by step, and that's what I'll do with this Siberia trip."

"You'll be traveling across the pages of history, that's for sure," said Jerry. "By the time you get to Vladivostok, I'll bet the Allies will be there, or they'll land soon afterwards. It should be very interesting to be there when it happens and to see what they are going to do."

They talked more, mostly about the present situation in Russia. The general consensus among the men working at the Embassy was that the Whites and their Cossack allies would eventually kick the Bolsheviks out. They weren't sure if that would mean that the Czars would be restored to their throne. Maybe there could be some form of democracy installed in Russia, although they weren't sure it would work. Most of the Embassy experts apparently didn't have much respect for the Russians' ability to govern themselves democratically.

"It will all be very confusing in Russia for a long time, Alex," said Jerry. The confusion is your chance to escape notice. You'll get lost in the crowd out there. Siberia is full of people going every which way. Nobody has any papers, and nobody is asking to see any papers. A few rubles will buy anything and take you anywhere. Just stay out of the line of fire. If you see soldiers of any kind, take off the other way."

Earl Johnston came over from the Embassy and joined them, and they got out more cake and poured more tea. Johnston had additional advice for Morrie.

He suggested that the trip from Vologda to Omsk would be fairly simple. The trains were uncrowded and they ran with reasonable regularity. After that, it would be more complicated. The line east from Omsk was jammed with Czech stragglers trying to catch up to the main body of the Legion, refugees of all sorts and released prisoners of war going the other way, trying to get home.

"Just play it by ear," said Earl.

"Play it by ear?" echoed Morrie. "Is that American rhyming slang?"

Bob and Jerry laughed, and Jerry suggested that, yes, it was rhyming slang, and it meant "say it with a beer." They explained the joke, to Earl, and he had to have some samples of Cockney rhyming slang from Morrie, and another hour went by.

Eventually they all went to bed, and for Morrie the night's sleep was fitful. Tomorrow the real adventure would begin. He had said that before, as he left Murmansk and as he left Archangel, but this time it was for real.

Nobody would be traveling with him. He would have no pass for his railroad fare and no introductions to people at the other end of the ride. He would be strictly and entirely on his own.

Bob and Jerry ate breakfast with him and then requisitioned a sleigh and pony. They went first to the Vologda railroad station, a different one from the station he had arrived at the day before. He would be leaving on a different line. This station was an immense yellowish building, and inside, lines of ticket buyers snaked around the cavernous hall.

When they got to the window, Jerry, who spoke passable Russian, talked to the ticket seller. There was a heated exchange, obviously more than would be necessary to purchase one simple ticket. Morrie wondered about the problem. Everything in Russia seemed to involve a problem of some kind.

"We've got a problem, Alex," said Jerry. "The regular train to Omsk doesn't leave until the weekend. There is a train tomorrow to Ekaterinburg, and from there you can probably catch a train to Omsk quickly. They run frequently from there. What do you think?"

Morrie thought quickly. He really couldn't impose on these people any longer, and he couldn't afford to go to a hotel to wait for the Omsk train.

"I'd like to get moving," he said. "Get me a ticket to Ekaterinburg. I'm really anxious to start."

"Suit yourself," said Jerry. He turned back to the clerk and bought the ticket.

"When you get to Ekaterinburg," said Bob, as they were walking back to the sleigh, "maybe you can rescue the Czar and be a big hero."

"Is the Czar there?"

"Sure, didn't you know? That's where he and all his family are being held in some private house."

Nextthey drove to the bank. Morrie would have recognized it as a bank anywhere. Funny, he thought, whoever designs banks must be the same person all over the world. They always look solid, substantial, and serious.

It seemed to Morrie as though bank designers created an atmosphere that was deliberately intimidating.

The Central Bank of Vologda had heavy wooden doors adorned with brass knobs and hinges. The brass hadn't been polished and had acquired a gray film. Morrie understood why nobody was polishing the doors as soon as he got inside. Everyone must be busy working as tellers. The place was jammed, and long lines of customers stood before every available window.

"Ever since the revolution it's been like this," Bob explained. "The people don't know what's happening. They come in and take their money out. They are then reassured and they put their money back in. Then something else happens and they get scared again and come back and withdraw it again."

This seemed to be withdrawal day. Everybody was leaving the windows with fists full of paper money of various colors, most looking torn and dilapidated. On some of the bills Morrie noticed things that looked like postage stamps. He couldn't help but compare the confusion here with the staid and austere quality of British banks. Here everything, including the money and the people, seemed worn out.

There was again a long discussion at the window, longer than Morrie would have expected from the simple transaction of changing British pound notes into Russian currency. Jerry and the teller were on the verge of shouting, but finally the deal was made and they smiled at each other.

"Let's go, boys," Jerry said. "I've got your dough for you, Alex, if you call this pile of dirty paper real money. I did the best I could. The teller wanted to give you all Bolshevik money, but that could be worthless tomorrow. I wanted all old money. He wouldn't do that. So we compromised and I took some of the new and he gave me some of the old."

Outside he handed the money to Morrie, explaining that one pile was Bolshevik money, and the postage stamps were changes of denominations as inflation boiled over. The other pile was the old Imperial notes. Even those had been in his terminology, "Bolshevized." An Imperial ten-ruble note had a stamp over it, meaning it was now worth forty rubles. There was also some Kerensky money, longer, narrower notes.

Morrie had been confused trying to convert kopecks and rubles into pounds, and vice versa, but now, with three different kinds of Russian money to learn, it was even more confusing.

Chapter Six

"Well, is our wandering Jew ready to start wandering again?"

Morrie had come over to the Embassy from the house where he had slept, and that was the questions with which Earl Johnston met him. Morrie momentarily bridled, but then realized that there was nothing unpleasant intended. Johnston meant the remark to be friendly.

"I guess I'm as ready as I'll ever be," Morrie said. "I owe you and the others here a great deal. You have been very kind to me, but I do admit I have a bit of a fright about it."

"I love your English," Johnston said. "You put it so delicately. We would say, I'm scared shitless, but you say, I have a bit of a fright."

They had breakfast, and an Embassy clerk came in with some dispatches. Johnston read them and exploded.

"I'll be Goddamned!" he said. "Listen to this, fellows. Trotsky, I guess he's the big cheese in Moscow these days, he sent this order a few days ago, April 7, to be exact. 'The movement of the Czechoslovak trains eastward is permitted.' Just two weeks ago there was this order." He leafed through the papers until he found the one he wanted. Dated March 20, it read, "the transportation of all Czechoslovak trains to Siberia must immediately be stopped."

They all shook their heads. The Bolshevik government had done a complete about-face in a little more than two weeks on the subject of whether or not they would permit the trains carrying the Czech Legion to pass along the tracks of the Trans-Siberian railroad. No wonder the situation in Siberia was chaotic.

"They'll probably do a reverse again in another couple of weeks," said Johnston.

"Now here's another little dilly," he said as he continued through the morning reports. "This was intercepted by one of our agents in Irkutsk. It's from the Irkutsk Soviet to the Kransnoyarsk Soviet, from some high muck-amuck named Jakovlev. Listen to this and try to understand these nuts. 'To the Krasnoyarsk Soviet, all Czechoslovak trains must be immediately and unconditionally disarmed. The Czechs may retain only a minimum of weapons needed for protection of their funds and supplies. All machine guns must be taken away. Each train may retain only fifteen to twenty rifles and a few rounds of ammunition. There is no need to negotiate this disarmament with the representatives of the Czechoslovak National Council.'

"Can you picture them out there, telling the Czechs that it's okay for them to proceed, but kindly hand over all your machine guns? How would you like to be the one trying to enforce that order?"

"It sounds to me like they're getting ready to doublecross the Czechs," said Bob.

"They'll never get away with it," said Johnston. "Those damn Czechs are too smart, too rough. They'll fight before they give up their weapons. The Bolsheviks need those guns, so they'll fight right back."

That's all I need, thought Morrie. I'll be out there in Siberia somewhere, and the Czechs and the Bolsheviks will be killing each other all around me. I may have to choose sides in this war.

"Let's go, Alex," said Earl Johnston. "I have to see somebody and the station is right on the way, so I'll take you over there. You about packed?"

"Nothing to pack. I'm ready."

On the way Johnston said that he knew a man in the Omsk Consulate, a man whose name was Harris. He wasn't a good friend, but he knew him, and it was at least a name to ask for if he found he needed a hand when he got to Omsk.

They said good bye at the station. Morrie tried to hide his fear and depression, but it was too heavy a load. Johnston gave him a pat on the back and the standard cheerful speech: "You'll be all right, nothing to worry about, just stay in the background." He waved and was gone.

Morrie made his way along the platform. He found the usual man with the green flag and showed him his ticket, and the man directed him, via arm and finger signals, to the correct car. He found a seat and tossed his small bag on the shelf above. This train seemed older, dirtier and smellier than the ones he had ridden before.

A typical Russian family sat across from him, and two middle-aged Russian ladies sat next to him. The father of the family smiled at him and said something casually. He obviously expected an answer and seemed a little put off when Morrie just smiled and shrugged. The man tried again. Morrie went through his pantomime of not understanding, and the man caught on.

"Ah," he said, as the light dawned. *"Amerikanski!"*

"Nyet, Angleterre."

The man then lost interest. Apparently he was prepared to be friendly and go out of his way for an American, but an Englishman was something else again. Americans had a certain mystique for some reason that Morrie did not understand. It would change later, but in 1918 the Russian people adored the Americans.

The train gave its first, reluctant lurch, and there was a small cheer from the passengers. Apparently it was still something of an event when a train left on time, as this one had. The hypnotic chug-chug, clackety-clack, was soon heard, and people settled back for a long, dull trip.

Morrie got up from his seat and started walking. He had just about reached the end of the train, and he considered whether to turn around and go back or to sit there for awhile, because it was emptier and hence more comfortable. He had begun to feel very depressed heading into an unknown wilderness. He was, in actuality, feeling very sorry for himself. Then his good luck reasserted itself. *"Pashalsta, shokalat?"*

He felt a nudge, and turned around to see a tall, good- looking young man next to him, offering him a chocolate bar. Without thinking, Morrie said "thank you" as he accepted the candy.

"Hey, English!" said the young man, with a big grin. "That's an unexpected treat. Where you from, friend?"

Morrie said he was from England, and the man stuck out his hand and said, "Glad to meet you! I'm John Alexander. I'm with the Y, you know, the Y.M.C.A. I'm on my way back from St. Petersburg. Petrograd now."

"I'm Alex Chernofsky, from London."

"Come on, let's sit together. I thought this was going to be a long, boring ride. The good Lord must have brought us together."

John Alexander draped his arm around Morrie's shoulder and they found their way to Alexander's seat. Morrie got his bag and rejoined his new friend.

"It's nice to be able to talk English," said Morrie. "My jaw is aching from all the *pashalsta*s and *spasebo*s and all that. I don't know how the Russians do it. It's the damnedest language on the jaw that has ever been devised."

They sat and drank tea and talked. It was an educational process for Morrie. John Alexander had been all over Russia. He had even been to Vladivostok and back on the railroad. He knew the answers to all the questions that had been building up inside Morrie's troubled brain.

They also talked about Morrie. Alexander had only been to London briefly, as he was travelling from the United States to his post in Russia. He wanted to know more about the city, and particularly about how the English were surviving under the wartime conditions.

Naturally, he was curios about what Morrie, an obviously healthy, soldierly-age young man was doing wandering around a remote part of Russia. Morrie gave him his time- honored story and was relieved when Alexander seemed to accept it without a second thought, or even a second question.

Morrie was curious about Ekaterinburg, since that would be his next stop.

"Great cheese," the Y man said.

"Cheese? Really?"

"Sure, why not? Ekaterinburg is the center of Russia's dairy industry. The making of cheese has become the city's foremost industry. Last time I was there, I had to buy a lot for our work with the Y, so I got to know the leaders of Ekaterinburg's cheese industry. A funny thing—except for one Russian Jew, they are all Danes. At least, they were; maybe now, with the Bolsheviks taking over everything, they've kicked the Danes out, but until recently the Danes ran things."

Morrie asked Alexander to explain just what he meant by "our work," when he talked of what the Y.M.C.A. was doing in Russia. Alexander told him that the Y was there to help whoever happened to need help. Right now that included just about everybody, so they had cars on most of the Trans-Siberian trains, dispensing food, medical supplies and kind words.

The two men did the jump- out- and- buy- food routine when the train stopped at Viatka and Perm, although there were some smaller towns where brief stops were made. There were tables with ladies ladling out soup and selling roasted chickens and other edibles at each of the larger stations. Morrie and his new friend each got on separate lines at Viatka and Perm, so they were able to share good meals after both stops.

"Where will you be staying in Ekat?" asked Alexander.

"I hope I don't have to stay there at all," said Morrie. "I'd like to catch the next train for Omsk. Do you have any idea when it leaves?"

"They run pretty often. It's only a day's ride from Ekat to Omsk. Look, as long as you're here, stick around a few days. After all, how often do you get to Ekaterinburg? It's a nice little city, and you might enjoy looking around, and we can put you up in our staff headquarters for a day or so."

"You sure it'll be all right?"

"Absolutely sure. My pal, Riley, runs things. He's a good guy and he'll welcome you with open arms. I'll be going on to Omsk in a few days, and I'd be pleased to travel with you."

"That's marvelous," said Morrie. "I would love to go on to Omsk with you." And he meant that, sincerely. His good luck was obviously continuing, at least for the next leg of his journey. An experienced Russian hand to travel with would certainly ease his way considerably.

Morrie noticed one strange thing about Russian trains, as he watched the stations. There were very few buildings near the stations at Viatka and Perm, as well as the other stations they had visited. The actual city or town seemed to be miles away from the station, which generally sat in solitary non-splendor in the middle of nowhere. He asked Alexander about that peculiar phenomenon.

"That, my friend," Alexander said, "is one of the great mysteries of Siberia. You will find it true all the way to Vladivostok. The stations are far outside of the towns. According to the legend, when the railroad was being built, the engineers asked each of the cities for a payoff to put the station in that city. Most of them refused, so, in revenge, the engineers built the stations far from the town.

"Ask a Russian to explain it and he'll just shrug his shoulders. It's the Russian expression, 'You can't explain the inexplicable, so why bother to try.' They're so used to the stations being far from the town that they don't really think about it anymore."

Morrie also asked Alexander about the Czechs, because he still had that conversation in Vologda fresh in his mind, when Earl Johnston predicted a battle along the Trans-Siberian railroad if the Bolsheviks tried to disarm the Czechs.

"I like the Czechs," Alexander said. "By and large, they are a very interesting group of men. They are generally better educated than the Russians, and they are more, well, more our style. The Russians are Asians, after all, and the Czechs are Europeans. Let's face it, there's a big difference."

"A lot of our Y people are traveling with the Czechs, and you and I could conceivably run into some. You will, somewhere between here and Vlad. Our Y cars are often hooked onto the trains taking the Czechs east. We just hook our *teplushkas*, that's their word for boxcars, onto their trains and supply them what they need. At least, if we have it."

Alexander had heard about the contradictory orders coming from Moscow and about the order to disarm the Czechs. He, too, predicted what he called "a blow-up." He went a step further: he said that the Czechs would destroy the Russians if it came to a face- to- face battle.

Morrie was dozing when the train screeched to a stop in Ekaterinburg, and Alexander shook him awake.

It was just dawn. They walked down the platform in a light, mist-like rain. Alexander spotted a friend who was there to meet him. He was tall-and curly-haired, with a face full of freckles. His name was George Green.

"How's everything here, Georgie?" asked John.

"Everything's hunky-dory, John. The sleigh is right outside. God, the road is bumpy. Spring is just about here, and the snow is melting fast. We'll have to put wheels on the old crate any day now." Alexander introduced John to Morrie.

They had an eight-mile ride from the station into town. Obviously this town hadn't payed the graft. The road was very bumpy, as George Green had predicted. It was pleasant for Morrie because he was with people who spoke his language. The moment of truth when he would be totally alone and on his own had been postponed for a few more days.

The sleigh pulled up to a small, neat wooden building, with the Y.M.C.A. triangle on the front door. The place was buzzing. Crates full of supplies crammed every room. Outside, men were loading them onto sleighs, while other men were unloading other sleighs and hauling crates inside.

Morrie quickly realized that Ekaterinburg was a very pleasant little city. It was in a bowl surrounded by the Ural Mountains. Green had said that spring was just about here, and on the distant slopes of the mountains Morrie could see wildflowers in bloom.

The only structures that he could make out on those far hillsides were the churches. He thought Ekaterinburg must be a very religious city because there seemed to be more churches than houses.

Alexander treated him as a long-lost friend and introduced him to the others, Jeff Pruitt, Greg Jolly and the Y Chaplain, Reverend Joseph Dugan. Riley, the head man, was away.

It was the first time the others had had a chance to talk to Alexander since his arrival. They questioned him about things in Petrograd and he, in turn, questioned them about the situation here in Ekaterinburg.

Morrie knew now that he had to get aboard the Omsk train the next morning. He said good bye to everyone, thanked Alexander for his kindness, and made his way on foot the many miles to the station. He kept to the side of the road and when he heard the sound of an approaching sleigh, he stepped into the ditch that always paralleled Russian roads. He skirted the few homes that were on the route to the station.

Morrie reached the station sometime after dawn. He turned up his collar and stayed away from the people on the platform. A severe storm had blown up, and it was almost impossible to distinguish the people from sacks of goods on the platform. Morrie found a niche in the station wall and crouched inside.

Soldiers appeared as the train pulled into the station. They marched back and forth, carefully scanning the crowd. Perhaps it was just a routine procedure.

Morrie saw the station-master wave his green flag and heard the first belch from the engine. He stood up. Timing his leap perfectly, Morrie grabbed on to the iron railing of the observation platform of the last car. The soldiers didn't see him in the swirling snowstorm. He was safe.

Morrie rested on the platform a few moments then went inside the car and found a seat. He dug out his ticket and stuck it in the slot in the seat in front of him. He then pulled his hat down over his eyes and pretended he was asleep. Morrie was finally alone and all on his own. He would have to make his own luck in the future.

Chapter Seven

Morrie slept for a while, waking when the conductor brushed his shoulder as he reached over to take his ticket and punch it. He woke again, quickly, at the first station. Rubbing the frost from the window and looking out, he spied John Alexander standing on the chicken line.

He then remembered that John had said he was traveling to Omsk and he had been looking forward to sharing the ride with the man from the Y.

He jumped up and went outside, yelling, "Hey, John, I made it." The Y man grinned and waved back. Morrie managed to grab a few eggs from the egg lady and joined Alexander as the tall man walked back to his car.

"Are you okay?" asked Alexander.

"No, not really. I'm very confused."

"Want to talk about it?"

"Now what?" He still had no alternative. On to Omsk and then on across Siberia to Vladivostok.

"Tell me about Omsk," said Morrie. He was shutting the door on the past and once more looking forward to the future.

"They're all living in boxcars in the railroad yards," said Alexander. "Most depressing thing I've ever seen. Hundreds of boxcars lined up with people, dozens of people, maybe as many as fifty people, living in one car. No sanitary facilities and no real water supply. They're melting snow for drinking water now, which is okay in the winter, but what's going to happen to them come summer."

"More refugees going nowhere," continued Alexander. "I don't know what they expect to find in Omsk, but I guarantee you it isn't what they will actually find. I'm sure they expect that they will have a job and a home but they are going to be homeless and they are going to wind up sharing a boxcar with twenty or thirty or maybe fifty other poor souls."

John and Morrie got off the next time the train stopped. This wasn't a food stop, just a stretch-your-legs stop. Morrie noticed a bunch of boys playing a game that seemed to involve throwing some white objects of various shapes and sizes on the ground and being concerned with the pattern that developed from the way these objects landed. He asked Alexander about it.

"I don't know the rules of the game," said the Y man, "but I can tell you that those things they throw are pig's knuckles. Those are toys for Russian kids. This damn country may be short of everything else, but they have a surplus of pig's knuckles."

Morrie noticed that the cars on the train were painted different colors, blue, yellow, and green. "It was," said Alexander, "a Trans-Siberian color code, with the different color denoting a different class." Blue cars were first class, yellow were second class, and green were third class. These were Trans-Siberian cars, although they had not yet reached the Trans-Siberian tracks.

Morrie saw a picture of a letter box that had been painted on one of the cars. He didn't need to have that explained to him: it was a post office car. There was still such illiteracy in Russia that pictures of things were common instead of words.

"These are the typical *moujiks*," said Alexander.

"What's a *moujiks?*"

"Sort of like a peasant, but really it means more than just peasant. It means a class of society. They call them untouchables in India. These are the majority of the Russian people, and damn few of them can read or write. They are the ones who get taken and put in the Army and shot and killed. They are the ones who do the dirty work and get the dirty end of the stick for their trouble. Maybe they're like your Cockneys, I'm not sure."

"How can you tell a *moujiks?*" Morrie asked.

"Look at their feet."

Morrie did. No shoes. They were all wearing cloths wrapped around their feet, fixed with straps just above the ankles.

After the train began moving, Alexander pointed out the houses of the *moujiks* along the tracks. Huts, really. No floors, except mud. Certainly nothing like electricity or running water or any plumbing facilities. Generally, just one room where everything happens such as cooking and sleeping.

"They are like children," said Morrie. "That's what they remind me of, children. Simple little kids playing in toy houses like grown-ups. Look at that one. Pigs are running in and out."

"You ain't seen nothing yet. These are palaces compared to the ones you'll be seeing out in darkest Siberia. You don't know what primitive means until you've been through there. They don't have anything out there, not one thing. The pigs live better than the people."

There was the now-familiar sight of the city's cathedral in the distance as the train came slowly into Omsk station,which as usual was far from the city. Alexander suddenly sat straight up in his seat as he looked out the window.

"Hey, would you look at that," he said.

"Look at what?"

"Trouble, that's what. Last we heard, the Russians were still in control here. Something's gone wrong."

Alexander said it could mean some difficulty getting off the train, because the Czechs were sticklers for formalities. Morrie had no papers, and even Alexander, figuring this was just a casual trip, only had some letters as proof of his occupation. He advised that, once the train stopped, they hustle their butts, as he put it, and hope that there was somebody from the Y there to meet them.

The Czech soldiers were lined up, standing rigidly at attention, and John and Morrie had to run the gauntlet of their curious, accusing eyes as they walked briskly down the platform. It was mid-afternoon, but when they reached the station itself Morrie noticed that the clock read twelve.

"Don't worry about the dumb clock," said Alexander, taking Morrie's arm and hustling him along. "It's okay. They keep all the clocks on Petrograd time anywhere along the Trans-Siberian. Don't ask me why."

They passed more rows of Czech soldiers and then Alexander spotted one of his Y.M.C.A. friends.

"Oh, there's Terry Comer," he said. "Great."

Comer saw them as soon as Alexander spotted him. They exchanged waves.

"Come on, Johnny. Move it," Comer said. "Let's get out to the *droshky.* All hell's breaking loose here, and we'd better get moving while we still can."

Alexander explained that Morrie was with him, and Comer gave him a nod, leading the way out a side door to where his vehicle was parked. The refugees were milling around, lost and confused and, consequently, angry. They were yelling at the Czech soldiers who were trying to herd them out toward all those boxcars that Alexander had spoken about. The boxcars were lined up for what seemed forever, and in and around them were swarms of people. Smoke drifted out of every boxcar door and chimney,hanging over the railroad yard like a gray film. There was still snow on the ground, though the weather was starting to warm as spring approached. The snow in the railroad yard was as gray as smoke.

Comer hurried them into the *droshky* and clucked to his horse, and they moved off. He adroitly maneuvered the animal and the sleigh in and around the hordes of people thronging the area around the station. It still took them some fifteen minutes to get clear from the traffic and move with any speed.

Comer was too busy to talk until they got away from the station and its throngs of people and vehicles.

"Okay" he said, "sorry I couldn't talk before. I was damn anxious to get us away from that mess. Things could get pretty sticky around here."

"What's been happening?" asked Alexander. "This business with the Czechs is new, isn't it?"

"Yes, but it's the real thing. The Czechs are running things in Omsk now. They control the city, totally."

Later, in the Y.M.C.A. building, which was next door to a large church in a lovely residential section of the city, Comer and some other Y officials welcomed Alexander and Morrie. Over some tea and biscuits they continued the saga of the Czech takeover.

"Well, it started with that business in Chelyabinsk," said a man named Chet Firebaugh, who, Morrie found out later, came from Mobile Alabama. Firebaugh spoke a brand of English that Morrie could only sporadically understand.

"What business in Chelyabinsk?" Alexander asked.

"Boy, you're really out of touch. I thought everybody knew about that."

He quickly sketched in the background of the Czech Legion's plight in trying to get to Vladivostok. Units of the Legion were making their way as best they could along the railroad. "They were strung out," said Firebaugh, "from Pensa in the west practically to Vladivostok itself in the east. There was an entire regiment, the Sixth, in Chelyabinsk.

"They were camped on a siding and wouldn't you know, along comes a train load of Hungarians just released as prisoners of war, going back west toward Hungary. Well, you know that the Czechs and Hungarians get along like cats and dogs. They absolutely despise each other.

"So wouldn't you know, one of the Hungarians throws a hunk of iron out the train window at the Czechs. He gets lucky or unlucky, depending on how you look at it. Anyhow, he conks one of the Czechs right on the noggin and kills him dead. Well, the Czechs get the train stopped somehow and they go through the train. They get the guy they think threw the iron, and they haul him off the train and beat him to death right there on the tracks."

Morrie was thinking that that was the railroad he was going to be riding any day now. This railroad had been described to him as a long and boring ride, peaceful but monotonous. It didn't sound very boring or monotonous at this point.

"So then the local Chelyabinsk Soviet gets into the act, and they arrest the Czechs they claim were responsible for beating the Hungarian to death. Next thing, wouldn't you know, a bunch of Czechs go into town, break down the jail door, and rescue their buddies. They go on and take over the whole damn city.

"Well, the word apparently spread. There must be a Czech grapevine. Anyhow, wouldn't you know, first thing is that the Czechs, wherever they are, take over whatever city they're near. It spread here to Omsk two days ago, when they suddenly marched in and booted the Russians out."

"Was there a battle?"

"No. The Russians knew that they didn't have chance. The Czechs have more men, more guns and more discipline. The Russians just quietly moved out of town. They're camped about four or five miles outside."

There were Y cars on many of the trains, and the Y representatives were wiring in reports. It was chaos all over. The American Embassy had recently moved from Vologda to Irkutsk, and the new American Embassy Consul-General, a certain Ernest L. Harris, was reportedly unnerved by the events. He had told friends that in his opinion the Czechs might take over all of Siberia.

"Why would they want to do that?" Terry Comer wondered. "All they want to do is go home. At least that's what we've always been told. Why would they want to control Siberia?"

"No logical reason," said Firebaugh. "When someone is confronted with the opportunity to rule, it goes against human nature to turn that opportunity down. It is very possible that given a chance to run Siberia the Czechs will take it, even though they have no right to do so." After a hearty dinner they talked into the night. From this meal, Morrie realized that he had been spoiled lately. The food in some of the places he had stayed in had been first- rate. This meal was hardly Spartan but neither was it elegant.

They gave him a room upstairs. This building was much larger than the one at Ekaterinburg. There were, he was told, twenty people working there; Eight of them were local women hired as secretaries and translators. Morrie went to his room soon after dinner, leaving the others still hashing over the politics of the day.

He wanted to think about himself and his own problems. He was now, obviously, completely committed to making the run to Vladivostok. He would get the details tomorrow, buy his ticket, make his final preparations, and be off as soon as possible.

Morrie fell asleep with those enigmas whirling around inside his head. The next morning, a rare day of sunshine with a hint of the coming spring season in the air, he joined his new friends at breakfast. It was as though they had been there all night. They were still talking about the politics of the moment.

There was a new arrival, a man named Peter Graft, who was just back from Irkutsk and had a startling report. A train heading east with a company of Czechs had apparently been ambushed by some Bolsheviks, and there was a pitched battle right there in the Irkutsk station.

I'm going to be going there, Morrie thought to himself; I'm going where people are shooting at each other.

The men all agreed that the situation throughout Siberia was getting out of hand. They realized that, as the Y representatives in the region, they were in for difficult times. They began talking about logistical matters, such as how to get enough supplies and medical materials to the right places and at the right times. Where was the greatest need, what should they order, and what was expendable?

The men asked Morrie about the British attitude toward the war, and he was back on familiar ground, talking about the English moral fiber and stiff upper lips, telling about the Zeppelin raids and how the country was rallying behind its fighting men. He also said that, as far as he knew, the average Briton in the street knew nothing about the situation here in Russia and, in fact, cared little about it. They would like the Russians to get back in the war, which would take pressure off the Western Front, but, otherwise, what was going on in Russian was of little concern to them.

After breakfast, John Alexander, who had an errand at the Consulate, asked Morrie to accompany him. It would, said John, give him a chance to see a little something of Omsk.

There were Czech soldiers everywhere, easily recognized by a small but eye-catching red patch on their caps. Morrie was impressed by the fact that, compared to the Russian soldiers he had seen, the Czechs were always neat and their faces were clean-shaven.

Alexander told Morrie that Omsk was unique in Russia, in that for many years it had been a depository for convicts. They had been sent to Omsk and many had stayed after their sentences, so roughly half the population was descended from these convicts. Omsk was also a place for internal exile. The Czar's police would send "undesirables" to Omsk, where they could live peaceful lives, provided they didn't try to leave. Dostoyevski had been an exile in Omsk and it was here that he wrote his "Memoirs From a Dead House." His was not a peaceful exile, however. They had beaten him so often and so badly that he barely hung on to life for some years, and the locals called him *"Pokoinik,"* the Deceased, even before he died.

Alexander told Morrie something he had already heard, that the butter industry in this part of Russia was controlled by Danes, and that there was one Russian Jew in the otherwise Danish-run industry.

Alexander pointed to an odd-looking character on the street.

"A Kirghiz," he said. "The Kirghiz are to Siberia what the Indians are to the American West. They've been here forever. They are basically nomads, raising sheep and cattle. I heard that in their economy a cow is worth eight sheep but a woman is only worth four sheep."

Alexander told Morrie that after he left Omsk on the train, he would see many Kirghiz settlements. They lived, he said, in what looked like half-coconut shells, round tents they just build wherever they camp.

When Alexander came out of the Consulate, after doing his brief errand, his face looked somber. He had heard disturbing news, he said. The feeling in the Consulate was that this trouble with the Czechs was going to escalate into a full- blown civil war. The Allies might become part of it in an effort to stop it from going wild.

Back at the Y, Alexander gathered the others and told them the news from the Consulate. Some officials of the Russian Railroad Commission, which had an American named John Stevens as its head, were traveling on the Trans-Siberian to Harbin to assess the situation.

"There was fighting at Marinsk. The Bols and the Czechs again, and Colonel Emerson of the Commission offered to arbitrate the matter. He managed to iron things out, so the Czech train got rolling again and the Bols let it go. No telling how many might have been killed if he hadn't been there."

The Whites were helping the Czechs here and there, and there were rumors that the Cossacks would also join them. The rebel leader, Semenov, was watching what happened, like a vulture watching the lions and jackals fight over a dead animal, knowing that whoever wins, he would eventually get his share.

Morrie wanted to ask them about his situation. Did they think it was safe for him to go across Siberia now, in view of all the trouble, all the fighting? This was obviously not the right time.

They were all talking, and realizing that he wouldn't be missed, he walked out of the Y building. He knew where he was going. He had noticed some Hebrew letters on a little building as he drove around with Alexander earlier that day. Perhaps it was that observation that made him recall Willie's advice.

Morrie walked toward the building. He thought it was a synagogue. It was right across from a Russian church, one of those big ones with onion-shaped domes. He tried to remember some of the Hebrew words he had learned for his Bar Mitzvah, but only a few unconnected words and phrases surfaced. They might be enough to prove to somebody that he was a Jew.

It must be a synagogue. When he got close to it he noticed a replica of the ten commandments in marble, old and dirty but clear enough, above the door. He opened the door and entered a large room.

It was exactly like the *shuls* his father had taken him to in London before he lost interest in religion. The heavy, musty smell, the wooden railings around the lectern, the balcony running around the room for the women. A faint light slipped in from the frosty windows.

An old man with a long white beard came out of a side door, as if in answer to Morrie's appearance. He said something in Russian. All Morrie could manage was to ask, in hesitant Yiddish, if this was a *shul*. The old man nodded.

Morrie tried to communicate. He said to the man, in a combination of English, Yiddish, and a little Russian, that he was from England and needed help. The old man listened politely, saying nothing, and then disappeared through the same side door he had entered. He came back in a few minutes, accompanied by a younger man with a small, carefully trimmed Van Dyke beard.

"*Britanski?*" The man asked. Morrie answered "yes."

"*Yevrey?*" Morrie thought that he was being asked if he was Jewish, so he again said "yes"

The man smiled and held out his hand, and Morrie took it. The man held it tightly, and led him outside and along the streets. They walked perhaps twenty minutes. Morrie tried to remember where he was going, memorizing landmarks in case he had to find his way back to the Y.

They turned in at a large house surrounded by an iron fence. The man knocked on the door and a young girl answered. The man said something in Russian, and the girl opened the door to let them enter. She led them into the living room and gestured to the sofa.

It was an elegant room. Morrie could see, through the door to the entry hall, a winding staircase flanked by a highly polished oak bannister. The little girl had gone up the stairs and she came down with an enormous man. Morrie immediately judged him as weighing more than 250 pounds. He had on a dark blue suit, and a gold chain was hung across his ample stomach. This was by far the best-dressed man Morrie had seen since his arrival in Russia. The big man walked right up to Morrie, who felt dwarfed standing next to him.

"*Britanski?*" He had a rich, deep voice, the kind of voice one expected in a man of that size. Morrie nodded.

"*Masla*," the man said, pointing to himself. When Morrie looked quizzical, the man repeated the word.

"Ah, I see," said Morrie. "You are Mr. Masla. I am Mr. Chernofsky, Alex Chernofsky, from London. Happy to know you."

"*Nyet, nyet.*" He said "*masla*" again a few times, accompanying the word with a little charade, as though he were churning butter. Then it dawned on Morrie that the man was saying he was in the butter business. Perhaps this was the Russian Jew he had heard about, the only person other than the Danes who was in the butter business in this region.

At that point, an attractive woman came down the stairs and joined them.

"How do you do?" she said, in perfect English. "You are from England? From London, perhaps?"

"Yes, I am. I'm Alexander Chernofsky. Happy to know you."

"It's my pleasure, young sir. I have not had a chance to practice my English in, my goodness sake, it must be six years now, since our last trip to your lovely country. We are the Polacheks, Monsieur et Madame Polachek."

She rang a little bell. A servant came, and Madame Polachek said some words in Russian. Morrie recognized the ubiquitous *chai* as the servant pattered off.

"Now, then, young sir," said Madame Polachek, "How may we be of service to you?"

She began to speak again before Morrie could answer. "My husband is a very open and frank personality," she said. He wonders why an English young man would be here in Russia in these times, these troubled times. Omsk is not a place where tourists visit very often, you know, and certainly these days are very discouraging to travelers."

"I can see that you would be puzzled by my sudden appearance," said Morrie, as he started to launch into his by now practically memorized, word-for-word story. He then stopped, realizing that it made no sense to tell these people an untruth. Why not tell them the real story? Surely they were not about to turn him into Scotland Yard. In the first place, there wasn't a Scotland Yard official within thousands of miles, and in the second place, they had no interest in seeing him imprisoned or shot.

He told them the whole story. They tsk-tsked when he talked about the anti-Semitism he had encountered in the Army,as it was a subject with which they were quite familiar. They laughed when he told about being deposited on the shore of Murmansk without knowing a word of Russian or having any idea where he should go.

The servant brought a tray with tea and little jam-filled tarts.

"You have done remarkably well so far, young sir," said Madame Polachek, as she poured. "What is it you would like for us to do for you?"

"I don't know what to do next," said Morrie. He explained that he had been planning to go east, to Vladivostok, but that recent reports about fighting along the Trans-Siberian railroad had discouraged and frightened him.

"I can't stay any longer with my friends at the Y," he said. "In the first place, I've imposed too long. Besides, they have certain rules about how long travelers are allowed to stay, and I think I have just about used up my allowed time there."

Monsieur Polacek, after his wife has translated those words for him, turned directly to Morrie.

"Moishe," he said, using the Hebrew equivalent of Morrie, and rattled off a string of spirited Russian, punctuated with gestures and smiles and pats on Morrie's knee. Madame Polachek said that her husband was suggesting that Morrie stay with them a few days. Monsieur Polachek had to go to Tomsk on a business trip and could use Morrie's assistance. Tomsk was about halfway to Krasnoyarsk, which was to the east, and toward Vladivostok. They would be going in the right direction.

As for Morrie's discouragement and fear about the situation along the railroad, Monsieur Polachek waved those worries away, as he would wave away a troublesome mosquito.

"It is nussing," he said, in accented English.

"He says it is nothing," his wife translated. "You have to understand that my husband is always the optimist. He never sees any trouble ahead. He thinks the Bolsheviks will—."

She stopped, remembering that there was another man in the room, the man who has escorted Morrie to their house.

"Thank you for bringing our guest, Misha," she said, and then, realizing that Misha spoke no English, she repeated her thought again in Russian.

Monsieur Polachek took out a few bills and pressed them into Misha's hand. He mumbled something, and Morrie understood that he was giving him money for the *shul*.

"I'm very grateful to you," Morrie said. "I think I will be going back to the *shul* with Misha, and I know how to get back to the Y from there. I've got a few belongings that I'd like to collect, and then I can come back here. You have really taken a load off my mind."

Misha led Morrie back to the synagogue, and from there Morrie found his way back to the Y building. He thanked his friends for their hospitality and told them that he had found a place to stay for a while before continuing his journey. He then went back to the Polachek house and joined them for a simple dinner. He learned at the dinner table that Monsieur Polachek was, indeed, the Russian Jew who was a major figure in the butter trade. Madame Polachek had gone to school in London which accounted for her fluency in English, and she wanted to reminisce with Morrie about the places she remembered fondly.

"I lived with a wonderful family in St. Johns Wood," she said, "while I was going to school. They were so kind to me. I am glad to be able to return their kindness."

She talked to Morrie about places he knew, along with some places he didn't know, because she had moved in circles that were above him. She was fascinated to hear about his life and his experiences, but she cringed when he talked about his days as a prize fighter, as though someone had struck her. When she translated to her husband however he wanted to hear more.

It was difficult for Morrie to communicate his boxing experiences to Monsieur Polachek, because obviously the translator knew that the gore would be lost in the translation.

Elizabeth, the Polachek's daughter, eagerly listened to the conversation between her parents and this exciting stranger. Strangers were a distinct rarity in her world.

Morrie said that he wanted to know about the Polacheks, and their lives. He meant that he was interested in them today, but Madame Polachek thought he was asking about their history, and so she launched into biographical details.

She was from Riga, in Courland, which later became part of Latvia, and was the daughter of a wealthy cloth manufacturer. She wanted to continue her education, but there was a Jewish quota in their gymnasium in Riga, so she was forced to go to Mittau. It was not a very good school, so her doting father sent her to London.

Her husband, she said, came from St. Petersburg. "Now they want to call it Petrograd, can you imagine a beautiful city with a beautiful name like St. Petersburg, and they want to call it with the ugly name of Petrograd?" She said that very few Jews were permitted to live in St. Petersburg, but the Polacheks were there because they were important in the economy of the city. They spoke German, like all the St. Petersburg elite; they felt that the Russian language was for the *moujiks*, while German was the language of the upper classes. They had met in Riga. Monsieur Polachek wanted to find a new business, because he was a younger son and his brother would run the family's timber business in St. Petersburg. He didn't fancy working for his brother, who was a bully,so he was looking for something new. But he took his new bride back to St.

Petersburg, because he had met a Dane there who wanted to get started in the butter business but needed a partner with capital.

Monsieur Polachek began talking animatedly when the conversation reached this point. His wife had trouble keeping up with him as he galloped along in his account of the butter business.

"The Czar's men," he said, "had for a long time been trying to get the Russian peasants to do more in the dairy business. We had many herds of fine cows, but the *moujiks* only made enough butter for themselves. They wouldn't accept modern machinery; they think the devil is in the machinery. So the Danes came in and made a fine living from our cows. This one Dane, however, needed money, and I was able to raise enough from certain family members so that he and I became partners. Eventually we went our separate ways, Knut and I, although we remain good friends."

Monsieur Polachek was very eager to talk more, as he was obviously in an area that he felt strongly about, Russian agriculture. His wife translated.

"This is a rich country, Moishe. Siberia is not the wasteland that people think. Our peasants are uneducated, true, but our land is fertile and there could be much progress here. I have my doubts that the Bolsheviks know that, but someday someone will come to power who will know. They will know that this is as good a land as there is for raising animals—horses, cattle, goats. Today there are eighty-five horses in Siberia for every hundred human beings. There are in the United States only twenty-two horses for every hundred humans. I think only the Argentines have more. They have more horses than people, I think it is 112 horses to every hundred people.

"I think you must have heard of the trouble the other day in Chelyabinsk."

Morrie nodded.

"Well, would you believe that between Chelyabinsk and Irkutsk, there are living more then three million horses?"

He sat back in his chair with the look of someone who had just told an amazing fact. That was precisely what he had done. Morrie was amazed, not simply at the quantity of horses in Siberia, but also at the fact that this man had all these statistics.

"Besides horses," Monsieur Polachek went on, leaning forward again, "Siberia has many kinds of animals. Foxes, black ones, blue ones, white ones, and those beautiful silver ones. We have trappers who make much money with these fox furs, and ship them all over the world. We have wolves, too, but they have no commercial value."

Morrie asked them what they thought of the revolution. He knew this was always a touchy subject in Russia these days, but he had told them his darkest secret, and so he felt a kinship. Monsieur Polachek had no hesitation about expressing his opinions on the subject.

"Russia was overdue for a change," he said. "There is no doubt but that there were, and still are, very bad conditions in this country. The peasant class was treated terribly. They are not given any education. The medical facilities for the lower classes are practically non existent. A baby born into the peasant class is doomed to a life of hard labor and no pleasure. Death may come by the time he is thirty-five years old, death from ill health."

He paused for breath, and to give his wife a chance to translate.

"My husband speaks for the two of us," she said to Morrie. "I want you to know that. What he says is what I, too, believe."

Monsieur Polachek then continued. He felt that the change, overdue and necessary though it was, was too rapid, too radical, and too bloody.

"They do not have to kill all the aristocrats," he said, "to help the peasants. If an aristocrat is shot, does that help send a peasant child to school? If an aristocrat is shot, how does that put meat on a peasant's table? These killings are not for anything except revenge. We are fortunate here, a little too far away from the center of things to be involved. We have had no killings here, no confiscation of aristocrats' property, thank God. I believe there will be fighting in Russia and Siberia for a long time. The Whites are getting help from the Allies, and the Bolsheviks have the might of Mother Russia.

"And then there are all those evil men who want to cause trouble, men like Semenov. That Semenov is nothing but a murderer, plain and simple. A Mongol and a murderer."

"Enough of this horrible talk of killings and war," said Madame Polachek, after she translated her husband's monologue. "I think it is time for our guest and ourselves to retire."

She had the maid show Morrie to his room, where he quickly fell into a deep sleep. It was, perhaps, the best night's sleep he had since he arrived in Russia.

In the morning, they talked more about the coming trip to Tomsk. Monsieur Polachek said that one of the biggest customers for his butter was the government prison system, which had its headquarters, at least for Siberia, in Tomsk.

A young Dane appeared later in the morning. He would be making the trip to Tomsk with them. His name was Kenneth Christiansen and he worked with Monsieur Polachek at the dairy.

"I am pleased to meet you, Mr. Chernofsky," said Christiansen. He went on to say that he used to visit England regularly, before the war, when the Polachek company sold most of its products to English grocery firms. "Did you know you were eating Russian butter in England?"

The station was full of refugees, as it had been when Morrie arrived from Ekaterinburg. The Czech soldiers were still in command, standing with rifles at the ready and guarding each entrance and exit to the building.

Monsieur Polachek asked the station master something, and the answer was a word that Morrie had heard frequently, "*Cechas.*"

Morrie asked Christiansen what it meant.

"I think literally it means within the hour," said the Dane, "but in Russia it means something like at the earliest moment, a very vague thing. It could be in five minutes or it could be tomorrow or next week, or maybe never. I think what he's really saying is that he doesn't have any idea when it's coming."

Morrie asked him how long the trip to Tomsk would take. Christiansen said that the distance was six hundred miles. They had to take a smaller train for the last forty miles or so, from Taiga north to Tomsk. He estimated that the entire journey would take about two days.

They waited on the platform, sitting on their luggage. Morrie watched the refugees. From where he sat he could see the endless rows of boxcars, and his heart went out to the children playing listlessly along the tracks. He could easily tell they were hungry, and many were obviously ill. He wondered why the Y people didn't help them, remembering the storerooms at Y.M.C.A. headquarters bulging with chocolate, food and medicine.

A whistle blew.

"Train coming," Christiansen said.

"Is it ours?"

"Can't tell yet."

But it was apparent, after it moved slowly through the station, that it wasn't theirs. It was an armored train, made up of flat cars with sandbags around the perimeters. Czech soldiers crouched behind them holding their rifles loosely but ready for anything.

"Don't say a word," Christiansen whispered. "Never know what might set these fellows off."

The armored train stopped, and Another train appeared on an adjacent track. This one was made up of boxcars. Standing at the open doors were Russian soldiers, former prisoners of war, who were being returned by the Germans. They made a sorry comparison with the Czechs. The Czechs were neat and clean, with their shoes polished and their equipment shining, while the ex-prisoners were grimly and poorly clothed, and many of them had no shoes at all.

The Czech train moved on, and on the last car Morrie saw the familiar inverted triangle with the Y.M.C.A. insignia on it. He could see a couple of Y men at the open door of the boxcar.

"*Amerikanski*," Monsieur Polachek said, pointing. There was something magical about Americans. You could tell from the expression in his voice that seeing Americans was a special event.

They waited on the platform for another hour. Morrie realized that they were fortunate that the weather was relatively mild. The station structure itself was jammed with refugees, and there was no way they could have fought their way inside. But it was almost pleasant waiting outside. A train arrived from the east with another string of boxcars. More open doors, with more tired, grim, unshaven ex-prisoners of war looking out. These were from the other side of the war. Austrians, Turks,and Hungarians, said Christiansen, being sent home after being held in Eastern Siberia.

"Look at the Czechs," he said. "They hate these fellows."

From the way the Czechs gripped their rifles tighter and the hard look in their eyes, Morrie could see that the Dane was correct. The Czechs did hate these men, and with good reason. Until a month ago, they had been battling them across the trenches. They were the enemy, and it would take more than a treaty to change that fact.

The station bell began to ring, and the man with the green flag walked along the tracks shooing the horde of refugees back. The train came slowly into the station from the west, and, in a magnificent puff of gray smoke, lapsed into silence.

The refugees and the other waiting passengers dashed toward the train doors, creating an elbowing, pushing, shoving mass of humanity. Polachek led his two charges to the only blue first- class car on the train, just behind the fuel car. Now that the train was here, his impatience vanished.

It was a comfortable unit, with seats that converted into sleeping berths for the night. The seats were upholstered in a dark blue velvet material that had obviously once been elegant, although it was now worn in several spots. Still, as he sat back in his seat and ran his hands appreciatively over the smooth velvet, Morrie felt that he was leading a very luxurious life.

Christiansen had brought along some newspapers, the Japanese *Advertiser* and the *New York Times*. Both were several months old, and contained no news that Morrie didn't know. Still, he enjoyed reading them, for it was the first time since his arrest in London that he had seen a newspaper of any sort. He asked Christiansen if there was any news from the Western Front. The reports in the newspaper spoke of tremendous Allied losses, of bloody battles in the trenches that seemed to have become a stalemate.

Polachek wanted to know what Morrie had said. Christiansen translated, and then relayed Russia's answer.

"He says that in this part of Russia they are not very concerned with the western front at the moment," Christiansen translated. He says it is the war in Siberia that is of more importance here. That's, natural of course. One is always more concerned with the fighting in his backyard than the fighting down the street."

"What does he think will happen here, then?" Morrie asked.

There was more talk between the two men.

"He says that the Allies will certainly intervene here in Siberia and fight with the Whites against the Bolsheviks. He says what is needed in Russia is a strong man to tell everyone what to do. The country survived so long under the Czars because the Czars ruled with an iron fist. The Bolsheviks are disorganized, he says, with their committees and their soviets. He says a committee cannot rule a nation. He says that if that man, Trotsky, (he hates Trotsky, but he admires his strength), if Trotsky can control the other Bolsheviks, perhaps the Bolsheviks will stay in power. If not, then he believes they will collapse, like Kerensky collapsed."

About an hour down the road toward Taiga their train stopped to let another train go by in the other direction. It had, Morrie noticed, large red crosses on its sides. He asked about it, and Christiansen explained that it was one of the American Red Cross sanitary trains, as they were called. Really, they were hospital trains, although they were called sanitary trains. The Americans man them, and they go back and forth along the tracks, helping people, soldiers, and civilians alike.

"There is plenty for them to do from here to Vladivostok," said Christiansen. "I doubt that there are a dozen doctors between Omsk and Vlad, if you exclude Irkutsk."

The sight of the Americans brought forth another dialogue between Polachek and Christiansen. Morrie waited patiently until they were through, for his private translation.

"He was talking about the Americans. He likes them. He says they are being totally neutral here in Siberia, and he thinks that is an admirable thing. They said they would be neutral, and they are being neutral. They are trying to help all sides. He says he doesn't trust the Japanese, of course he wouldn't, because the Russians and Japanese have long been mortal enemies. He doesn't think the French are being very decent here, and he doesn't like the fact that the English are supporting the French."

Polachek made a sudden statement and leaned over and patted Morrie's knee.

"He said he apologizes if you are offended by what he said about the English. He meant no offense."

"It's Okay," Morrie said, and Polachek smiled. He held out his hand, and Morrie shook it.

Polachek said that their first station the next morning would be Novo-Nik. That was how everybody referred to the city of Novo-Nikolaievsk. He said it was one of the two or three cities in Siberia that apparently paid the graft demanded by the railroad builders, and hence the Novo-Nik station was in the middle of town.

The attendant made their seats into berths, and they went to bed. The train noises and the motion combined to lull Morrie into a quick sleep, but it was not a sound one. Whenever the train stopped, the change in sound and feeling roused him. He would look out the window at the action on the platform, and then fall back asleep when the train began moving again.

In Novo-Nik, there was an unexplained delay that stretched to more than four hours. As at Omsk, there were Czech soldiers, rifles at the ready, on guard on the platform, so Christiansen and Morrie didn't stray too far and Polachek didn't even get off the train. The younger men needed the exercise, so they walked up and down the platform, stopping to buy food and tea from the omnipresent *babushkas*.

Since the Novo-Nik station was in the middle of the city, Morrie could see some of the sights, such as they were, from the platform. Christiansen pointed out a large building from which a large American flag fluttered. That was, he said, Novo-Nik's Commercial Club, which during the war had been taken over by the Americans and was now the American Red Cross hospital. Christiansen wanted Morrie to see Novo-Nik's main street, called Nikolaievsky Prospekt. He said it was one of the most beautiful streets in all of Russia.

It was getting dark, so Morrie could barely make out a few buildings and a broad boulevard lined with tall trees. "When spring comes," Christiansen said, "and the leaves come back to the trees, that street is absolutely beautiful."

"The Bolsheviks changed St. Petersburg to Petrograd," Christiansen said. "Before they're through, they'll probably change this to Trotskygrad or Leningrad or something like that."

The Novo-Nik station was full of activity. Trains were coming in and going out, and on most of them Morrie could see there were Y cars attached. He remembered the stocks of cigarettes, soap, and chocolate at the Y headquarters in Ekaterinburg, and noticed that some of the babushkas were selling merchandise that looked suspiciously like that in the Y cache. He reasoned that, in all probability, the Czechs, who were the main recipients of the Y's largesse, were turning around and selling the goods to the women on the station platform, or exchanging them for food and drink.

When the train began moving at last, the three men talked about the area they were crossing. It was heavily wooded, and Polachek said that it could be developed into a prime agricultural area "if we ever have a government that has the good sense to realize it, and to do something to help."

One problem, he said, was that the *moujiks* were people who, in his estimation, had no ambition to better themselves. He explained that they were descendants of the convicts who were sent to Siberia over the centuries, and they still had the convicts mentality. They were just putting in their time until they died.

"The only people in this part of Siberia with any ambition," he said, "are the Jews. If there is a small business here that is thriving, you will find it is owned by a Jew. So, of course, the Jews are hated. It is always jealousy that inspires hatred, you know. The *moujiks* want what the Jews have, some money, a better house, but they haven't the brains or the drive to get it. So instead of working, they hate. It's much easier to hate than to labor."

Inevitably, over a small bottle of vodka, the conversation turned to politics. In the quiet and privacy of their compartment, Polachek was able to unburden himself regarding his views about the revolution that was going on in his country.

"I sympathize with their goals," he said, "and I sympathize with their plight before the revolution. The conditions the peasants lived with under the Czar were certainly intolerable. Now they are behaving as badly as the Czar. They're killing and stealing and imposing laws that control the human mind and spirit.

"The tragedy is that here in this magnificent country there appears to be no alternative, no middle ground between the extremes of the Romanovs and the extremes of the Bolsheviks. You have kings in your two countries, Denmark and England, but you have democracy, too. Look at America - my God, why can't we have a democracy like America?

"The only alternative we seem to have now are these villains, Semenov, Kolchak, or Denikin. They are worse then Nikolai ever thought of being, worse then Trotsky and his hoodlums, worse than you can possibly believe. They are just murderers, criminals who call themselves General or Admiral, call their gang of thugs an Army, and make people believe they are an authority.

"That is what will turn this country to Bolshevism- the fact that the only available alternative is much, much worse."

They neared Taiga, and Christiansen explained that the need for them to change trains there, for the four-hour ride north to Tomsk, was an example of the railroad graft situation at its worst. When the Trans-Siberian railroad was being surveyed, it would have been natural to have it go directly from Omsk to Tomsk. Tomsk was the center of education in Siberia, the site of Siberia's only university. So the railroad planners approached the Tomsk citizenry with the proposal of building the railroad through that city, for a price.

"Tomsk was too proud to pay them even a kopeck," said Christiansen. "So the railroad was built miles to the south."

Taiga station was a duplicate of the others that Morrie had visited recently, full of Czech soldiers and tired refugees. There were more Mongols and Tatars among the throngs of people along the tracks, however. This was a sign that they were getting into the heart of Siberia, with its diversity of people. Morrie noticed their high cheekbones, sallow complexions, and Oriental eyes. They were also dressed differently, in distinctive Astrakhan hats and quilted coats.

There was an hour's wait before the Tomsk train arrived. They watched the refugees and the soldiers, who paraded ominously back and forth along the platform. It was clear that, here at least, the Czechs were in control, and that didn't sit well with Polachek. He said, and Christiansen translated, that the idea of foreigners taking over was anathema to him. He was a very patriotic Russian and he would rather have seen Bolsheviks or even Semenovites in control here than any kind of foreigner.

The short, fifty-mile leg from Taiga to Tomsk enabled Morrie to see why people had been telling him about the incredible poverty of the *moujiks*. The train passed sights that Morrie could never have imagined.

He saw the little villages, which consisted of a single mud street lined with shacks of such flimsy construction that Morrie wondered how they could survive the next rainstorm, to say nothing of ice and snow. Pigs roamed at will, and the people just seemed to be sitting, waiting, passing the time between birth and death. Even the children sat. They were not playing. They looked up as the train chugged by, but none of them waved at the train, as children do everywhere. Instead, they just looked for a moment, then looked back again to the mud and the pigs.

"*You see why the Bolsheviks will win,*" said Christiansen. "These people just don't care who runs things. It's all the same to them. The people of Russia are like this, with the exception of those who live in Moscow, Petrograd, or the other big cities. Most will bow to whoever orders them to bow."

The train tracks followed the river Ob from Taiga to Tomsk, and the station was at the river's edge. A troika was waiting to take Polachek and his party to his hotel, the Europe. Polachek had a private room, but Morrie and Christiansen shared a room. They were greeted at the hotel as old valued customers, because Polachek made the trip almost once a month.

From the window, Christiansen pointed out the university. He said that there were actually two parts to it, the university itself and the Polytechnic Institute. He said that Morrie would see it closer tomorrow, because that was where Polachek did some of his business im Tomsk.

"We sell them butter," Christiansen said. "And the university here is growing very fast. The Bolsheviks have closed the universities in Russia proper, so many of the students there have come here. There are now some fifty-five hundred students here and that's a lot of butter!"

Chritiansen said that they would go to the university in the morning and to the prison in the afternoon. He said that Morrie should just listen, but do no talking; if Morrie spoke English it would just make people start wondering, and wondering people ask questions. It would save a lot of difficult answers if he didn't say anything.

It was, as it turned out, a disastrous meeting for Polachek and his business. The morning session with the university administrators went fine. They simply renewed the contract for butter for another term. But there was sorry news at the prison. It was good news for the prisoners, but bad for Polachek and his cows.

They wouldn't be needed after another month. The prison housed, primarily, Hungarian and Austrian prisoners of war, but they were gradually being released and sent back home. Within another thirty days, the prison officials said, they would all be gone. The few prisoners who remained - "common convicts," the prison officials called them- would get no butter.

Morrie couldn't follow every word of the discussion, but he got the definite impression that the Russian authorities were jittery. They fiddled with their papers, they looked nervously out the window, they seemed unsure of themselves. Afterwards, as the three made their way back to their hotel, he asked Christiansen if his impression was accurate.

"Yes, very accurate," the Dane replied. "They are nervous about the Czechs. They do not know who is their boss, really. They are employed by the Russian government, but here the Czechs are in charge. The Czechs hate the Hungarians and the Austrians, so they are afraid they will invade the prison and try to kill all the prisoners.

"If that happens," he said, "the prison authorities will run out of there as fast as they can and leave their prisoners."

They left the next morning, taking the Tomsk-Taiga train. As they neared Taiga, Polachek said to Morrie that he would pay him a salary for his help on their trip. Morrie said he hadn't done a thing, which was true, but Polachek insisted that he had done a service by carrying a briefcase, which was also true.

"I tell you what I will do" Polachek said. "Instead of paying you a salary, I will buy you a ticket on the railroad from Taiga to Irkutsk. Does that seem like a fair deal to you?"

Polachek said he would like to invite Morrie to stay in Omsk with him and his family, but it wasn't safe. The revolution was coming, he said, and any day now the Bolsheviks would decide that he was ripe to be plucked.

They have their eye on my dairy and my house," he said. "I do not wish for you to be mixed up in my troubles. You are going in the right direction, away from Moscow, away from the revolution, toward Vladivostok and toward the freedom of America. Go there, my boy. I would go there myself if I was younger, believe me."

He told Morrie that the train from Irkutsk to Vladivostok passed through Harbin, and that it would be a very interesting city to visit. It was, he said, half-Russian and half-Chinese, and a little Jewish. Many Jews had fled there when the pogroms erupted, those who couldn't go west to England or America.

Christiansen took some money from Polachek and bought Morrie his ticket to Irkutsk in the Taiga station. They stood on the platform, talked and drinking tea. The Omsk train came in first, and Polachek and Christiansen got on board. Christiansen said that Morrie's train, heading east, should arrive in about two hours.

"*Do zvidaniya*" said Morrie. Polachek laughed and Christiansen complimented him on his accent. Morrie embraced the two men, and they boarded the blue first-class coach, immediately behind the fuel car. Morrie waved to his two friends as the train left he then turned to face reality.

The station platform was, as usual, packed with refugees. Morrie realized that he, too, was a refugee.

Chapter Eight

Morrie felt hot for the first time since he had arrived in Murmansk. He took off his coat and hat and sat on them, using the wall as a back rest. He looked across the fields on the other side of the tracks and realized that there was no snow in sight. The winter was finally over.

He went into the station, stood in line, and eventually found himself facing an impatient ticket clerk.

He produced his ticket.

"Irkutsk," he said. "Irkutsk."

"*Nyet* Irkutsk," the clerk said, shaking his head vigorously. "Krasonyarsk *da*. Irkutsk *nyet*."

That was clear enough. No train to Irkutsk, only to Krasonyarsk. He knew enough of Siberian geography to know that Krasonyarsk was a little more than halfway between Omsk and Irkutsk, so Krasonyarsk was in the right direction. He could probably go to Krasonyarsk first, then to Irkutsk.

"Why?" He asked the ticket clerk, accompanying the word, which he knew the clerk could not understand, with his best play acting, shrugging his shoulders, holding out his hands, raising his eyebrows. That, to him, connoted "why?"

"Irkutsk nyet Czechs." The clerk must have understood the gestures.

Morrie went back outside to the platform. His wall resting spot was taken, of course, so he stood and looked across the web of tracks. There were eight sets of tracks and on one, about four tracks over from where he was, he saw a train. It was an armored train, full of soldiers, but what caught Morrie's eye was the last car on the train. It had the now-familiar insignia of the Y.M.C.A., the inverted triangle.

157

Morrie didn't waste a second on thought. He grabbed his bag and dashed headlong across the intervening tracks to that Y car. The sliding door was open and a young man was leaning against the side of the door, watching him approach.

"Hello, up there," Morrie said.

"You're talking English," said the young man in amazement.

"Give me a hand up," said Morrie, and the man helped him climb into the car.

"Thanks. My name is Alex Chernofsky, and I'm from London, and I"m a friend of John Alexander and all the fellows in Omsk."

"Old John? He's a pal of mine. Welcome to my happy home. I'm Bill Geller."

Naturally the young American was astonished at the sudden appearance of an Englishman scrambling across the tracks in Taiga in the heart of Siberia and climbing aboard his car. Morrie explained as quickly and vaguely as he could, and Geller didn't seem to want more. He was, apparently, just grateful for somebody to talk to in his own language.

Morrie asked him about the trains.

"I can tell you there is no train service to Irkutsk," said Geller. "There is fighting between Irkutsk and Krasnoyarsk, so they've stopped running any trains. Too dangerous."

Bill heated up some hot chocolate and broke open a tin of biscuits from Sweden that had somehow turned up among his stores. While they talked, another Y man named Sam Orick joined them. Morrie had to repeat his story for him.

"Looking for a ride east?" asked Orick.

"I have a ticket to Irkutsk,"said Morrie, holding up his precious piece of paper, "but it doesn't seem to do me much good. Can I hitch a ride with you blokes?"

"Glad to have you," said Orick, who appeared to be the man in charge. "This isn't going to be a vacation trip. This train, as you may have noticed, is full of Czech soldiers, and they are armed to the teeth. We're headed east, where the Whites and Semenov and the Cossacks are also well armed. The Bolsheviks are also somewhere around here. There is probably going to be some heavy fighting between all that."

Orick and Geller told Morrie that he was welcome, although the only accommodations they could offer was a spot on the floor. They said they really could use an extra hand, so they were pleased to have him. They would feed him and give him a blanket and a pillow, but that was as far as they could go. "That," said Morrie, is more than enough."

Morrie made himself at home. The two Y men showed him their stock of stores, which was an truly amazing cache. There were cartons and cartons of cigarettes and chocolate, which seemed to be the Y's main stock in trade. There were other things, too, everything from toilet paper to bandages. Plenty of coffee and good old Eagle Brand condensed milk, which to travelers in Russia and Siberia was almost a staple.

"What do you do with all these things?" asked Morrie, surveying the well-stuffed storeroom.

"When we get to a station," said Orick, "or to a train that is stopped and full of troops or prisoners, we hand these things out. Sometimes we just open the door. We're really just errand boys, bringing these things to those who need them, and we hope that we help a little bit in easing the pain and the suffering of these poor people. You know, they are having a rough time of it, and that goes for everybody—the Bolsheviks, the Czechs, the prisoners, every last one of them."

"We're doing more for them than their own governments are doing," added Sam Orick. "I don't believe any of the soldiers or prisoners have had a decent meal in the last couple of months. When we come along, with our chocolate and coffee, they love it. It may not be the most nutritious food they could get, but it keeps them from starving to death."

"We're also equipped to do some first aid things," said Geller. "Not anything major, of course, but we have bandages and antiseptic, and Sam and I have had some first- aid courses. We're better than nothing."

The two men suggested that Morrie rest a while, because they had some work to do. The work consisted of making up some baskets, just so they would be ready in case they were needed. While they did that, Morrie studied a map tacked to one wall of the car. He was able to trace the route he had already taken, which was beginning to embrace a sizable chunk of the vastness that was Russia and Siberia.

But there was still an even more sizable chunk left to go before he would arrive at Vladivostok. It looked to him as though he was roughly halfway there. He estimated he had already traveled around three thousand miles, with another twenty-eight hundred left to go.

He saw from here that the next important landmark was Lake Baikal, which was just beyond Irkutsk. After that it would be on to Harbin and then the final leg to Vladivostok. "Here, Morrie, grab this." Orick held out a big basket to Morrie. "We might as well do some good while we're just sitting here. There are a lot of soldiers out there who could use a bit of assistance."

The three men jumped down from the car, closed and locked the door behind them, and then proceeded down the train. When they came to a boxcar with soldiers in it, they called out "Hey, you, up there!" The Czechs would peer down with puzzled looks on their faces, but those looks quickly changed to delighted amazement when the three strangers began throwing up bars of chocolate, cans of soup, and the other unexpected treats.

All the baskets were empty in a very few minutes. Other soldiers in other cars, curious about all the noise and laughter, were holding hands out and yelling "*prosim, prosim*," which Morrie understood to mean "Please" or "Hey, how about me, you blokes?"

When they returned to home base Morrie noticed a few holes in the car's side.

"Bullet holes?" he asked.

"Yes," said Orick.

"Were you in the car when that happened?"

"Yes. It was back in Ufa. Just as we were pulling out, the Bols opened up on the train. Only one of the Czechs was hurt, a bullet in his hand. The train kept moving and we were well out of range in a few minutes. We passed a Red Cross sanitary train a little while later, and put the wounded fellow on that train. I never figured, when I signed up to work with the Y, that anybody would be shooting at me."

The three men had some hot chocolate and more of those Swedish biscuits then Geller said he was going to try to find out what was happening.

Bill came back with the welcome news that the train would move in about a half-hour. There was more news that Bill and Sam also felt was welcome. Gadja was going to be with them.

"Who is Gadja?" asked Morrie.

"He is the Czech railroad commander," said Bill. "If anybody can get these trains through, it's him. He's on the train just ahead of this one. Gadja will be in command of the Czechs if there is any fighting, and from what I understand, they aren't in any mood to take any more from the Bolsheviks. They've been stalled by the Bolsheviks, who are pussy-footing about the issue, and the Czechs are just going to move on through, no matter who's in the way."

They said that Gadja was violently anti-Bolshevik, and probably Anti-Russian. He was a hard-nosed officer and Morrie could tell that Bill and Sam had a lot of admiration for him. They seemed to be more confident, now that they had heard he was running things.

The train started moving in less than the anticipated thirty minutes. Morrie could hear the sound of cheering from the men in the cars ahead of them. He looked out the rear of the train and saw the refugees scrambling to get on the train behind them, which had some flat-bed cars. They were apparently designed to help them move along their tragic route.

The two Y men spent the next half-hour on their inventory. They were required to keep track of their supplies and to note how much had been given out, when, and to whom. It was a nuisance but they realized it had to be done. Morrie tried to help by counting cartons and they welcomed his assistance.

After the train started off, Morrie got his blanket and pillow. He found a nice, quiet niche in the store room and slept. The sudden squeal of the trains's brakes and the jarring as the train stopped woke him abruptly. He went out into the main part of the car.

"Anything wrong?" he asked. Bill had opened the door and was peering out into the blackness.

"I think we're in Marinsk," he said. "That's about halfway to Krasnoyarsk."

Morrie leaned out and saw, from a tiny puddle of light from some lanterns, a small, green station house and a water tower. The train was still edging slowly forward, but suddenly there was a hissing sound followed by a loud explosion. Morrie could see a fountain of sand spraying into the air from one of the sandbags that circled the car just ahead.

"Hit the deck!" yelled Orick. "It's gunfire!"

They heard shouts and the pounding of boots on the wooden station platform. Bill cautiously slid open the door on the other side of the car and peered out.

"The Czechs are chasing them across the platform."

Morrie and Sam got up then and joined Bill at the slightly opened door. They could see running figures in the distance, but they couldn't make out their nationality. Sam said that the chasers were the Czechs and the chasees were Hungarians and, surprisingly, some Germans. What Germans were doing in Siberia was anybody's guess, but everything in Siberia at this point in time was so confusing that anything was possible.

The running figures vanished in the gloom, and for a while there was nothing but silence and the slight hiss of the escaping steam from the railroad engine.

Then the Czechs came back. They all headed for their cars, but two of them peeled off from the others and came toward the Y car. When they got close enough, Morrie made out the fact that one was supporting the other, who had blood oozing from his sleeve, dripping down his arm and hand.

"We've got us a casualty," said Sam. "Lend a hand, Morrie."

The three of them jumped down and helped boost the wounded soldier into the car. They had him lie down and Sam tore off his jacket sleeve.

"Morrie, in the back of the car, get us some bandages. Quick."

The three worked together well. Fortunately, the wound was not serious. The bullet had grazed the upper arm, and really amounted to nothing more than a deep cut. The man was understandably afraid, and in a state of semi-shock. Bill expertly washed and bandaged the wound, and then they sat him up and gave him a glass of strong tea, and the man gradually calmed down. His face, cold and clammy and sweaty, slowly dried off and his color returned.

"Thank you," the man said in English, when he had recovered enough to be able to speak. "Where is rifle?"

He was concerned, now that he had his wits about him again, with the whereabouts of his most precious possession, his rifle. The wounded soldier's friend had leaned it against the car's side, so Sam brought it over to the soldier.

"Good," the soldier said, giving his weapon an affectionate pat. "Is good."

"Did you see that gun?" asked Sam. "American. How about that? We send the Russians guns and then we have to duck bullets from those guns. That's just dandy."

The soldier's buddies were standing patiently on the platform, waiting for their friend. When he felt well enough to walk the Y men helped him down. The soldiers, one by one, came over and shook the hands of Bill, Sam, and Morrie, and each one ritualistically said the same words:

"Thank you, dear sir, for help to us."

Sam asked one of them what the shooting was all about. He was told, in mixed Czech, German, and English, that the Bolsheviks had been waiting in ambush and even had a cannon, and the battle had been short but intense for a while. There were Magyars, as the Czechs called the Hungarians, Austrians, and even a few Germans.

That was the end of the Battle of Marinsk, as Bill and Sam called it. They made up some mock medals and gave one to Morrie and said he was now a veteran of the Battle of Marinsk.

Sam said, "You are entitled to certain benefits as a veteran of the Battle of Marinsk, not the least of which is a chance to ride with us for a few more days and perhaps undertake another battle. Congratulations, private."

He kissed Morrie on both cheeks as the train started up again en route to Krasnoyarsk.

Chapter Nine

The Marinsk-Krasnoyarsk leg of the trip was uneventful. The train rolled for three hundred miles without stopping, and in the Y car the three young men cleaned the blood from the floor, inventoried the supplies, and had a sound sleep.

At the Krasnoyarsk station, Morrie and the others had a much-needed chance to stretch their legs. They walked ahead and found the soldier they had treated, who was still so grateful that he embraced them all. He had a friend, an English- speaking Czech soldier named Paul Cecek, who had spent several years in Chicago.

"Were there any other casualties besides your friend?" asked Bill.

"It was very surprising, but not a one," said Cecek. "I think we killed a few of the enemy, however. We captured their cannon. See, there it is."

The cannon, small but lethal, was stashed on one of the flat cars, with sandbags all around it.

There were other Czech troops on the platform, and Cecek explained that these men had been further east, in Irkutsk, and had found their way through a line of Bolshevik troops to reach their confederates here in Krasnoyarsk.

"Do you expect trouble ahead?" asked Sam.

"Yes, most probably," said Cecek. "The railroad is clear for a few hundred *yersts* but, from then on until Irkutsk, it is in the hands of the Bols. They hold Irkutsk now. General Gadja is afraid that they will blow up one or more of the tunnels."

"Then we'd never get through," said Bill.

Morrie wanted to know what tunnels he was referring to. Bill explained that, beyond Irkutsk, as the railroad curved south to clear the southern tip of Lake Baikal, there were a series of tunnels through the mountains in that area.

All that was left between Morrie and total poverty were seventy-five rubles, in assorted types of Russian currency. If he had to go off on his own, separated from the Y car, he would soon be one of the starving refugees he had seen so often along the way.

Krasnoyarsk had its share of those pitiful figures. Here there were more Mongols than before, and a smattering of Chinese, with their long queues hanging down their backs. The voices were speaking a dozen different languages. Morrie had never realized that Siberia was such a melting pot of different races and cultures.

They left Krasnoyarsk, heading east along the road to Irkutsk. It was, for a time, another journey without incident. The train chugged along peacefully for the rest of that day, and through the night. There were a few stops, mostly for fuel and to water the engine, and then they moved off again. Morrie was acquiring tremendous respect for the people who ran the Trans- Siberian railroad. Given the conditions that existed, soldiers, refugees, and all that, they were doing an incredible job in keeping the trains moving.

The peaceful trip ended in a burst of gunfire, heavier than at Marinsk. It was almost dawn, and a faint light from the rising sun illuminated the scene as the three men cautiously peeked out of the car door.

"It looks like another ambush," said Bill.

There was a station ahead, and Morrie clearly made out flashes coming from the muzzles of many rifles aimed at his train.

Now there was another, nastier sound added to the cruel chorus; a machine gun, maybe two, chattering away. Then came the boom of a cannon, and the Y car shook from the reverberation of the sound. Behind him he heard cans falling from the shelves as the car continued to tremble on the rails.

The firing started to rake the train and was getting closer to them. Instinctively the three of them fell to the floor. A few bullets plowed through the wall of the car and on across, over their prone bodies, and out the other side. Morrie could make out slender splinters of light coming in through the bullet holes in the door.

They heard the sound of Czechs dropping off their cars, their feet crunching in the gravel, and their shouts as they attacked. The machine guns stopped. The rifle fire grew fainter and the voices faded in the distance.

"I guess we can get up now," said Bill. "The Czechs sound like they have them on the run."

They stood up and looked out, but there was nothing to see. The platform was empty of soldiers and there were no Czechs on the flat cars. The battle had moved away from them.

Bill went over to a corner of the car where there was a small table with a wireless key attached to it. He began to send a message.

"What's that?" Morrie asked. Sam explained that it was the wireless to the other Y cars and to the Y headquarters. Bill was asking them to send a sanitary train here, because with all that firing there were bound to be a lot of casualties.

They waited silently for almost an hour, with only an occasional pop of a rifle to break the stillness. Then the Czechs began straggling back to the train. A few headed directly for the Y car. These were the injured, seeking help.

There was a bad leg wound. A bullet had shattered the bone a few inches below the knee. The soldier's leg was covered with blood and he was screaming with pain and fright. They had him lie down. When Bill applied Iodine to the open wound, the man fainted, which was the best thing that could have happened.

His companions said they had chased the enemy into the village, and after a short, house- to- house engagement, chased them out the other side of the village and up into the hills. They said the enemy were mostly Bols, but their commanding officer appeared to be German.

The slightly wounded soldiers, and those who were uninjured, left the Y car and went back to their command. The man with the shattered leg stayed on in the Y car, and Bill and Sam explained that they would pass him along to the first sanitary train they met. Meanwhile, they would care for him as best they could.

The train began moving again, but slowly. It was as if the engineer wanted to see what was ahead before he ventured too far. He was at the front of the train and therefore he was the most vulnerable. He was being understandably very cautious. They had only traveled an hour or two, covering barely thirty miles, when they pulled off the main tracks and onto a siding. There was a tiny station, and across on another set of tracks there was a train with the distinctive markings of the Red Cross. This was the sanitary train that they had been looking for.

Sam ran across and got help. Two of the Red Cross men had a stretcher and they took the wounded man, who was still unconscious, over to the sanitary train, where there were doctors and reasonable facilities.

"Tell this poor guy's buddies that he'll be at our hospital in Irkutsk," said the Red Cross man. "That is, if we ever get there."

"What do you mean by that?" asked Sam.

The Red Cross orderly explained, as though he were talking to a small child, that at last report, Irkutsk was in the hands of the Bolsheviks and the surrounding territory was in the hands of the Czechs, so there was bound to be trouble.

"We're afraid that one side or the other will blow up the tunnels around the lake. That would totally stop the railroad. Everything between here and Irkutsk would back up. Nothing would move."

He patiently explained about the two famous Lake Baikal boats, the *Baikal* and the *Angara*, and what they meant to the people who lived near the lake.

The *Baikal* had been important to lake commerce as a ferry until the railroad came along in 1900. She had been built in England, Newcastle-upon-Tyne, and then taken apart and packed into seven thousand crates, with each piece carefully numbered. The crates went from England to St. Petersburg by ship, then overland to Krasnoyarsk, and then shipped down the Yenesei River and up the Angara River by barge. It was reassembled when all the crates reached the lake. The engines, boilers, and the rest of the boat's mechanical parts had been Russian-built, but these, too, had been sent to the lake in crates.

"Now," the Red Cross man continued, "these famous old boats have been commandeered by the Bolsheviks. They have lashed cannons to the decks and are taking pot shots at passing trains, especially trains with Czech troops aboard.

"It sounds like it'll be a swell trip," said Bill. "We have to go through a bunch of tunnels that might or might not be open and then go around a lake with a boat shooting at us. Nothing like a spring vacation in beautiful Siberia, right?"

They laughed, but it wasn't exactly uproarious laughter. They then went back to their car, which was pretty messy after the day's events, and tried to clean it. The train began moving again, but the engineer was still obviously afraid of what might be ahead, and so was proceeding very slowly.

The train stopped a quarter-mile or so before every little station, and the Czechs sent a scouting party ahead to make sure there were no more ambushes. There weren't.

The Czech commander would talk to the station master at each station. He would tell his subordinates the latest news, and soon rumors swept through the train, eventually reaching the Y car. The rumors were generally the same, involving trouble ahead around Irkutsk and Lake Baikal. The assumption was grim. Irkutsk was the military headquarters for the Bolsheviks in Siberia and that would be the Czechs' main target, should they elect to turn this unpleasantness into an all- out war. That probability was strengthened by the report that the Czechs were in control of Vladivostok and were launching a westward drive. This pincers movement, Czechs coming from Vladivostok in the east and Krasnoyarsk in the west, would converge on Irkutsk very soon.

"We appear to be headed for the middle of the damn thing," said Sam.

They got out a detailed map of the Lake Baikal-Irkutsk area. There were thirty-nine tunnels beyond Irkutsk, between the towns of Baikal, on the southern tip of the lake, and Kultuk to the east. Block any one of those tunnels and the railroad would grind to a permanent halt.

The train had been moving so slowly that it took them a few minutes to realize that it had completely stopped. They slid open a door cautiously and looked out. No station this time. They were sitting on a broad empty plain with nothing in sight in any direction.

Then they noticed that the Czech soldiers were jumping down from their cars. Bill ran up and spoke to one of the men who had been in the car with the soldier with the shattered leg, and then reported back with the news that this was as far as the train was going.

"They are going on foot from here to attack Irkutsk," Bill said. "One of the tunnels is blocked. The Bols exploded a bomb inside the opening, and it's impassable. The troops are going on foot, some along the tracks, some others across those mountains up ahead, to the tunnels."

"What about us?" asked Morrie.

"We walk too. No choice."

It was, at best, the Czechs explained, a two-day march from where they were into Irkutsk, longer if they were fired on en route. When they reached the city the Czechs would attack. The men would go with the Czechs into Irkutsk if they won the battle. They would presumably be able to get aboard another train beyond Irkutsk and proceed east, once the tunnel was cleared. But what would be their status if captured by the Bolsheviks?

"Theoretically," said Bill, "Sam and I are neutrals, as part of the Y.M.C.A. organization. I don't know about you, Alex. You have no papers and God knows what they will make of an Englishman out here."

"Might shoot you as a spy," said Sam, clapping Morrie on the back.

"It's not a joke," said Morrie. "That could happen, you know. Let's just hope the Czechs win this bloody battle."

They crammed as many supplies as they could into bags: Chocolate bars, Eagle Brand milk, soap, toilet paper, and cigarettes, and then stuffed more of those items into their pockets.

The three of them promised that, no matter what happened along the way, they would stick together and take care of each other. Sam and Bill both said how glad they were that Morrie was with them. He hadn't told them that he had military training, but somehow they sensed that he knew more about military matters than they did. They deferred to him. It wasn't a responsibility he particularly desired, and yet he found himself in charge of the three-man unit.

They let the soldiers take as much of the supplies as they could carry; there was no point in leaving it sitting in the middle of Siberia. There were some commands in Czech and the soldiers assembled alongside the train. They marched out, half moving straight ahead following the railroad bed, the other half cutting off at an angle toward the distant mountains.

"Which way should we go, Morrie?" asked Sam.

"Let's follow behind the troops on the tracks," said Morrie.

"I don't particularly fancy doing any mountain climbing."

They agreed that that was sound thinking. Morrie's first command had been basic, but wise. They began walking.

The Czechs, trained soldiers and in good condition, strode along at a good clip. Bill, Sam, and Morrie were able to keep up, but it was difficult for them. Fortunately, the terrain was flat and the weather was ideal for walking, not cold but certainly not hot. The Czechs stopped for a ten-minute break every hour, and the three in the rear sank gratefully to the ground and gobbled a chocolate bar for energy, then smoked a cigarette, which sapped their wind, although they were blissfully unaware of it.

Morrie was happy that they were, at least for the moment, on the side of the Czechs. The Czechs and the Cossacks saluted each other, although they did not speak each other's language, and embraced and raised sabers and rifles, yelling threats to their mutual enemy.

The meals for the three young men were simple at best. Still, they were probably eating better than the troops with whom they were marching. They had brought some soup with them, and that formed the basis of lunch and dinner, augmented by chocolate bars. They lit fires, which served the dual purpose of protecting them from the wolves and from the hordes of mosquitoes that had infested the area.

A thunderstorm drenched them in the middle of the second night on the road, and the next day they had to slog through mud. They were, therefore slowed considerably. The two- day march turned into three days, with the last day and a half being thoroughly unpleasant.

Late on the third day, they came to a river. There was a small village along its western bank. The people in the village had run indoors at the sight of the advancing army, because to them an army meant pillaging and confiscation, rape and, quite likely, murder. The Czechs did none of these things. They were not necessarily any less inclined to those pursuits, but they were under strict discipline.

That night the soldiers, together with the Y men and Morrie, slept inside two ramshackle old barns. Bill, Sam, and Morrie gave the villagers some chocolate bars, and some old ladies came back with some fresh bread and a few bags of salt. It was all they had.

Perhaps the bread and salt had another significance. Morrie remembered how, back home in the East End of London, when a family moved into a home, their friends and relatives would bring them bread and salt. It was a kind of ritual welcome. Perhaps that tradition had its origin here in Russia and the old ladies of the village meant the bread and salt as a gesture of welcome.

At noon the next day, the men came to a bluff. The city of Irkutsk lay below them, and railroad tracks wound down a gradual hill. The city seemed very peaceful from this vantage point. The Czech commanders, equipped with binoculars, reported that they could see no sign of any fighting. They waited there until the rest of their forces, who had taken the mountain route, joined them. They cautiously approached the city together.

The Czechs were greeted at the outskirts by some of Gadja's men, who came out to give them the welcome news that the Bolsheviks had quit the city.

"Irkutsk is ours!" shouted the Czechs.

The reports stated that there was heavy fighting around the lake. A couple of the tunnels were blocked. The Bolsheviks, firing on the railroad from the lake boats, controlled that portion of the main line.

Morrie stood there admiring the sight of Irkutsk that he could see from the hill. The houses all seemed to be made of wood, neat and painted white and yellow. There was the obligatory cathedral with its onion-shaped dome. The Irkut river meandered through the city glistening in the sun, and Morrie could see a few small boats on its shiny surface.

There were hills all around the city, and most of them were covered with white birches. The combination of their snow- white bark and flut-tering green leaves completed the beautiful picture.

Bill had been to Irkutsk before and was convinced it was the most beautiful city in Siberia, perhaps in all of Russia. He pointed to a bridge.

"We'll have to cross that bridge to get into the city. That bridge is over the Angara, which is a tributary of the Irkut. When we get there you'll see the clearest water you've ever seen. Absolutely crystal clear. You can see right down to the bottom."

They found when they approached the city, however, that what had looked so lovely from the hills above now showed signs of damage. The Bolsheviks, before abandoning the city, had systematically wrecked it. The bridge over the Angara was now impassable so the Czechs commandeered some small boats and were rowed across. The Irkutsk citizenry, led by the city officials, greeted them warmly as they disembarked.

Bill and Sam, with Morrie tagging along, detached themselves from the Czech army at this point. They felt that their duty was to try to find the Y people in Irkutsk. They walked along the city streets, searching. They found a line of people queued up outside a bakery, and Bill approached them.

"*Amerikanski*," he said, and gave a passable imitation of a tall building with a flag fluttering from the staff on the roof. He was trying to find the location of the American Consulate. His charade worked.

"*Spasiba*."

They walked a short distance and arrived at the Consulate, which was about two blocks away. It was a large square wooden building with a guard stationed at the front gate.

The guard greeted them in Russian, according to protocol, and was visibly pleased when they responded in English. What was more astounding to him was that their English was American English.

"What can I do for you fellows?"

"We're with the Y, and we're looking for the other Y people. Do you know if there are any in Irkutsk right now?"

"I wouldn't know," said the guard, "but why don't you go inside and talk to Henry Probst. He's Mr. Harris' secretary. Harris is the Counsel here, and if anybody would know, it's old Henry. Nothing goes on in Irktusk that he doesn't know about."

They went inside and found Probst, a younger man than they had expected after the guard's build-up. The guard was right, he did know about the Y people who were in Irkutsk and Sam and Bill were both overjoyed to learn that a man named Jim Hassenger, who they both knew well, was just down the street. Probst insisted that they stay for some tea and cake.

"Sit down for a few minutes," he said. "You fellows look like you've been on the road for days."

They told him that that was exactly the case, they had been walking for three days. Probst was interested in learning about their experiences. Morrie could see him filing all the information away in his mind, and in return he told them about the situation in Irkutsk. They then explained Morrie's situation.

"Your friend is at the Dekko Hotel," Probst said. "There is no Y head-quarters here, just Jim Hassenger. He has a room at the hotel, and that's where he handles all his Y business.

"Let me see if I can get Mr. Harris to invite you three to stay for dinner. You can then go over and see Jim afterwards, and he can find rooms for you at the Dekko."

As they sat for dinner, Probst told them that he had gotten word to the Dekko Hotel, and rooms had been reserved for the three of them for the night.

Harris, the Consul, who looked the part with a full head of snow- white hair and a contrasting black mustache, sat at the head of the table. He offered them vodka, which they accepted, and proposed a toast "to the good old U.S. of A."

He wanted to know something about his guests. Sam spoke for Bill and himself, explaining that they worked for the Y.M.C.A. and were based in Omsk. They were riding one of the Y cars to Vladivostok and back, and told how they had to abandon their car and join the Czechs marching to Irkutsk.

Harris wanted to know all the details of the two attacks on the train that they had survived. He was somewhat disappointed when they couldn't give them any concrete information about the size of the attacking force.

Harris loosened up over dinner, and after a glass or two of Armenian brandy he was positively courtly. He gave them the news that American troops, according to an announcement only a few days before from President Wilson, would be coming to Siberia, via Vladivostok. They were en route from Seattle at the moment.

"Great," said Bill. "Leave it to us Yanks. We'll straighten out this mess."

"Absolutely right, young man, and we'll have help there, too. French and Japanese troops are coming. The Japanese are already there."

They talked a little about the Japanese. Harris was suspicious of their motives. He felt that they had their eyes on Manchuria and might use this situation to put their hands on it. They were lending their support, both spiritual and physical, to Semenov, and it was Semenov who was doing their dirty work for them.

"The Japanese are certainly not being neutral," said Harris, "but we have given our word, our sacred word that we will respect the neutrality of the Russian people. We firmly believe that it is the right of the Russian people to choose their own government.

"My colleague, Mr. Nash, the British Consul, believes that we should be backing the Whites against the Reds, as his government is doing. He and I have gone round and round on this issue. The root of Britain's decision to back the Whites is purely economic. There are millions of pounds invested in Russia by British concerns and they are afraid of what a Bolshevik government might do to that investment. Our concern is humanitarian, not economic."

Morrie felt like applauding. This was so obviously a political speech that he thought that Mr. Harris probably expected a rousing ovation as he finished.

"You are absolutely right, Mr. Harris," said Bill.

"Yes, indeed," said Sam.

"How about you, Mr. Chernofsky?" asked Harris." As you're a subject of His Majesty, I would be interested in knowing how you view the current situation here."

"Well, sir," said Morrie, who also had a few glasses of brandy, "I certainly agree with your president's desire to let the Russians chose their own form of government, but I think that will be difficult from what I have seen of the Russian people. They are like little children. Most of them can neither read nor write. The ones I've seen, with some rare exceptions in the upper classes, don't know a thing about politics, and they don't care a fig about it, either. Like children, they follow whoever makes the biggest promises to them and I think the Bolsheviks are the best promisers.

"The Czars obviously didn't care about them. They suffered under the Czar, so they welcome a change. The Whites are basically the same people who used to work for the Czars, so they don't want them. Semenov and the other petty leaders are murderers, and they know that. The Cossacks are murderers too. That pretty much leaves the Bolsheviks. It just seems to me that the Russian people, the *moujiks*, the common people, will go with the Bolsheviks. They are simply the lesser of a whole bunch of evils."

"An interesting assessment, Mr. Chernofsky," said Harris. "Have you ever thought of a political career when this dreadful war is finally over?"

"No, sir," said Morrie.

Henry Probst joined them. He had been on some official errand that kept him from dining with them. He gave the latest intelligence about what lay ahead for them around Lake Baikal and the crucial tunnel area.

Gadja and the main force of the Czechs were deployed along the railroad between the villages and Baikal and Kultuk. They were under constant fire from the two boats on the lake, the *Baikal* and the *Angara*. The *Baikal* was the larger of the two; it was a huge, ferry-like craft that had been built in England and could be used as an ice-breaker on the lake in the winter. The *Angara* was smaller, but faster. The *Baikal* had been equipped with a cannon, and was devastating the troops on shore along the railroad.

Probst said that the Czechs were advancing west along the railroad, from Vladivostok toward Chita. If Gadja and his men could clear the path and open the railroad from Irkutsk to Chita, then the Czechs would control some four thousand miles of the Trans-Siberian. That would almost certainly mean the end of the Bolsheviks' chance of controlling Eastern Siberia. The war depended on what happened barely a dozen miles from where they were sitting, puffing on cigars and sipping brandy. It all depended on who controlled the tunnels along the southern shore of Lake Baikal.

Harris began nodding off, so Sam tactfully suggested that they call a halt to the evening. He said that he and his friends were tired, which was certainly true enough. Probst kindly volunteered to drive them to their hotel in his *droshky*.

The Hotel Dekko was a solid, square stone building, three stories high, on Irkutsk's main street, Bolsholiskaya. The rent of the room for one night took precisely half of Morrie's remaining funds. They all agreed to meet in the hotel restaurant for breakfast, at which time they would make their presence known to their Y friend, Jim Hassenger.

Morrie was tired, but he was worried about what he was going to do next. It seemed obvious that he would have to stay here in Irkutsk for some time, because as things now stood, they certainly couldn't proceed along the railroad. He was practically broke, and seemed to have no prospects for making any money. As he mulled the problem over in his mind, he tossed and turned rather than slept. He came to the conclusion that he would do here what he had previously done, successfully, in Ekaterinburg. He would try to find some Jewish families to help him.

He realized that he probably had enough rubles to buy himself breakfast and a little something for lunch, but that was it. If he couldn't find some friendly Jews to help him, he was going to become one of those refugees he had been pitying as he made his way across Siberia.

Chapter Ten

Breakfast in the Hotel Dekko dining room was slow but pleasant. Morrie, although he didn't tell this to Bill or Sam, realized that it might be his last decent meal in some time. He savored every mouthful. He also enjoyed being with his good friends and their friend, Jim Hassenger.

Hassenger explained the Y's situation to them. There was no Y establishment of any sort in Irkutsk; Jim and his hotel room office were it. The Y had applied to the Russian government, asking permission to set up a headquarters in the city, but so far they had heard nothing. That, Hassenger said, was typical of the way the Russian government was reacting to most things these days. They didn't say yes or no. They just didn't say.

"So it looks like we'll just stay on here for a time and see what develops," said Bill. "How about you, Alex? Are you okay? Got enough money?"

Morrie felt that he had imposed enough on these two.

"I'm fine," he said. I'm going to go out after breakfast and head for the first synagogue, and they'll help me."

"Why in the world would you go to a synagogue?" Phil asked.

"For some help. I speak a little Yiddish and...."

"You must be kidding. You're Jewish?"

"Sure. Didn't you know?"

"Of course not. You don't, I mean, we never had any idea. Not that it matters, of course, but we just never even thought about it."

They said they just assumed, from the way he talked, that he was an Englishman. Morrie said he *was* an Englishman, but he was Jewish, too. Bill and Sam were still shaking their heads in surprise over this revelation. Morrie understood that they had nothing against Jews, it was simply that they were stunned by the fact that Morrie was Jewish. That was all there was to it.

179

Morrie was smiling as he left the dining room. It had been sort of fun to see those shocked faces.

At the desk in the lobby, he asked the clerk for directions to "synagoga." That was, he hoped, the way to say synagogue in Russian. The clerk appeared to understand. He led Morrie to the door, pointed off to the right, waved his hand vaguely in that direction, and said "Novosibirskaya." Morrie assumed that that was probably the name of the street on which the synagogue was located. He said thank you to the clerk and walked off briskly in that direction.

He noticed, as he walked along, that the people he passed seemed better dressed than anywhere he had been so far in Russia. There were attractive shops, and the horses pulling the droshkys and carts appeared to be better fed than most horses he had seen. The whole city had an air of prosperity that he had not hitherto encountered in Russia.

He stopped an elderly man at the first corner, a broad, tree-lined boulevard, and asked "*Pashalsta*, Novosibirskaya?" The man smiled, obviously amused by Morrie's accent, and nodded. He said "*Da*" and held up two fingers. Morrie understood him to be saying that Novosibriskaya was two blocks further on.

He wasn't sure which way to turn after he reached that second corner. He stood, looking in both directions. There was a large building to his left about half a block away, so he decided to look at it more closely. When he got in front of it, he could see he had guessed correctly.

This was plainly the synagogue, but it was not a plain synagogue: it was, in fact, very imposing. The face of the building was fine white marble, trimmed in gold, and there was a large, graceful dome on top. The front entrance, a set of massive carved wooden doors, was reached via a flight of steps. Only the familiar Hebrew letters on a small tablet near the entrance identified the building.

Morrie climbed the steps, opened the door and went inside. There was a beautiful lobby, more white marble and more gilt trim, with richly upholstered benches lining the walls. Morrie proceeded into the sanctuary itself. There was not a soul in sight.

He spotted a small door in one corner, and Morrie went over and knocked softly on the door. A man with a long black gown responded. In his uneasy Yiddish, Morrie explained who he was and that he needed help.

"*Helfen*," he repeated. "*Helfen. Helfen, selt azoi gut.*" Help, please.

When had he arrived in Irkutsk, the Rabbi asked. Morrie replied that he had arrived last evening, and volunteered that he was staying at the Hotel Dekko. He said he had very little money and was desperate for help. He needed to find a place to stay and a way to earn money for his food.

This was a lot of information to convey in his very shaky command of the language. He wasn't sure that the rabbi really understood every word, but he appeared to get the drift, for he kept shaking his head and murmuring "*Orim jungel*," which Morrie understood to mean "poor boy." It was what his mother would say when he had fallen and hurt himself.

The rabbi began speaking. Morrie got the message that he should return tomorrow. Meanwhile, the rabbi would seek help for him. Morrie thanked him and returned to the hotel.

Morrie had a day to himself. Bill and Sam said they would show him Irkutsk, and the three friends took a long relaxing walk. Phil was anxious to show Morrie the Angara River. The water was amazingly clear. They went to the bank, and cupped their hands and drank. It was delicious, cool, sweet, and pure.

"I can't believe this is Siberia," said Morrie. "It's surely not the Siberia I've always heard about or seen myself."

He looked around. The houses, without exception, were painted sparkling white and had green metal roofs. The city looked green and white, a color scheme that was pleasing and restful to the eye. The river, with its clean and clear water, meandered through the town, and the little bridges were all tiny duplicates of larger spans and gave the city a touch of beauty.

They stopped for some tea, purchased from a man with a samovar strapped to his back. They drank it by the edge of the river, stretching out on the grassy bank.

"This has been the best afternoon I've spent in Russia since I got here," said Morrie. "It's hard to believe that people are shooting at each other only a few miles away."

When they got back to the hotel they found there was a new arrival, Rick Stirling, another Y man, was just back from investigating the situation at the lake. He said that it looked bad for the Czechs there, because the Bolsheviks, from their vantage point on the two lake boats, could command the railroad. Nothing could move. The Russian cannon on the *Baikal* had a bead on the tracks and there was no way the Czechs could silence that gun. They had tried to make a run for it at night, crossing the open tracks under cover of darkness. But the train made so much noise that the Russians heard them, and they had the range down so accurately that they didn't need to see the train to fire at it. That attempt resulted in the loss of a train and about twenty-five men.

"How about the tunnels?" asked Jim.

"So far, only one has been blocked," Stirling said. "But the Bolsheviks have planted explosive charges inside several others. They're sure to explode them if it looks like they're going to lose, and then it'll be months, maybe a year or more, before the railroad is passable through that area."

Morrie went to bed realizing that it was very possible he might be marooned in Irkutsk for a long time. He didn't know what he would do if the people at the synagogue weren't able to help him. "Please, God, let me get out of here soon."

He, Phil, and Sam parted in the morning. Morrie thanked them, but they also thanked him. They said he had been a big help to them, and that made him feel good. They embraced each other warmly, Russian fashion, and then Morrie walked back to the synagogue.

The rabbi was waiting with two gentlemen, who were dressed neatly in well-tailored business suits.

"My name is Boris Tiomkin," said one, in a thick accent, but one that Morrie was able to understand, because it sounded like most of his parents' friends back in London. "And here is my friend, Alexander Shtein."

"How do you do? I am Morrie Kotler."

"Mr. Kotler, a pleasure I"m sure. You are from London?"

"Yes, sir, I am."

"A fine city, London. I was there once, but years ago."

Tiomkin explained that he was in the tea business and had gone to London to learn about tea. He said he thought Russian tea was better than English tea, and wondered what Mr. Kotler thought about this important question.

"Well, sir, it took me some time to get used to Russian tea, but now that I am used to it, I find I like it very much."

Tiomkin smiled. This was obviously a matter of great importance and pride to him, and to have an Englishman say that he liked Russian tea very much was a great triumph.

"The rabbi tells me," he went on, "that you have no money and no place to stay."

"A few rubles left, sir. That's all."

"We will help you, never fear," he said. "Excuse my friend, Mr. Shtein, for his silence, but he speaks only Russian. No English. No Yiddish. He is here to say that he, too, is willing to help, but first I will help. You will come to my home. You will stay a few days. We will talk and see what can be done."

They drove in Mr. Tiomkin's droshky to a large home, right up on the banks of the Angara. The river at that point was narrow and plunged over some rocks, so there was the constant and soothing noise of the water bubbling its way over the rapids.

They went downstairs, and Tiomkin beckoned Morrie into his study.

"Tell me about your voyage through my country. Tell me what you have seen, what you like, what you don't like, and why you are here."

It was a large order, because Morrie had already been through a lot in Russia, had seen a lot, and had formed many opinions, pro and con. Certainly Mr. Tiomkim was curious, and this was the least Morrie could do to repay his kindness and hospitality. So he launched into his story, telling the tea merchant the truth and giving him most of the details of his "voyage," as Tiomkin had called it, from Murmansk to Irkutsk.

Tiomkin frequently interrupted with questions. He would also offer brief comments at appropriate points in Morrie's narrative.

Morrie talked for about an hour, after which Tiomkin said, "That is a remarkable story. You have been very lucky."

"Yes, I realize I have been lucky."

Tiomkin apparently felt that one good story deserved another, so he promptly launched into the tale of his family. They had, it seemed, been in the tea business here in Irkutsk for more than three generations. He said that Irkutsk was the tea capital of all of Russia.

"I thought tea came from India or someplace like that," said Morrie.

Tiomkin laughed.

"My dear young friend," he said, "you misunderstood me. I did not mean that we grow tea here. The ground here never really thaws, but we import it and process it. You know the Russian word for tea is *chai*, and that is the same word we have for China. Tea and China are almost synonymous. Caravans crossed the Gobi desert from China with their black bricks of tea for centuries, and those caravans ended up here in Irkutsk. Do you know that any real tea connoisseurs say that sea air ruins the flavor of tea? They insist on what they call "overland tea" that is brought from China on land, rather than by sea.

"Today," he continued, "most tea is brought from China to Odessa by ship. Not the Irkutsk tea, however. That still comes overland, through the Gobi Desert and then north to Irkutsk. Now, there is a new industry in the area, gold. That precious metal has been discovered nearby and there are mines scattered all over."

Tiomkin said that his family had trouble with the Bolsheviks, who had taken all their horses and they were pleased now that the Czechs were in power, nobody knew how long that situation would last. Everyone was worried, thinking of ways to protect themselves and their possessions from what they considered the inevitable return of the Bolsheviks in Irkutsk.

A delightful meal was served at the dinner table. Tiomkin wanted to know about the condition of Jews in London. Morrie answered, and Tiomkin translated for his wife and children. Tiomkin asked Morrie if he knew of the street where Tiomkin had stayed when he had made his one memorable visit to England so long ago. The Russian remembered the precise address and fortunately it was a street that Morrie was familiar. He described it perfectly and rattled off the names of the nearby streets. Tiomkin was delighted; for perhaps two decades, he hadn't had a chance to talk about that visit to London with anyone who could respond.

"You are a fine young man," he said. "I would like my friends to meet you. Perhaps they can help you. I will have my wife plan a tea in the next few days, and we will invite them here. I must warn you, though, that they are nosy people and will ask you many questions."

Morrie visited the tea warehouse with Tiomkin almost every day. Heavy aromatic bricks of pressed tea lined the walls in stacks at least twenty feet high. The workers were curious- looking men, stocky, almost all Mongol in appearance, with a strange reddish cast to their complexion. They hustled the bricks to the processing room.

"Are those men Chinese?" Morrie wondered.

"No, they are Buriats," said Tiomkim. "They are a kind of nomadic people centered around this region of Siberia. They come and they go. Wanderers like us Jews. Like you, Morrie. They are good workers, but one day they will just leave. No explanation, they just have something in them that makes them leave after a while."

Tiomkin said that the notorious Semenov, leader of a band of outlaws he called an army, was reported to be half Buriat. The other half, the Russian said, was villain.

Tiomkin's plant processed sixty million pounds of tea annually. It arrived in boxes during the winter and in raw unwrapped bricks in the summer. Tiomkin's men and machinery then repackaged it for domestic consumption and shipped it to all parts of Russia. They exported it throughout Europe before the war, but now they were limited to domestic distribution.

On the third night of Morrie's stay with the Tiomkin family, they had the tea party Tiomkin arranged. Morrie was introduced as his guest to their friends.

Most of the guests, all part of Irkutsk's old and solid Jewish community, were in the tea business. A few had ventured into the new gold trade. One was in coal and another in marble.

Each one left an envelope in a silver dish that Madame Tiomkin had provided on a side table near the front door. Morrie wondered about the custom. Were they leaving their names?

Morrie was ashamed of his appearance. His clothing had naturally grown shabby during the weeks he had been traveling. These people were all beautifully turned out, the men with impeccable suits and the women in lovely gowns. They greeted him warmly, and, as Tiomkin had warned, they were full of questions. They were most anxious to hear about the Czechs, who were now in control of their city. Their curiosity was understandable. There had been rumors, of course, of Czech atrocities, and they wondered if Morrie had found them to be bestial. He said that as far as he could tell, they appeared to be civilized and not given to cruelties.

They were also interested in Morrie's reaction to Russia and the Russian people. He was able, with honesty, to praise the Russian countryside, and felt that the Russian people he had met had, by and large, been hospitable and friendly. He had encountered little or no unpleasantness. He did say that he felt that the peasants appeared to be very downtrodden, and that said he thought their conditions could definitely be improved.

"Oh, well, they're just *moujiks*," said one well-fed lady. He didn't want to start an argument but the lady's reply seemed to be the sort of thing that breeds revolution.

"The young man is right," said another lady. "*Moujiks* they may be, but they have a right to an education, to medical treatment, to sanitation."

"You talk like a Bolshevik," said the large lady and turned away.

He was interested in learning about anti-Semitism in Siberia. The consensus was that it existed, but was far less virulent than in Russia proper. They wanted to know about the same in England. He said there was some, but not the violent sort, just the kind that prevents Jews from joining certain clubs or becoming residents of certain exclusive areas.

After the guests had departed, the Tiomkins gathered up all the envelopes from the silver dish and handed them to Morrie.

"What are these?"

"Open them. Look and see."

Inside each envelope was a sheaf of ruble notes. It then became clear: this was their form of hospitality. This was what the Irkutsk Jewish community was doing for one lost soul.

"This is too much," he said. "I can't believe you would do this for a total stranger."

"You are not a stranger," said Tiomkin. "You are our brother."

During those five weeks in Irkutsk, Morrie often went back to the Hotel Dekko and visited with Bill and Sam. He felt as though they were his oldest and best friends.

The reports from the lake and the tunnels were very discouraging. The two lake boats, in Bolshevik hands, still dominated the southern tip of the lake and the railroad tracks that skirted it. The Czechs were building a huge raft in a small stream. They hoped to put cannons aboard the raft, float it out into the lake under the cover of darkness, and sink the boats. They could then go to work on clearing the tunnel, a chore that could take months.

"Months?" asked Morrie. His heart sank. He was happy and comfortable with the Tiomkins, but he couldn't stay there for months.

"Afraid so," said Bill. "That is, after they can get to the tunnel, which they can't do yet."

The idea was that the raft would be a surprise, but if the Americans, and now Morrie, knew about it, probably half of Irkutsk also knew. Any surprise element would most likely have vanished. Morrie didn't say so, but he thought to himself that the Bolsheviks, if they had any sense, would probably sink or burn the raft before it could be put to use.

One day Bill said he was going to go down to the lake and invited Morrie to join him. Bill had hired a droshky, and they reached the Baikal station, or what was left of it, in about two hours. The station had been bombarded by the lake boats and was a pile of useless rubble.

"We can hitch a ride on one of the hand cars," said Bill. When a couple of Czech soldiers, lugging cartons of food, hopped aboard one of the cars, Bill ran over and negotiated a ride, and quickly the little hand car was skimming over the rails. Morrie and Bill volunteered to take a turn at propelling the vehicle, an offer that the Czechs promptly and gladly accepted. It was harder work then it looked, and producing blisters on Morrie's hands, which had become unused to manual labor.

The route took them through several of the tunnels, mostly short but at least one was long, and with no light visible from either end, they were somewhat frightening. Eventually the group pumped their way out into the sunlight again.

Finally, they came to the tunnel that was blocked. The Czech soldiers were trying to clear the rocks and other debris, but they had only a few shovels, and the work was proceeding very slowly. Morrie could see how, at this rate, it would take months. One of the lake boats would suddenly sail over and begin shelling the area, and new slides and new debris would accumulate.

Bill said that they were making progress. Furthermore, another crew was working from the eastern side. They now felt that they could have the tunnel cleared, barring any drastic action by the enemy, in perhaps three more weeks.

Bill suggested that they walk around and see how the work was progressing at the other end. It meant a bit of mountain climbing, but it turned out to be fairly easy, as the slopes were gentle and not too high.

The work appeared to be going at a brisker rate at that end. There were more men, heavier equipment, and a more orderly and efficient system. Morrie's spirits rose. Maybe they would have this tunnel cleared in a few weeks.

From the top of the mountain, as they crossed back, they saw the two lake boats clearly in the distance. They were steaming slowly and menacingly toward the shore. One of the Czechs spotted them and blew a whistle, and the soldiers took cover. Morrie and Bill scrambled up behind an outcropping of huge boulders. There was a distant bang, a whistling sound, and a thud. The guns were aimed at the western end of the tunnel, and Morrie could hear the distant sound of men yelling. It seemed to him they were yelling more in anger than pain. There was a crunching noise, which he took to be the sound of earth and rocks and trees falling.

The boats withdrew as quickly as they had come. They had each fired no more than two rounds. They obviously had no ammunition to spare. They had the range down exactly, so with those few shells they had, it turned out, undone days of work.

Perhaps the Bolsheviks were unaware of the work proceeding from the eastern end of the tunnel. They never attempted any attack on the men shoveling over there. While they could keep the work on the western end from proceeding, the debris inside the tunnel was being removed anyhow.

A few nights after Morrie and Bill had visited the lake, the Czechs did manage to launch their attack raft, and, towed by Cossacks in canoes, hauled it within range of the *Angara*. The Czech gunners had blasted several gaping holes in her hull before the Bolsheviks could get up steam to sail out into deeper water. The *Angara* managed to beach itself, but she was out of action. For some reason, the *Baikal* was not used again without the *Angara* to help, so the work of clearing the tunnel was able to proceed from both ends.

It was announced after three weeks that the railroad was about to resume normal operations, as the tunnel was completely cleared. There was no more threat from the two boats.

All the Tiomkins came to the station with Morrie, and all, with the exception of Madame Tiomkin, who remained reserved to the end, hugged and kissed him. Madame Tiomkin shook hands and smiled, which was in itself a major concession. Morrie was very moved when Tiomkin put his arms around him, in a mighty bear hug, and kissed him full on the lips. Morrie knew by now that Russian men exchanged kisses, but it was still difficult for him to accept. He had exchanged more restrained good-byes, the previous evening, with Bill and Sam, who had given him enough chocolate bars to hold him for a month. Madame Tiomkin, despite her seeming aloofness, had pressed a large and over stuffed basket of food on him.

He boarded the train for Vladivostok, via Chita and Harbin. He had his ticket, some money left over from the gifts he had received at the party, and plenty to eat. It should be a pleasant, relaxed trip.

He settled back in his seat, third class, because even though he had money, he wasn't about to waste it. His fellow passengers were a crazy-quilt assortment of ethnic types; Russians, Chinese, Mongolians, and Buriats. Their languages, customs, clothing, and food, were different, yet they all smiled pleasantly at him and at each other.

Morrie pulled out a chocolate bar and relaxed. It would be a long trip, but it should be a fascinating one. The train began going slowly though the thirty-six tunnels, and Morrie counted them. Between the tunnels, he had breath taking views of the lake. He was somewhat higher than he had been on the hand car, and the view was correspondingly better. He could see fishermen out on the water now, where there were none when the armed boats had been terrorizing the lake.

The tracks took the train almost on a roller- coaster ride as they climbed and then descended assorted dips and rises. Eventually, after they had gone through the last tunnel, they found themselves at lake level. The tracks then veered sharply to the east, away from the lake, and Morrie craned his neck for one last look at the body of water he had come to think of as "my lake." When he could no longer see it, he felt a sadness, as though he had left a good friend behind.

His attention was captured by new sights, new diversions. This time it was a huddle of Cossack tents, round-domed and grayish in color, made from some sort of animal hide. The Cossacks, when they spotted the train, jumped on their horses and, with shrill cries, raced the train for a half mile or so, waving and grinning. They wore their great sheepskin coats and tall, furry astrakhan hats.

The terrain began to change, from the mountains and evergreen-strewn hills that bordered Lake Baikal to a flat, more barren area of plains.

Morrie had become an experienced Trans-Siberian railroad traveler by now. He could tell, when they pulled into a station, whether the stop would be a long enough for him to jump off and stretch his legs and buy some food, or whether it was destined to be too brief to do more than walk up and down for a few minutes. The tip-off was always to see whether or not the babushkas were there with their tables of food.

Morrie peered out of his window when dawn came, and the scene changed again. This was dry country, desert- like, with only a few tufts of some sedge-like plant to show any green against the vast stretches of brown and gray. No more farms, no more Cossacks. Now there were Chinese coolies, busily working on the tracks and the station buildings along the barren, depressing landscape.

They came to Chita, a city with a quaint history. Deep in Siberia, it had an Italian name and an Italian past, for it had been established, many years before, by some Italian gold prospectors. They had built a replica of an Italian mountain town on the flat, harsh Siberian desert, trying to make the wilderness seem less alien. Morrie had learned from Tiomkin that the Chita station, as usual, was a few miles from the city itself.

Tiomkin had told him of the chalets with red tile roofs, the town square with its cobblestones and fountain in the center. The only thing Morrie could spot from the distance was a typical Russian cathedral, with its golden, onion-shaped dome shining in the sun. Italianized Chita it might be, but this was Russia, and a Russian Orthodox Cathedral, apparently, was mandatory.

Morrie didn't waste much time searching the horizon for signs of the Italian influence on Chita. There was too much to observe right beneath his window, on the platform, where he saw hundreds of Japanese soldiers mingling with the inevitable refugees and a sprinkling of Cossacks. The diminutive Japanese contracted sharply with the Cossacks, who were almost always burly and tall, their height accentuated by their tall fur hats.

Morrie was anxious to get off the train, not merely to exercise his legs, even for a brief moment, but also to study these new people more closely. He reached up to grab his bag to take all his possessions with him, when suddenly the conductor ran through the car waving his green flag and excitedly shouting words that Morrie couldn't understand. His gestures were clear enough, however as he practically pushed Morrie back into his seat, and the rest of the passengers sat back down. It was apparent that, for the moment at least, no one would be permitted on the platform.

The reason soon became obvious. There was the beat of a drum and the platform magically cleared, with the people and soldiers, and Japanese and Cossacks, stepping back to allow a clear passage down the center. The drummer, pounding steadily on a huge instrument with what looked like a horsehide stretched across it, led the way. He was followed by a troop of Mongolian soldiers, holding scimitars aloft, escorting a squat man with a huge mustache and a fierce scowl. His skin had a slight reddish tinge to it, something like the color of the Buriats that Morrie had seen im Tiomkin's tea warehouse, only a few shades lighter.

"Semenov!" shouted the people on the platform, and many of the people in Morrie's car picked up the chant. "Semenov! Semenov! Semenov!"

The troops disappeared down the platform, and everyone was then permitted to get off the train. It was as though the frightening procession had never occurred. Morrie realized, after the fact, that he had witnessed a figure in Russia's current history, the infamous rebel leader Semenov. He wondered what the Russian people saw in the man, so obviously a cut-throat and murderer. He reasoned that Semenov was an alternative for the *moujiks*, who wanted no further dealings with the Czar, with the Whites who were bent on restoring the monarchy, or with the Bolsheviks, who represented a brand of government that frightened them with its novelty.

Morrie walked back and forth along the platform getting some needed exercise. There would be many things for him to watch, as the train would now be traveling on tracks belonging to the Chinese Eastern Railroad. An engine from that line was shunted onto the train, replacing the Trans-Siberian engine. Chinese conductors and engineers as stokers replaced the Russians who had been on the train.

When Morrie reboarded, he found that the Chinese workers had cleaned his car. It was almost as though it were brand new. Somehow, in the brief stop, they had managed to wash it throughly, and it looked and smelled immaculate.

There were, now, more Chinese riding with him. The sing-song babble of their voices sounded odd after so many weeks of hearing the heavier, more guttural sound of Russian. They were intrinsically friendlier than the Russians. They invariably smiled at Morrie and bowed, and some even offered to shake his hand ceremoniously when their paths crossed.

It took a half- day to reach Manchouli, the border town. It was actually in Manchurian territory, and it served as the point of entry for the railroad.

Morrie had been a bit apprehensive about crossing into another country. He was afraid there might be a rigorous control policy, and since he had no papers, he dreaded that possibility. His fears seemed justified when, as the train braked to a stop into Manchouli station, a tough-look-ing official in uniform, accompanied by two armed guards, climbed aboard the train.

The inspection, if that was what it was turned out to be perfunctory. The official strode swiftly through the train without looking left or right, and nobody was even asked to show any papers. The train was underway again in perhaps two minutes.

Morrie could see little of Manchouli from his window. He detected what he took to be the main street, a dusty thoroughfare with no trees, a few shack-like structures, and, amazingly, an endless procession of little tables along the curbs, where Chinese were drinking tea and staring curiously up at the train. The train began to climb soon after leaving Manchouli. These mountains, Morrie learned later, were part of the Hingan Range. They were different from the glorious ones around Lake Baikal: these were brown and treeless. Gradually, as they climbed higher and higher, that changed too, and soon the mountains were carpeted with green. The train had apparently crossed over some invisible barrier. There was no rain and no trees on the western side, but now a pelting rain proved there was plenty of life-giving moisture and, therefore, many trees.

The train tracks snaked down from the mountains in circles as they began descending toward Harbin. The train had to proceed slowly because many of the curves were sharp. The drop- off on the side was incredibly steep, and Morrie wondered how many trains had gone over.

The last station before Harbin seemed like a pleasant little town. Morrie never did find out it's name, for the name on the sign identifying it was in Chinese characters. He couldn't tell how long they would be stopped, so he didn't get off. He was looking out his window and survey-ing the soft landscape when he saw a procession of Chinese men file past.

They walked into the field, across from the tracks, and formed a semi-circle. The leader was wearing a long white gown, flowing to the ground and tied at the waist by a black cloth belt. Down his back hung a longer than usual black queue. Another man in the group, attired in a quilted black jacket, carried a long, saber- like sword. He stood there, leaning on his sword, while the leader seemed to be making a speech or saying a prayer and the others were listening intently.

Then, so quickly that Morrie almost doubted that it had actually happened, the men seized one of their number and held him down in a prone position, and the man with the sword swung it up and down. The victim had been beheaded.

Morrie looked away, but it was too late. He had seen the grisly action, seen the expression on the victim's face and the blood spurting from the severed head held aloft by the executioner.

Morrie ran to the platform between the cars and vomited. He shook his head, trying to erase what he had seen from his memory. But it would not erase, and it never really did. A Chinese passenger, standing at the doorway, shook his head sympathetically. He then pantomimed the explanation for what Morrie had just witnessed. He stuck his hand in Morrie's pocket, making believe that he was withdrawing some money, and Morrie understood. The victim had been a thief, and apparently in Manchuria, justice was quick and sure.

Another incident, while the train was still halted in that station, convinced Morrie that Manchuria would be a hard place for criminals. He had gone back to his seat when two Chinese soldiers raced up to the train, pounded up the stairs, and dashed down the aisle. Without a word, they seized a Chinese passenger, jerked him to his feet, and ripped open his coat. Wrapped around the man's waist was a wide, thick sash of blue silk material. The soldiers roughly began unwinding the silk, which spun the man around and around like a top.

There must have been at least fifteen yards of silk in the strip that eventually lay on the floor of the car. One soldier gathered it up and the other took the man by his ear, hustling him off the train. The Chinese man who acted out the theft for Morrie caught his eye, smiled, and slowly drew his finger across his throat. The message was clear. Justice would again be swift, sure, and deadly.

Morrie's first glimpse of Harbin was hardly reassuring. The station platform was jammed with a confusing mass of people: Japanese soldiers, Chinese workers, Russian refugees, and Westerners looking out of place in their business suits in the midst of this Oriental setting.

Morrie stepped off the train into this hustling, bustling, elbowing, yelling multitude. He approached one of the Westerners, crossed his fingers that the man spoke English, and said, "Excuse me, sir, do you speak English?"

"Yes, young fellow, I most certainly do. Can I be of assistance to you?"

Morrie shook the man's hand warmly. He asked the man if he could direct him to a good but inexpensive hotel in the city. The man, who introduced himself as George Peterson, said that he would do better than just give Morrie the name of such a hotel. He was waiting for a friend and as soon as the friend arrived, he would be driving into town. He would be happy to give Morrie a lift and deposit him in front of a hotel that he recommended highly.

Peterson was, he explained, a member of the U.S. Railway Advisory Commission. His friend, a fellow commission member, arrived, and they went outside where Peterson had a cart with a Chinese driver waiting.

The roads were dirty and dusty. There was heavy cart traffic and, hence, heavy clouds of dust that they meandered through. Peterson and his friend, veterans of Harbin's dust clouds, routinely held handkerchiefs to their noises. Morrie quickly followed their lead.

Peterson pointed out the sights, such as they were. Morrie was particularly intrigued with his first sight of Hulan, the Chinese part of the city. The Russian part, Harbin proper, was separated from Hulan by the main road. Peterson said that the hotels in Hulan were considerably cheaper, but advised Morrie against staying in them for reasons of sanitation and language. The Hulanese hotels had no plumbing, nor did they have anyone who spoke English.

Peterson dropped Morrie in front of the Modern Hotel. It was on the main street, and he got a small but adequate room for fifty rubles a night.

He still had about four hundred rubles left from the money that the Tiomkins' guests had given him. He could stay for about a week before he would have to move on or find some other source of revenue. His first mission was to sleep. All those days on the train, without being able to stretch out, had left his body and his mind weary to the point of exhaustion. He was the first customer when the hotel dining room opened for breakfast. As he ate, his mind wandered. He knew that he had to find some source of income. He could perhaps go on immediately to Vladivostok, but there were two arguments against that course.

First, Vladivostok was the terminus. What then? He had no idea where he would go from there. Always he had been striving to get to Vladivostok since he arrived in Russia, but he had never given much thought to what he would do once he got there. Reaching Vladivostok marked the end, and he was reluctant to face that end without some plan of where to go next. He wanted to delay the inevitable day when he would have to make the decision.

After breakfast he set out to explore. He walked an hour or so, aimlessly, looking at the low wooden buildings with Chinese and Russian signs, neither of which he could read. He observed the parade of unusual men and women he passed.

Morrie came to the cathedral, which looked like all the other cathedrals in Russia, even though this one was technically in China. He walked around it. The cathedral's neighbor was one of the typical wooden Harbin buildings. This one had a sign he could read: U.S. RAILWAY ADVISORY COMMISSION

Peterson, the man who had driven him from the station to the hotel, was part of this group. Perhaps later, if he needed assistance, he would visit him. It was good to know where he worked.

Morrie decided to visit the Chinese city, Hulan. As soon as he ventured across the invisible barrier into Hulan, he stepped into another world. This was China. The Chinese he had seen in Harbin were Russianized in their clothing and mannerisms, but the ones he saw in Hulan were old

Chinese, wearing traditional clothing, queues and skullcaps. There were stalls in the street selling Chinese medicines, foods, and good- luck amulets. The streets were narrower.

He kept hearing one word over and over. It sounded like "hoydia," and he later found out that it was a word that was peculiar to Hulan and, to a lesser extent, Harbin. It was locally coined, part Russian and part Chinese, and had come to mean everything from its original meaning, "worker" or "coolie," to "hello" and "goodbye," and it could also be used, with the right inflection, as a cuss word.

He was intrigued with a display of bracelets at one stall, fabricated from silver coins. It suddenly occurred to him that perhaps these might be a source of income to him. He knew from what Peterson and his friend had said last night that most foreigners in Harbin were afraid of venturing into Hulan. There was still some fear of Chinese as being heartless criminals: the threat of Tongs and the works of Sax Rohmer and his "Fu Manchu" had left Westerners with the impression that it would not be worth a person's life to go into Hulan, or any other Chinese enclave.

Morrie realized that the foreigners would love these exotic and beautiful bracelets. They could then go home to wherever they came from and show off the jewelry they bought from the Chinese.

Morrie looked at the bracelets closely, as the Chinese man behind the stall excitedly tried to strike a bargain. Each of the coins had a square hole, and they were strung on a delicate but sturdy silver chain.

He decided that he had to take a chance. He gestured to the stock of bracelets on the man's tray. There were a dozen there. He made a sweeping motion, indicating that he would like to buy them all.

The stall keeper understood, but didn't know what to say. He could bargain with the best of them, for one chain or perhaps two. But twelve? That was something new in his experience. He shrugged his shoulders. Then he swept all the bracelets up and motioned for Morrie to follow him.

He took Morrie around a corner and up a flight of rickety stairs. Three Chinese men were in a room on the second floor, sitting on the floor and busily working on the jewelry the man sold in his stall on the street.

"Hoydia, Chi-jo," said a young girl. She was obviously half-Chinese and half-Russian or some other non-Oriental strain. She had long, blue-black hair, a complexion the color of sand, and slightly slanted eyes, although they weren't the jet- black eyes of most Chinese, but a grayish-green color. The total effect was smashing, particularly since she was wearing a dress such as Morrie had never seen before. It was form- fitting red silk, tight around the neck and slit generously up the side.

Chi-jo started to explain and the girl, Po-li, bowed to Morrie, who bowed back.

"Ah, you wish to buy bracelet in quantity," she said, in accented but very easily understood English.

"Yes, I do. I think I can find buyers for them among the Westerners in Harbin."

Morrie bought a half-dozen bracelets. Po-li bent over a tray and carefully selected the finest examples of the bracelets. She wrapped each one swiftly but delicately in rice paper.

"I will sell these to people in the Russian city," said Morrie. "I will come back for more, and other kinds of jewelry, too."

"I will await your next visit," said the girl.

Common sense returned to Morrie once out in the fresh air. He had bought the six bracelets for ninety rubles, fifteen rubles per bracelet. He carefully studied the landmarks, so he could find his way back again. There were no street names or addresses, at least none that he could see. He memorized the location of the building by its relationship to particular trees, rocks, and buildings that had distinct markings.

The next morning Morrie went to the building where he had seen the sign for the headquarters of the U.S. Railway Advisory Commission. He went in, found George Peterson's office, and knocked on the door.

Peterson was surprised, but seemed pleased to see him. They chatted for a few moments, mainly about how Morrie was settling in and whether or not he liked the hotel that Peterson had recommended. Morrie took one of the bracelets out of his pocket and carefully unwrapped it.

"Hey, that's a beauty," Peterson said. "Where did you get it?"

"I had it made by a fellow in Hulan."

"You went to Hulan? And found that? Well, you are a daring young man."

"Just like to explore a bit. Stumbled onto this chap who makes the bracelets."

"How much did it cost you? I bet it was a pretty penny."

"Fifty rubles, what's that, about five of your dollars?"

"About that. Say, do you think you could get me one for that price? The wife would go crazy for it."

Morrie handed Peterson the bracelet. He said he was in no hurry, and he'd go back to Hulan in the afternoon and get another one for himself. Peterson gratefully handed Morrie the fifty rubles. Peterson then showed the bracelet to some of his associates, and before he left, Morrie had orders for three more bracelets.

He went back in the afternoon with those three bracelets and pocketed his money. The Americans asked him if he'd mind taking dollars, and, of course, Morrie was delighted. Dollars were a much safer currency than the flighty ruble.

He went back to the hotel with his American dollars. They were smaller than the rubles, but the paper was much better quality. He knew that, if he wanted rubles, he could get, on the quiet, at least three times the official exchange rate of ten to one. If he could sell a few bracelets every day, making thirty-five rubles per bracelet, he would easily be able to afford to stay in Harbin for a while.

That is, if he wanted to stay in Harbin.

Where would he acquire the needed customers? Because of the war, Harbin was not flooded with tourists. But he knew one place where there were many foreigners, and that was the Y headquarters. Morrie asked at the hotel desk if they knew where the Y.M.C.A. was located. They didn't, but they said that the man who sold cigarettes next door knew everything and spoke English. Morrie went next door and asked the little old cigarette merchant. He was obviously a man of a mixed ethnic background. He smiled, bowed, and nodded. He then drew a neat but tiny map on a piece of rice paper with a white-tipped quill pen that Morrie could easily follow.

Morrie didn't know any of the workers at the Y building, but they were cut from the same mold as Bill and Sam. He was immediately accepted when he mentioned that he had traveled with them from Taiga to Irkutsk.

The Y secretary, Roy Foster, asked all the inevitable questions over tea and the inevitable chocolate bars. "How was the trip? Were the Czechs pleasant? How about the Bolsheviks? And, by the way, what's a young English boy like you doing in the wilds of Manchuria?"

Morrie had enough experience in the fine art of answering questions that he wouldn't reveal too much of his own precarious position.

He mentioned that he was in the jewelry importing business. It wasn't exactly importing, because he was crossing no legal boundaries, but he was bringing them in from the Chinese city. So, in a sense, he had gone into the importing trade.

Foster was intrigued with the bracelet that Morrie showed him. He wanted one to send to his mother back in Iowa, and another for his sister, who was going to a school for nurses in Chicago.

Morrie was in business. The next day he went back into Hulan and, after a few terrifying moments when he thought he couldn't find Po-li's building, reestablished his relationship with the beautiful girl and her lucrative jewelry products. She had other things for him, gold rings decorated with jade, pendants carrying Chinese characters she said were very lucky, and earrings to match the original bracelets.

They struck a bargain, and when Morrie left that day he had a full suitcase. They had included the suitcase in the bargain. The jewelry was all neatly placed in little rice- paper wrappings.

A codicil to the bargain was that Po-li had said, with a demure smile, that she would be happy to show him the sights of Hulan. Morrie said that he would like very much to take her to dinner at the finest restaurant in Harbin.

It turned out to be a very small establishment, only six tables, at the edge of the river. It was presided over by a large lady of obviously mixed blood who was the cook, the waitress, the maitre d', and the cashier. She handled all her jobs with ease, keeping the six tables of customers happy and well fed.

"Have you lived in Harbin all your life?" Morrie asked Po-li.

"Yes. Born here. Grew up here."

"But you didn't learn English here." It was more of a statement than a question.

"Yes, learn English here, too. I was very lucky girl, I think. There was a missionary here, from American church. Her name was Miss Austin, and she came to our school and she said you and you come with me, and I was one of the chosen."

"She just took you, like that?"

"Just like that. Me and three other girls. Most girls here never go to school at all, but my mother wanted me to have education, like my father."

"Who was your father?"

"A Russian. I never made his acquaintance. He went off a few days after I was born. My mother says it wasn't because of me. He had to go back to Russia, not to Siberia, to real Russia. He was, maybe he is a minster in church."

She said all of this without emotion. She drank her Chinese tea, nothing stronger, and talked about her history as though she were discussing the price of tomatoes.

"My father was a man of intelligence, and my mother said I should go to school. Miss Austin took me and the others and taught us in her house. I do not know why. Maybe just out of the goodness of her heart, which was very good."

Po-li said that Miss Austin made some effort to teach her religion, too, but when Po-li said she wasn't very interested, Miss Austin stopped without protest or argument. So Po-li grew up learning the good things the missionary had to teach her, without converting to Christianity. She remained a Buddhist, although she wasn't, she said, particularly devout. "Now, please to tell me all about yourself."

Morrie told her as much as he felt she should understand. Obviously, in her limited experience, some of the background of his adventures would make no sense. They scarcely made sense to him, and he had lived through it all, so how could he expect her to grasp the nuances of his desertion and subsequent deportation? Harbin became Morrie's temporary home in the days to come, which stretched into weeks. He made some friends, and Peterson invited him to a party at his home. He met a Russian there named Boris Kamaroff, who said he had a spare room in his house and would be delighted to rent it to Morrie. So Morrie moved out of the hotel and into the Kamaroffs' house.

Morrie also was making money, in several ways. The jewelry business was the cornerstone of his finances, but it wasn't his only source of income. He quickly learned that there was good, if not precisely legal, money to be made in the world of exchanging money. He juggled his rubles and his dollars and wound up every day with a sheaf of bills of many nations and many denominations. He bought a large and sturdy Russian leather wallet to hold it all, which he tied to his belt with a large Russian leather thong. Thoughts came to mind of the beheading incident but Morrie was too busy to worry.

Kamaroff had been a lawyer in the employ of the Czar's agents in Harbin, and he still had considerable prestige in the city. He and his wife, who felt that their days were numbered because of their association with the Romanov family, were very anxious to learn English. They felt that they would have to flee Harbin if they were to survive, and a knowledge of English would be imperative to that escape. Their best bet was to get out via Vladivostok, either to Alaska, Canada, or the U.S. Morrie's rent was reduced to nothing in exchange for him giving the Kamaroffs English lessons. Morrie spent his days buying and selling jewelry, then exchanging rubles for dollars or vice versa, and constantly amassing money. His wallet was bulging with bills.

One evening, as he walked home to the Kamaroffs, after a successful day of jewelry and money trading, Morrie decided to stop and get some butter. He kept a few things of his own in the Kamaroff's kitchen. They had given him a shelf in the cold room so he could have a bite to eat if he felt hungry at non- meal hours.

There was a short line at the butter merchant's shop, and Morrie stood patiently in line. The man in front of him gave the proprietor a large- denomination ruble note and was given a slab of butter and his change. Morrie asked for "*masla*" and took his slab, handing the proprietor a fifty-ruble note.

"Nyet," said the Chinese owner, in that peculiar Chinese-Russian accent that was spoken only in Harbin. He made as though to take the butter back, but Morrie yanked his arm back.

"You took the money from the man ahead of me," he said. The Chinaman screamed "Nyet, Nyet" and was obviously on the verge of going berserk. Morrie couldn't understand the fuss.

He tried to reason with the proprietor, but the man made a mistake. He shoved Morrie, and for the first time since his days in the army, Morrie lost his temper.

He was back in the boxing ring and somebody had punched him. He knew one thing: he had to counter punch.

Before his reason could return, he lashed out quickly with a left and a right, sending the Chinaman flying through the window of his shop. There was an explosion of glass, and all around the figures of the witnesses froze. For a few seconds nobody moved or said a word, their activity halted by the shock of the moment.

The victim of Morrie's attack sprung to his feet, blood coming out of a cut on one ear where he had broken the window, and from the corner of his mouth where Morrie had hit him. He yelled something Morrie couldn't understand and produced a long, curved dagger out of a fold in his sleeve.

"AYAA!" he yelled, as he sprang at Morrie with his dagger raised. Morrie turned to run, but the dagger's downward thrust caught him lightly across his backside with a long, shallow cut. It didn't impede his running, and he made great speed away from the area. The Chinaman, eager but definitely out of condition, gave up the chase very soon, and Morrie ran alone in the only direction he felt was safe.

He knew where he was going, and that was to Po-li's house. He had a feeling that the Chinese butter merchant would take his story to the police, telling them about the English madman who had attacked and hit him and smashed his window. Surely he would exaggerate the story. The Chinese police, who did not particularly like foreigners, would look for him, and everybody knew about the Englishman who was staying with the Kamaroffs.

He would stay with Po-li, a course that seemed safer. Morrie found Po-li's house and told her the story. She called her uncle when he told her where he had been wounded.

Chi-jo bathed and bandaged the long cut, and then Po-li gave Morrie a glass of rice wine to buoy his spirits.

Chapter Eleven

He must have fallen asleep. Perhaps they had put something in the rice wine. He woke with something warm and moist caressing his face. It was a dog. He was riding in a cart.

He remembered the fight with the butter merchant, fleeing to Po-li's house with his backside on fire from the slash of the merchant's wicked dagger, and her ministrations, along with those of Chi-jo. Was it Chi-jo who was driving this *cart*?

He turned around and, silhouetted against the black sky, saw the even blacker shape of a man.

"Chi-jo?" he called.

The black shape turned. It was a stranger, who then turned back to his duties of chauffeuring the cart.

Was he being kidnapped? Held for ransom? Sold into slavery? Or just being benevolently rescued?

He felt inside his shirt and was pleased to feel the reassuring bulk of his wallet. At least he hadn't been robbed. He saw that he was wearing his own clothes and nothing about his person seemed to have been disturbed. When he absently touched his face, he realized that he had quite a growth of beard, perhaps two days' worth. Had he been unconscious for that long? They must have really drugged him.   He felt a little woozy and weak, and had a slight, dull headache, but otherwise seemed physically fit. He thought about jumping out of the cart and making a run for it, but where would he run? He hadn't the foggiest idea where he was, or in which direction he had traveled from Harbin.

Morrie leaned back and quickly fell asleep again. The drug, or whatever it was, was still obviously in his system.

The next time he woke, it was morning. A cloudy day, a bit crisp as autumn was fast approaching. Summers in Manchuria, he had learned, were short. Now, in the middle of August, the winds from the north were beginning to be nippy. Morrie pulled his coat tighter around his shoulders.

He looked around but there wasn't much to see. They were on a rut of a road that wound between some low, grass-covered hills. There was no sign of life except for a few large, graceful birds of prey that circled continuously overhead, looking for some unsuspecting animal to grab.

"Hoydia," he said to the driver.

"Ah, hoydia," the driver said, without looking around.

Morrie wanted to ask him where they were going, but even when his mind was functioning properly, he didn't know the words, and right now he was still fuzzy.

"Harbin," he said. It was all he could think of to say.

"Ah, Harbin," said the man and pointed back the way they had come. End of conversation.

After another hour or so, they pulled into the courtyard of a small structure. The driver got down, motioned for Morrie to get down, and offered an arm to help.

The man gestured for Morrie to follow him, and they went inside the tiny building. It reminded Morrie of the houses he had seen on his first days in Russia as he journeyed from Soroak to Suma. It seemed like a lifetime ago.

The house was apparently an inn of some sort. A Chinese lady with no babushka on her head, but with the Chinese equivalent, bustled in from the back and bowed to the driver. They sat down and the lady brought tea from a steaming cauldron on the stove along with pots of rice and a broth with leaves of some sort floating in it. Morrie fumbled with the chopsticks but managed to get enough in his mouth.

They stopped at another inn of the same sort later that day, and finally, in the evening, just as the sun was setting, they came to a good sized village.

'Tsitsihar," said the driver. Morrie had no idea what he was saying, but later he learned that Tsitsihar was the town they had been heading for all along.

The driver knew where he was going, steering a devious course through the narrow streets of Tsitsihar. Morrie stared at the people curiously, but they were even more curious: he could easily have been the first white man they had ever seen. They were all Chinese, but with a slightly different tilt to their eyes that bespoke of some infusion of white blood some time in their ancestral past.

Finally the cart pulled up to what must have been the only mansion in Tsitsihar. It was actually not a mansion at all, but compared to the tiny huts that were Tsitsihar's norm, it surely was manorial; it had two stories, and that in itself was sufficient to set the place apart. Then, too, it was set back from the main road, and a curved, paved driveway led up to a front door that must have been imported from Italy or France. The building itself was ordinary, made of the same stone as the other buildings in the town, but the door was extraordinary. It was one and a half stories tall, made of heavy carved wood, with a huge and elaborate gold knocker in the middle in the shape of an eagle's talon.

The driver, with obvious delight, lifted the eagle talon and let it drop. It made a mighty boom. Three times, the driver knocked on the door. Boom! Boom! Boom! He laughed at the sound, and people ran down the street to watch and listen, marveling at the thunderous sound of the door knocker.

The door opened with an appropriate squeal of its huge and obviously rusty hinges.

And there stood Po-li.

"Mr. Kotler," she said. "How are you feeling? Please to enter."

Morrie was astounded. How had she gotten there ahead of him? It turned out that she had ridden on horseback. What was she doing here? This was the home of her grandfather, a very rich man by Tsitsihar standards. What was Morrie doing here?

"You have been poisoned," she said, leading him into the main room, which was dominated by a huge fireplace with a carved wooden mantel. "Messer Zhiang, the butter merchant, had poison on the dagger that he used on you. Chi-jo could tell when he examined your bottom- side that there was poison. So we quick found the antidote, but you were unconscious for some time. Messer Zhiang, he is a very foul man, he is an evil man, and he was going to have you made into fertilizer for his carrots, so Chi-jo and I decided to smuggle you away in a cart and bring you here to my grandfather's for the sake of your safety and your life."

Morrie was to stay here while, in Hulan, efforts were going forward to placate Zhiang, the butter merchant. His decency could be purchased, of course, but that was expensive. Rather, Chi-jo was attempting to negotiate with some business concessions. Morrie never learned what they were, but presumably they had to do with a better location for Zhiang's butter stand. When those negotiations were completed, Chi-jo would send word, and then it would be safe for Morrie to return to Harbin.

Morrie went to bed in the upstairs bedroom he had been assigned. It was Spartan but adequate. It had a bed with no linens, merely a rough, itchy blanket, and a washstand with the one fancy touch, a magnificent porcelain bowl decorated with hordes of multi-colored butterflies.

Morrie slept well. While it was still dark, Po-li shook him awake.

"Hurry," said Po-li. "Messers Zhiang has sent people here to kill you."

Morrie jumped up.

"Why is he so upset?" He quickly threw on his pants and shirt. "It was just a couple of punches, nothing that terrible."

"You dishonored him in front of his friends and relatives," said Po-li. "He must kill you or at least make a very fine attempt."

She urged him to hurry, and then she led him down the back stairs as the angry boom! boom! boom! of the gigantic front door knocker shook the house. She pressed a spot on the wall of the dining room. A panel slid open, and there inside was a damp, dark stone staircase going down at a steep angle.

"Here is a lantern," she said. "Go down the stairway. You will find a long passageway. Cannot get lost, no place else to go."

Morrie shuddered and she laughed.

"Go to the end of passageway and there is a room with fresh air. This passageway and hidden room my grandfather made so the robbers would not find him. Very many robbers in these hills, in old days."

She squeezed his hand, gave him a polite shove, and shut the door behind him.

The steps were slippery from some seeping source of moisture, and the walls, when he touched them to maintain his balance, seemed slimy. He walked down carefully and went straight ahead. The passageway must have been a few hundred yards long, and he walked quickly. The darting shadows around him had to be rats, he thought, so he walked quickly as directed, hoping they would pay him no attention.

The room, when he reached it, had two chairs and a table. He put his lantern on the table and sat down. He could feel the fresh air coming from above. There was air to breath, but he had no food and nothing to drink. Then he heard the sound of trickling water, so he followed the sound and discovered a spring bubbling out of the wall onto the floor, and then flowing out of a hole at the base of the rear wall.

He scooped up a handful of the water and found it cool and delicious. Morrie wouldn't die of thirst, and neither would he suffocate. Starvation was the only problem.

A rat scurrying along the wall was his only companion. What would he do in this gloomy, dank, and frightening cell for days? He wondered how long the oil in the lantern would hold out. Morrie shook the lantern and was pleased to hear a reassuringly full gurgle from the bottom, where the fuel was stored. He turned the wick down so only a slight light survived. The prospect of being in this place in the pitch blackness was terrifying.

He heard strange, thumping noises above him. They must have been footsteps, but it was impossible to tell. They sounded heavy enough. Perhaps the room's stone walls exaggerated any sound, but those footsteps echoed and re-echoed in the gloom.

He then clearly heard voices coming down through the air hole that Po-li's grandfather had so ingeniously constructed. They were talking in Chinese and they were gruff, angry, excited. Then he heard Po-li's voice, soft and placating.

She suddenly stopped speaking Chinese and began speaking in English. Morrie realized that it was safe for her to do so, because the others obviously couldn't speak English. Between her Chinese sentences she threw in a few English words, directed at the strangers, and Morrie understood that she was sending him a message.

"Go back out passageway," she said, in and among many Chinese words. "These men have already searched house so it is safe to go back to your room."

Morrie had the presence of mind to listen carefully at the door before he opened it and stepped back into the dining room, into something approaching civilization. It was totally quiet. He crouched low, so he could not be seen by anybody looking in the windows, and made his way as quickly as possible back up to his room.

He sat down on the bed and waited. Eventually, Po-li knocked softly.

"All right for you to come out now," she said. "Messer Zhiang's men have gone."

"What did they want?"

"Only to kill you."

"I hope you talked them out of that foolishness."

"Yes, they have agreed to spare your life. On one condition however."

Morrie was amazed. Over that minor incident, when all he wanted to do was buy some butter, people were setting conditions over his life or death.

"What condition?" he asked.

"Is very sad for me to say this," she said. "You must leave Harbin immediately. Messer Zhiang says it is an affront to his good name and that of his family and ancestors for you to be seen in public in the city where you disgraced him."

Conflicting thoughts tumbled through Morrie's mind at that ultimatum. What a ridiculous, absurd man! He wouldn't be run out of town over the price of a slab of butter. What could they do to him? A mental image of that curved dagger, with its tip oozing poison, brought him back to reality. Surely some sort of accommodations could be reached, yet from Po-li's tone, the decision was final.

"When do I have to leave?" he asked.

"As soon as possible," she said.

"Well," said Morrie, "I had to leave sometime and now is as good a time as any."

That, of course, was the truth. Even though life in Harbin was good, comfortable, even enjoyable, he had always known that sooner or later he must proceed on his way to Vladivostok. He was hardly on a time schedule.

"Yes," she said, "I suppose now is as good a time as any. Where will you go?"

"Vladivostok," he said.

"And after?"

"I hope to get to the United States," he said. "The problem is that I have no papers. I don't know how I'm going to get there."

This conversation took place as they sat on the edge of the bed in the room that Morrie had slept in.

"Let me go and see about arranging our trip back to Harbin," she said. "Will you join me downstairs and we will have something to eat before we begin our journey."

He almost said that he had to pack, except there was nothing to pack. Still he needed a little time by himself to compose his thoughts and control his emotions.

They left in an hour, in the same cart and with the same driver who had transported Morrie out to Tsitsihar. They stayed in the same little inn he had stayed in before. When he got back to Harbin the cart deposited him at the Kamaroff house. He found those good people worried to death over his sudden and unexplained disappearance.

"I had a chance to go out into the countryside," he said, "and it seemed too good an opportunity to pass up. It happened suddenly and I wasn't able to let you know. Terribly sorry."

Then he dropped the bombshell. He would be leaving immediately. Another sudden decision, he said, and a firm one. It was time to be moving on: winter was coming and he wanted to get settled in Vladivostok before the severity of the cold weather was fully upon the land. A lame excuse, he knew, but they appeared to believe him. They said how sorry they would be to see him go.

"I would like you to have this," said Po-li as she handed Morrie a small package. "I hope you remember Hulan and Po-Li in the happy years of your life."

"And this is for you," he said. He had time to buy a present for her. Since she was in the jewelry business, he thought, it made no sense to buy her jewelry. He had found a little stand where a man was selling scarves, which the men said were imported from Paris. Morrie doubted that there was any way for Parisian scarves to find their way to Harbin in the middle of a war, but Chinese merchants were ingenious, so anything was possible. He had bought her one in vivid blues and purples.

"Thank you," she said, unwrapping the scarf and tying it around her neck. "I will wear this only on large days."

He opened his package. She had given him a ring with a lovely jade cameo, with a Chinese character on it.

"What is the character?" he asked.

She turned to go and, just before she shut the door on his final glimpse of her radiant face, she said, "Always."

He stood there a few minutes, staring at the wooden door.

The next day, with his bulging wallet lashed securely about his waist, he boarded the train for the ride from Harbin to Vladivostok. It was the last leg of his trek across Siberia.

Chapter Twelve

He got on the train as though he belonged there. He could speak enough Russian now to make himself understood, and he walked with an air of confidence.

As Morrie strode along to his first class car, he noticed that the Harbin platform was full of Japanese officers and soldiers. He paid them little attention, and they seemed to sense the fact that he was a man of stature, so they stepped back to let him pass. Perhaps it was his tall astrakhan hat. It made him look even taller and, to the short Japanese, he seemed to be a towering figure.

Morrie found his car and his seat. He had splurged on the first-class ticket, but this wasn't a long trip, only some three hundred seventy-five miles, a journey of perhaps ten hours. So he felt he deserved to spoil himself a little. After all, he had been through a lot in the past few days, and this was the last leg of his personal Trans-Siberian travels. He had no idea what the future held for him once he arrived in Vladivostok. So why not go first class? It might be his last chance for such frivolity.

Morrie took off his hat and coat and carefully placed them in the overhead rack. He had a sack of food, given to him by the Kamaroffs as he departed. He sat down, reached inside, and pulled out some rich, prune-flavored pastry. He could feel the comforting bulk of his wallet strapped inside his jacket, and, for the moment Morrie was content.

The train started moving. Morrie finished his pastry and got a cup of tea from the tea urn. The Chinese railroad was still sufficiently Russified so that it had a Russian-style samovar in each of the first-class cars. He sat back in his blue velvet seat.

Morrie talked to the man across the aisle, who turned out to be a flax merchant from Courland, on the Baltic Sea. Obviously, he was a man of substance. Morrie could now carry on a conversation with such a man as an equal, and the flax merchant listened to Morrie's opinions about the world situation with grave concentration. The man spoke English with a German accent. He believed the Bolsheviks would inevitably be defeated by a combination of "right-thinking true Russians" and the intervention of the Allies. He told Morrie he thought that Admiral Kolchak was the man who would lead Russia out of its present state of confusion into a promising future.

Kolchak was, like Semenov and Denikin and Horvath, one of the local leaders who had sprung up and had attracted a coterie of followers. The flax merchant made him sound like someone who deserved being followed: he described Kolchak as a man of education, an explorer, and a naval hero of the war against Japan in 1905. Morrie let the man talk, only half-listening as his mind wandered. He couldn't help but compare this trip to some of his earlier ones in third-class cars, traveling with refugees and goats. Now he was sitting on a blue velvet seat, sipping a cup of excellent tea, and chatting socially with a wealthy and educated man.

"I must be becoming a snob," he thought to himself, "but I do enjoy traveling first-class. I do enjoy nice things."

He was snapped out of his reverie by the flax merchant handing him a newspaper.

"Read it," he said. "I believe it will emphasize some of the points I have been making."

It was a copy of the English-language *Japan Advertiser*, and Morrie seized it eagerly. It had ben months since he had seen any sort of current newspaper. He read an article by Peggy Hull, an American newspaperwoman with Newspaper Enterprise Association, with a Vladivostok dateline. She was writing about the thousands of Allied soldiers in that city. British, French, Czech, and Japanese troops were already there, the Canadians were due momentarily, and, of course, there were the Yanks.

He returned the paper to the flax merchant, who had dozed off and was snoring softly. Morrie turned and looked at the panorama outside his window. The terrain was flat and barren, with only a few trees in thick clumps. The train slowed as it passed the stations, giving Morrie an opportunity to glimpse the confusion that appeared to be part of the station landscape. Japanese soldiers, Chinese peasants, and Russian officials were milling around on each platform.

"We will be in Vlad in about an hour," said the flax merchant. Suddenly, Morrie's confidence disappeared. Now, once again, he was nervous, uncertain about what awaited him when the train arrived in Vladivostok. The train was his last link with things that he had any knowledge of. When he stepped off into the Vladivostok station, he would be entering a new and unchartered area.

Naturally, the unknown is frightening. He began talking to the flax merchant again, because the gentlemen had said he had often been to "Vlad," as he invariably called it. Morrie questioned him about the city, its habits, and its peculiarities.

"I like Vlad very much," the man said. "I should prefer Riga, because it is the city nearest my home, but Vlad is friendlier. It is newer, of course, and more modern, and it has a vitality about it that is exciting. Now, with so many of your countrymen there and with the Americans and everybody speaking English, you will feel right at home."

The man stopped then and beckoned Morrie to come over to his side of the train. He pointed out the window.

"There is the Pacific Ocean," he said. "Well, it is not really the Pacific, you know, it is the Sea of Japan, but that is an arm of the Pacific."

Morrie looked excitedly at the water that lapped lazily up to the grassy plain in the distance. He marveled at how far he had come, from the roaring, frigid North Sea to the Pacific, which seemed to live up to its name.

Morrie began to see more and more buildings and then the port itself as the train drew closer to the city. There were many ships of all sorts and sizes moored to docks and anchored in mid-harbor. Among them were dozens of warships . Morrie saw the flags of France, Japan, the United States, and, yes, there was the good old Union Jack.

This was a bustling port. Workmen were running around, and horses were pulling huge crates. Trains shunted up to the dockside. Soldiers were marching in tight formation.

They went around a curve, and then Morrie saw the largest ship he had ever seen. The American flag at its staff. Morrie must have gasped audibly at the enormity of the craft, for the flax merchant came over to look and identified it as the *Brooklyn*, an American cruiser. It was, he said, the flagship of America's Pacific fleet, under the command of Admiral Knight.

"I was aboard her once, on business," he said. "Fine ship. Served the best ice cream I have ever tasted."

Then they arrived in the station. Morrie saw the familiar sight of Czech soldiers on guard. He then saw some British uniforms, and he became paranoid. Could they be looking for him? Might they start asking questions if they heard his accent? He decided to keep his mouth tightly shut until he was well out of the station area.

He got his things from the rack and said goodbye to the flax merchant. Morrie walked off the train into the unknown.

It was late afternoon. He had money, so the first item on his agenda was to find someplace to stay that night. He could look around and begin to make some proper plans the next day.

He followed the crowd off the train, down the platform, into and through the station, down the stairs, through a long tunnel, and finally out into the street. They probably thought he was just another Russian, Morrie decided.

He walked along the sidewalk, and immediately one facet of Vladivostok's character was brought home to him. There was a diversity of ethnic types such as in no other city Morrie had visited. There were Chinese, Japanese, Mongols, Buriats, and Russians, as well as many European soldiers and naval personnel. The normal population was about forty-seven thousand, but now there were over a hundred and fifty thousand people from all over the world.

The flax merchant had recommended the Alexsander Hotel, so Morrie, after walking around aimlessly a while, just to absorb a bit of the flavor of the city, hailed a horse-drawn droshky and had the driver take him there. It was only a brief ride, and Morrie went through the lobby, noting happily that English seemed to be spoken more than any other language. He checked into the hotel with no problem. The desk clerk, who spoke English very well, gave him a room on the fourth floor.

Now it was time to look ahead. The next leg of the journey would be even more difficult. How was Morrie ever going to get across the Pacific Ocean to Canada or the United States? He had no papers. This was still war- time, and there was no international shipping except for war supplies and troops.

One day at a time, an hour at a time, step by step—that had been the way he had made it from Murmansk to Vladivostok, and that would have to be the way he made it from Vladivostok to whatever turned out to be his destination.

Morrie figured that he had enough money to last him perhaps two weeks, judging from the cost of the hotel. He would have to find a way to make some more money, explore a little, and get to know the city, which everyone had told him was one of the most exciting cities in the world.

He skipped breakfast and wandered out into the bustling streets. He was again struck by the diversity of languages, the variety of ethnic types, and the incredible mixture of costumes that paraded up and down the Svetlanskaya Prospekt, which was obviously Vladivostok's main avenue.

Morrie came back to the hotel for lunch and quickly discovered that the Aleksander's bar was, very obviously, one of the city's busiest at the noon hour. The patrons were lined up, three or four deep, all the way down the lengthy bar.

Morrie found a place where he could catch the eye of one of the bartenders.

"Piva," said Morrie using the Russian word for beer.

The bartender nodded, got a glass from the tap, and handed it across the crowd to him. Morrie knew that the going rate for a beer was two rubles, so he handed two bills to the bartender and the man nodded satisfaction.

Morrie's "Thanks, friend" was overheard by a husky, middle-aged man who spun around to look at the newcomer speaking English with an English accent.

"You're an Englishman," the man said. It was a statement, not a question.

"That's right,"

"You with the Middlesex Regiment or the Consulate?" asked the man. It was obvious to Morrie that, judging by his accent, an American.

"Neither. Just traveling through."

"Oh, come on, Traveling through? That's a hot one. You can tell me it's none of my business if you want to, but don't hand me any nonsense about traveling through."

Morrie laughed.

"Okay, I won't. The real truth is that I'm the king himself, traveling incognito, just to get the lay of the land."

The man stood up, laughing. He stuck out one huge hand and said that he was a newspaperman and his name was Carl Ackerman.

"Come on over here to one of the tables, kiddo," he said. "One way or another I'm going to get the truth out of you, even if it means buying a bottle of genuine bourbon and getting you so drunk that you'll spill the truth all over the goddamn floor."

Morrie followed the big man to a table and sat down and introduced himself. "I'm Alex Chernofsky." Morrie told the man that he had just gotten in and that the truth, hard as it might be to believe, was that he was just traveling through, that he had been traveling for more that a year. Under Ackerman's prodding, Morrie told him as much of the story as he felt he could safely tell.

"Incredible, absolutely incredible," the newspaperman said. "I want to really talk to you, get a story about the trip. It's too damn noisy here, so how about you meet me for dinner. It will be on my paper, the *New York Times*. We can really go into all the details. OK?"

"Fine with me. Where?"

"Right here in the Aleksander. Only decent food in the whole damn city, right here."

Ackerman led him back to the bar and introduced him to some of his friends, other journalists from other important American newspapers. Ackerman was careful not to divulge any details of Morrie's story; he wanted to keep this to himself. A British sailor was sitting next to Morrie at the bar. The bartender asked the sailor if he could speak Russian, and he answered "Gaw blimey. I can't speak me own language."

The reporter's questions were incisive. Morrie found himself telling him details that he had almost forgotten about the journey. Ackerman was particularly intrigued by Morrie's experience along the railroad when the Czechs came under fire and fought back. Some vague rumors of that had reached Vladivostok, and Morrie was the first actual eyewitness to those events. Ackerman wanted to know even the smallest detail.

Morrie shrugged and decided that when it came time to tell Ackerman how he happened to be he in Russia in the first place,

there was no harm in telling the truth. "I've told a made-up story so often," Morrie said, "that I've almost come to believe it myself. Here's the real truth about how I happen to be here. I'm an Englishman, born in London, and I...and..."

He faltered. He just couldn't bring himself to say that he was a deserter from the British Army. Another story quickly popped into his head.

"...and I joined the Merchant Marine when I was just a lad. Wanted to see the world and all that. There was this miserable sod of a mate who had it in for me, so I jumped ship in Murmansk. I know that wasn't very smart. Murmansk is no garden spot, you know, but I really believe that if I'd stayed aboard the old tub, that mate and me would have had a killing row. One of us was going to die, and he was meaner than me."

Ackerman said he wanted to tell Morrie's story. Morrie said that was fine, but asked the reporter if he would please use a made-up name. He didn't want his parents to read that fictitious story.

Morrie said that he had relatives in the United States, in St. Louis. His hope was that he could get there some day. Morrie asked about St. Louis but Ackerman was not favorably impressed. He himself was a New York resident but if he had his "druthers"—and what in God's name, Morrie wondered, was a "druther"? he'd rather live in San Francisco than anywhere in the world.

They then talked about the war situation, about the political situation in Russia. Whenever any two people got together in Russia during that period, that was always the ultimate topic of conversation. Ackerman, the pragmatist, felt the Bolsheviks would eventually take over the country because they had control of the purse strings, and, in his view, whoever ruled the economy ruled the nation.

"All I know is what I've seen," said Morrie. "And what I've seen tells me that this country is in a muddle, and it needs some strong leadership to get it moving again."

"This fellow Lenin appears to be a real strong man," said Ackerman. "So is his right-hand, Stalin. People who call themselves 'iron' and 'steel' have to be tough, right?"

Ackerman thought the Japanese, who now totally outnumbered the Allies in Vladivostok, might go so far as to annex the city and its surrounding territory, and there was little Russia could do to prevent it. The Allies might try to stop it, but nobody really believed that this backwater city was important enough to start another war.

So they talked, and solved nothing. They developed a sturdy respect for each other, and Morrie began asking Ackerman for advice. He wanted to know about job opportunities, money exchange, all those practical items he had to find out about in order to make a living in this strange new city. Ackerman was pessimistic. There were thousands of refugees, and unemployment was sky-high. There was a flourishing black market in money, true, but the authorities were cracking down on it, and they were arresting anyone they caught trading money illegally. Morrie had the optimism of youth and inborn bravado, and felt he would be able to survive. Still, discretion being the better part of foolhardiness, he thought it might be wise to stick with his good luck charm, the Y.M.C.A. He asked the journalist where the Vladivostok Y was located.

It was on the fourth floor of the Churin department store, tucked away in a corner behind the department where expensive samovars were sold. As Morrie walked in, he saw a couple of rickety desks and a few battered file cabinets.

"I'm Jerry Talkin," said the man behind the desk. "How may I serve you?"

Morrie told him that he knew some of the other Y fellows. When he mentioned their names Talkin beamed. These were old friends. Talkin dragged a folding wooden chair out from under the desk, opened it, and gestured for Morrie to sit down.

Morrie had to answer the usual questions and gave the standard answers, and then he asked Talkin for help. He wanted, first, a place to stay that was cheaper than the Aleksander Hotel. Talkin said he'd check around but thought he could find something.

"Come back tomorrow, Alex," he said. "I'll probably have an address for you."

The rest of that day Morrie did the touristy things he had seldom had time to do as he was making his way across Siberia. He bought a couple of postcards and sent them back to his parents and sister in England. He had his photo taken by an American Signal Corps photographer, standing between a Cossack and a Mongolian in front of a hat store. The store sign had pictures of hats, since most of the people could not read. This photograph was later filed away in the National Archives in Washington D.C.

Morrie was intrigued by the Chinese he saw, who looked like the Chinese from Harbin but were dressed differently and spoke a different language. Morrie's unskilled ear could hear the difference. He later learned they were from someplace called Chefoo, and they were the East Asian equivalent of migrant workers. Some ten thousand of them came up from their home city every year to Vladivostok, generally finding work around the docks. They also worked in the road- building gangs.

The next day, thanks to a tip from Jerry Talkin, Morrie found a comfortable room with a family named Markov on Aleutskaya Street. Markov had been wiped out by the Bolsheviks. He had once owned the Churin department store, where the Y's headquarters were located. He was presently going through the legal process of trying to get it back, now that the Bolsheviks were out of Vladivostok. Russia, no matter who ruled it, was a country riddled with red tape, so that process would take a very long time.

Morrie spent the next week getting acclimated, looking around for a business opportunity and, simultaneously, an escape. "Escape" wasn't the precise word, but it was the one Morrie used when pondering his future. He wanted to "escape" to Canada or, even better, the United States. He would say he wanted to "visit" those countries, but to himself he knew it was an escape, pure and simple.

He went out to Point Ulis, where he had been told the Czechs were billeted. He thought there might be the off-chance of running into someone he had met on the train or on that long hike to Irkutsk. But these Czechs, while friendly, were unfamiliar.

The week passed, and Morrie could find no way to make money. He went back to Talkin at the Y. He was about to ask him if he had any ideas for employment, but Talkin spoke before Morrie could ask the Question.

"Alex," he said, "I'm so glad you dropped in. It occurred to me last night that you might be just the person we need. Have you got a job yet?"

"No, not yet," said Morrie.

"Good. Well, I mean that's good for us. We've got a problem down on the docks. We have a feeling there's too much pilfering going on. We expect a little, but it's getting out of hand."

"What would I have to do?"

"Well, we need someone just to be there on the docks, keeping an eye open. My own feeling is that if the workers see there's somebody there, looking official, that will be enough. They aren't basically thieves, but the opportunity is just so glaring that they can't resist it. I figure you could do that, mingle with the workers, look around, make your presence felt."

"Sure. I could do that."

And so Morrie began working on the dockside, in the warehouses that flanked the docks, keeping his eyes open. Whenever shipments of goods for the Y arrived, which was almost once a week, Morrie was at whatever dock was indicated.

Most of the workers were Chinese, some from Harbin but most from Chefoo. Morrie liked them very much, and the feeling was mutual. There was an insurmountable language barrier, but they overcame it with smiles, laughs, and pantomime conversation.

Morrie wasn't making a fortune, but it was enough to pay the Markovs the rent for his room and buy himself some food. He looked forward to the weeks when the Y's goods were being unloaded at the pier across from where the *Brooklyn* was moored. Morrie would then fraternize with the sailors from that ship. It was good to talk and joke with them. One day, after he had mentioned that he had done some boxing back home in London, he sparred with one of the men. They taught him to throw and catch a baseball. He threw the ball overhand, making a loop as if he were playing cricket. That caused a lot of laughter on the dock. The sailors started to look forward to the weeks when he worked there as much as he did.

"Hey, Alex," one of the sailors said one day, "come over here. I want to show you something."

He led Morrie to a quiet, inconspicuous place behind some crates, and then asked Morrie if he had any rubles for dollars. Morrie quickly made a deal. He realized that the profit from that quick transaction was more than he made for a week's work on the dock for the Y.

He didn't discourage that sailor from telling his friends about the "limey," as they called him, who could give them a break on buying rubles.

Morrie soon had a thriving business, and his wallet was bulging with dollars. Gradually, he began adding English pounds, French francs, and Italian lire to that cache, as word spread about Morrie and his mobile bank. He changed the pounds, francs, and lire into rubles, and as soon as possible into dollars. It was the dollars that he wanted to keep. He knew that they were the currency for his escape.

He met Carl Ackerman from time to time for a beer or a meal. Ackerman kept him abreast of the political situation, which changed like the wind every day. The Allies were off in western Siberia, looking for Bolsheviks to fight, except for the Americans, who were staying strictly neutral as President Wilson had promised. Vladivostok remained calm, although beneath the surface everyone was jittery over the uncertain future. The Japanese, in their stiff white summer uniforms, were firmly in control of the city and ruled it with an unnatural moderation.

It was October 26th, with winter settling in throughout Vladivostok in earnest, when a troop transport arrived bearing hundreds of Canadian soldiers. They would be stationed at East Barracks, Gornostai and Second River. *The Empress of Japan* docked and Jerry Talkin asked Morrie if he would be there when she tied up and supervise the distribution of Y goods, the inevitable chocolates and cigarettes they would give to the Canadians as they came down the gangplank. He had that added to his duties recently.

The band from the port was playing "Onward Christian Soldiers" as the big white ship tied up, and it was still playing that same hymn when the last of the Canadian troops had marched off the vessel. Morrie thought they looked like fine young men, and he admired their crisp, neat uniforms, with the natty purple patch on the shoulder.

Two weeks later, as Morrie was walking to the docks early one morning, the city suddenly erupted. People were shouting and laughing, and the ships in the harbor were all blowing their horns. A group of American soldiers were hugging each other and drinking beer, though it was early in the morning.

"The war's over! The war's over!" they shouted.

Morrie reversed directions and ran to the Aleksander, where he knew Carl Ackerman and the other journalists had their unofficial offices in the bar. They were there, as he knew they would be, and he heard all the details about the armistice from them. They were all typing away furiously, typewriters set up at the little bar tables along the side wall. Ackerman asked Morrie to do him a favor: take his copy down to his office. Morrie read it as he walked the few blocks and found that it was basically a reaction story, how the people in Vladivostok had reacted to the news that the long, bloody war had finally ended. He marveled at Ackerman's ability to include so many details, while not even leaving the Aleksander bar. He didn't understand the technique of journalism.

Ackerman had shrewdly mentioned in the story, however, one factor that Morrie himself had realized. The end of the war with Germany did not mean the end of the war now going on inside Russia. That war, between the Whites and the Allies on the one hand, and the Bolsheviks and all the splinter Russian groups on the other, would still be going on for the foreseeable future.

Most of the celebrating that morning in Vladivostok was being done by foreigners. The natives were restrained, because they knew there was still much killing to be accomplished before their land could know peace.

There was a general air of celebration in the city for three days, climaxed by a gigantic victory parade along Pushkinskaya. Morrie and Jerry Talkin watched and cheered as the soldiers from the Allied nations paraded smartly down the broad avenue. The Japanese, Czechs, Americans, British, Canadians, French, and others all had their flags flying and bands blaring. They strutted down the thoroughfare, and the crowd of Russians, Chinese, and Mongols cheered them.

Three days after that glorious occasion there was another upheaval in the ranks of the anti-Bolshevik Russian hierarchy. Admiral Aleksander Vasilevich Kolchak assumed the title of "Supreme Regent," which really was meaningless because there was very little for him to regent over. He set up his headquarters in Omsk and, while he was recognized by the Allies as the ruler of Russia, he was really only ruler of those Russians who were actively campaigning against the Bolsheviks. There was some friction even among them. He had the supposed support of the Cossacks, General Denikin, and the always-vocal Semenov, but other factions actively opposed him.

Kolchak appointed a man named Ivanov-Rinov as the Commandant of Vladivostok, a meaningless appointment since in point of fact the Japanese were running the city. Still, the Japanese let the new appointee have some authority, and he promptly started a reign of terror, jailing or shooting men accused of being anti-White or pro-Red. Stories reached Vladivostok of Ivanov-Rinov's hooligans terrorizing outlying villages and trying to press the villages' young men into the army.

Vladivostok changed from the extroverted, cheerful city that Morrie had first encountered, into a dreary place, beset by bad weather and a cruel government. Winter increased its grip on the city and the icy winds tore down from the north.

Morrie stayed busy, working on the docks for the Y and doing his money-changing business. Two more Canadian ships arrived in January bearing mostly supplies for the Canadian troops who were already there, but with some things for the Y also. Morrie supervised the unloading of the Y goods from both the *Teesta* and the *Protesliaus*. The latter ship was two days late, limping into the Vladivostok harbor after losing one of its propellers to a small iceberg not far out of port.

Morrie, while waiting for the *Protesliaus* to dock, began talking to some of the Canadian soldiers assigned to assist the arrivals from the new ship as they came ashore. He had become a familiar sight on the Vladivostok docks in his distinctive black fur hat and black fur coat. Everybody knew Morrie, and dozens of the Canadians had already done business with him.

Two soldiers, part of the 259th Battalion, struck up a conversation with Morrie, and the three started throwing a ball around, mostly to keep warm. They were Ronald Perry and Stan Churchill. They would play key roles in Morrie's future, although none of them knew it at the time.

Morrie had done his best to stay away from the British troops, and it was a relief to speak English to the Canadians. Ron and Stan mentioned, during a conversation with Morrie, that the Canadians favored the British Lee-Enfield rifle over the Canadian Ross. Morrie's thoughts suddenly flashed back to Salisbury Plain, where he had trained with the Post Office Rifle Brigade. He had carried a Lee-Enfield while he was a "Squarebasher."

The Y.M.C.A. organized entertainment for the Canadians at the Vladivostok Commercial School. They were warned, however, not to go up to Kopeck Hill, the red light district, as one person was killed there almost every night.

The Y and the Knights of Columbus established canteens in all the barracks, and Morrie helped out at the Y canteens. There was also the "Casino" at East Barracks where concerts and movies were shown.

One night, Ron and Stan invited Morrie, to see a Canadian lieutenant perform "Salome's Dance" at the East Barracks. The same officer later produced a show called "The Roadside Minstrels." His name was Raymond Massey, and he later became a famous movie star in Hollywood.

Morrie changed a little money for them, although he knew this was risky business. They invited him to East Barracks, where a camp show was scheduled for that night to welcome the newcomers. Morrie, Ron, and Stan, in the weeks to come, became good friends and Morrie became a regular visitor to the 259th's barracks at Gornostai. He liked the Canadians in general, and these two in particular. He found the Canadians were as friendly as the Yanks.

Morrie had begun to be invited to many parties throughout Vladivostok as a representative of the Y, and as often as possible he asked Ron Perry and Stan Churchill to come along with him.

Ron and Stan, at one party, ran into another old friend from home. His name was Ross Owen, and he worked for the Canadian Pacific Railroad, in the shipping division. He was, Morrie learned, in charge of all of the

Canadian Pacific's ships that were running between Vladivostok and Canadian ports.

"I worked the *Empress of Japan* said Morrie. "I was at her dock the first time she came here. Somebody told me she stops at Yokohama on the way back to Canada. Is Vladivostok a regular port of call for your service between Vancouver and Yokohama?" Owen replied that they just added Vladivostok with the war going on, but still Vancouver-Yokohama was their bread and butter. "We have to stop at Yokohama, anyhow, because that's where we get our coal."

"There's plenty of coal mined here," said Morrie. "Why can't you get your coal here?"

"There's coal, sure, but no coaling facilities for the big ships and no repair equipment in this port. No, it makes sense for us to stop in Yokohama before crossing the ocean."

That conversation started the wheels churning in Morrie's head. Perhaps he would have to go to Yokohama first, before attempting to cross the Pacific.

As 1918 faded into history, the political and military status of all the Allied armies in Siberia was very confusing. The Canadians had never gotten involved in any of the fighting and neither had the Americans. The Canadian government was adamant about not being involved in what had come to be called "The Intervention." In February, 1919, the Canadians decided to withdraw their focus entirely from Siberia.

An impromptu soccer league sprang up about that time, and Morrie helped the Canadians organize a team. One day, with himself starring at center forward, the Canadians beat the French team 2-0, and Morrie was the hero. He celebrated at the Aleksander bar after that heady triumph with his friends, Ron and Stan.

The two Canadians were excited about something else. There were rumors that their unit was soon going home. They didn't know when, of course, but they figured they had a good source of information from their old friend Ross Owen of Canadian Pacific's shipping division.

Morrie started walking home after the Canadians left, when he met some American soldiers. They had a friend with them who Morrie didn't know, and they said that this friend had urgent need of some rubles. Could Morrie accommodate him?

He had begun to wind down his money exchanging, because, since the new regime had taken over, they had started to crack down even harder on illegal money transactions. These were American soldiers, and he might need a few more dollars to implement his plan.

"Let's go around the corner," said Morrie, "where it's a little less crowded."

Morrie led the way and pulled out a roll of rubles worth about ten dollars. Four Russian soldiers suddenly dashed out of a hiding place and surrounded them. Two held their rifles on Morrie as one of the others grabbed the money out of Morrie's hand. The fourth motioned the American soldiers to move, and they ran without a backward glance.

The soldiers then roughed Morrie up, shoving him against a wall and twisting his arm behind his back. They then began marching him off, one of them holding each of his arms.

Morrie realized that he was in serious trouble. They were taking him away, either to jail or be shot without a trial. Neither alternative was particularly pleasurable, but jail was certainly the better option. So he was somewhat relieved to find himself marched into the jail, next to the Vladivostok post office.

They marched him through the door and up to a counter, behind which sat another soldier, who addressed him in Russian. He didn't understand, and that seemed to anger them all. They grabbed him and pushed him down the corridor and into a cell.

Another prisoner lay on the stone bench and looked up when Morrie appeared. He said something in a language that Morrie recognized as Czech.

"English," Morrie said, pointing to himself.

"You are from England, true?" the Czech said in heavily accented English, taking a little interest now in his new cellmate. "Prague. And you?" "Yes, London." I am Thomas Pick. "I'm Alex Chernofsky. Why are you here?"

Pick shrugged. He said he had been arrested and thrown in jail for a crime called "slandering the government." He had been lecturing at the university where he was a professor of economics, and had said that some of Kolchack's men were nothing but murderers. He was jailed for that statement.

Morrie told him about his crime and realized that he was fortunate in one respect. He didn't have his big wallet with him when he was arrested. He had left it safely under his mattress in his room at the Markov's house.

"How long have you been in this place?" asked Morrie. "Not long, Pick answered. I think tomorrow will be three weeks."

That might not have seemed like very long to Pick, but it seemed like an eternity to Morrie. He had been in jail before, and even though it hadn't lasted more than a week or so, it had seemed like forever. He couldn't stand three weeks. Maybe he could tell them he was an American, and they would deport him to the States.

They told each other their stories. Pick had taught economics in Prague, and then had joined the Czech legion. Anyhow, he was lecturing and so he went overboard and began criticizing the Russian government, and here he was sitting in jail.

"They are not mistreating me," he said. "No beating, no torture. The food is not good, but what jail food is good? It is eatable, is that the word? No, edible, and it has not yet made me sick, so it's okay." As Pick talked Morrie began to assess his situation. The American soldiers with whom he had been doing business wouldn't tell anybody, because that would incriminate them. None of the people who might be able to help him, like the Y people or Kamarov or anyone else, would likely find out for days that he was in jail.

"You're not listening to me," said Pick.

"Sorry. My mind was wandering."

"Understand, under the circumstance, I was saying that we might be luck'y."

"Luck'y? Doesn't seem very luck'y to me."

Pick edged closer.

"I think maybe we have a friend here. Just this morning, before you came, I heard a voice I am positive I recognized. The man at the front desk. Describe him for me, if you would be so kind."

Morrie had only had a quick glimpse of the soldier who was at the counter. It was the soldier who had gotten angry when Morrie didn't understand his Russian.

"I just saw him for a few seconds," Morrie said. "He was sitting down, so I have no idea if he was tall or short. He was round-faced, a lot of curly hair, that's about all I remember. He did seem to have a Czech accent."

"Did he wear eyeglasses?"

"Eyeglasses? I think maybe he did, the kind that just pinch on his nose, nothing going over his ears."

"That's him!" Pick was exultant. He jumped up. "I knew I recognized his voice. That's my old friend Koretz, Paul Koretz. You described him perfectly. He and I were old school chums back in Prague. He must have come in with the Czech troops, and the Russians assigned him to this post. I will contact him tomorrow morning, and we'll be all right. I'm sure of it."

Morrie wasn't very confident that Pick's old school chum, if indeed that was him at the desk, would or could do anything for Pick, and why would he do anything for Morrie?

Morrie hardly slept, but with no idea of the time, when his attempts at sleeping were brutally ended by the sound of a volley of gunshots.

"What was that?" he blurted out.

"The firing squad."

"The firing squad? Who are they shooting?"

"One of the prisoners, I imagine. They haven't officially charged me yet, and certainly they haven't charged you. The Russians, if nothing else, are sticklers for form. Nobody would dare get shot until they have gone through the formalities of officially charging them, putting them on trial, and convicting them. So this isn't going to be our day in front of the firing squad."

That was slightly reassuring, but the sound of that firing squad echoed in Morrie's worried brain for hours.

There was no more thought of sleep. He sat up on the edge of his cot, watching the window high over his head for the first sign of the light of dawn.

Through a small opening at the bottom of the door their breakfast appeared, but it was a repeat of last night's meal, another portion of that alleged soup. Morrie wasn't hungry, so Pick ate his portion.

"Now's the time," said the Czech, rubbing his hands together eagerly. "I am going to take a chance that my friend is at the desk now. I'm going to ask the guard to take me to the toilet. It's just beyond the guard's desk."

Pick called out, and the guard opened the door, grabbed Pick's arm, and led him down the corridor. Morrie waited in the cell for more than an hour before the door opened and Pick came back. He was smiling broadly.

"I knew everything would be all right as soon as I heard his voice" said Pick. "My dear, dear old friend, Paul Koretz. As they dragged me past his desk, I yelled at him, and he saw me and nearly fainted from surprise. We hadn't seen each other in, well, it must be at least fifteen years. He remembered my name instantly. He insisted that I come over and sit with him, and we talked about old times. I knew you would be worried, but I felt I had to humor him. So everything is all right. We are both going to be released before lunch."

Morrie couldn't believe what Pick had just said. Why would this old friend turn a man free whom he didn't even know? It made no sense.

Pick said that Koretz was making out the release papers now, and as soon as they were completed, the two of them would be released. The time seemed to drag, and whenever there were footsteps in the corridor, both of them stood up, certain that this was the moment of their freedom. It took several hours before their door was opened and two Russians guards motioned for them to move out of the cell.

"As you go past the desk," Pick whispered, "don't even look at Koretz. Ignore him."

Morrie still couldn't believe his good fortune as he left the prison, he said a fond farewell to Tomas Pick, and then ran back to the Markovs' house. He was sure of one thing; he wouldn't do any more exchanging of money.

Now he was determined to put his hazy plan into operation as soon as possible. This life was getting too risky. He had to escape.

Chapter Thirteen

There was only a small wooden plaque to indicate what was inside the building. "Canadian Pacific Railroad Company, Shipping Division," it said.

Morrie went in and asked the receptionist if he could speak to Mr. Ross Owen.

"Who shall I say is calling?" she asked.

"Alex Chernofsky. He may remember me. Tell him I'm a friend of Ron Perry and Stan Churchill, and that we met at a party one evening."

Owen came out of his office with a big smile and a hearty handshake. He remembered Morrie very well, and he was happy to see him again. "What can I do for you, young fellow?" he asked.

Morrie explained. He had rehearsed this speech carefully, so it was almost a recitation. He said he had gotten to know the Canadian lads very well, and he was dreading the day when they would be shipping home, although he knew that day would be a happy one for them. He said he knew that Canadian Pacific would be providing the ships to take them home and, if it wouldn't be giving away any secret information, did he know when they would be going, and what ships would be taking them?

Owen laughed. He said it was all very hush-hush when they came to Vladivostok, because there was a war on then. But things were different now, and the shipping orders would not be a secret this time.

"We have the ships ordered," he said. The *Empress of Japan* and the *Empress of Russia* will be the ones we'll use. The government has also chartered the *Monteagle*, so there will be three in all. They all should be here, ready to go, in about two weeks. Does that answer your question?"

"Yes, sir. It means in about two weeks I will be one lonely English boy."

"Now how about telling me what's really on your mind."

Morrie stuck to his story, even though he could tell that Owen figured correctly that he had another motive besides the one he had expressed. Morrie couldn't tell anyone about his plan. Now, though, he had the information he needed.

Morrie went back to the Aleksander Hotel and looked up Carl Ackerman, who was a fixture at the bar. He asked the reporter if the withdrawal of the Canadian troops was definite and official, and Ackerman assured him that it was true. They were going home and it would be soon.

Now Morrie had to work fast. He went to the Canadians' barracks and found Ron and Stan.

They said they had been worried because they hadn't seen him for a couple of days. He told them about being imprisoned, and his lucky break in getting out.

"You ought to get out of this country," said Ron. "It might get pretty rough for you here after we leave. The Y.M.C.A. will be out of here when we and the Yanks leave. You can't do any more money trading. What will you do?"

"You're absolutely right," said Morrie. "I do have to get out of here, and soon. That's why I came to see you fellows."

"What can we do for you?" asked Stan. "You know we'd help you if we could, but there's nothing we can do."

"Yes you can. You can take me with you."

They were stunned. So was Morrie, now that he had said it. His words just sat there, and the two Canadian soldiers stared at him dumbfounded.

"How can we take you with us?"

Morrie leaned in and talked in a low voice, as rapidly and as convincingly as he could.

"I'm going to ask a huge favor of you chaps," he said. "This is my plan. Your ship stops over in Yokohama for about two days, to take on coal. You'll get shore leave there. I've checked and it's customary. I'll be on the docks there. You bring pieces of a spare uniform with you. I'll put it on and come back on board with you."

They both jumped in with objections. Ron said that there would be routine inspections aboard the ship. Morrie said he would make believe he was sick, and stay in the cabin all the way. Stan wondered how he would eat. Morrie said they could bring him scraps, leftovers, from their meal. He wouldn't need much. He said he'd probably be seasick anyhow, and not want to eat at all. They both wanted to know how he would get to Yokohama. Morrie said that was his problem, but he had it all figured out. Ron said what about getting back aboard the ship in Yokohama, but Stan said that would be no problem, because they wouldn't be checking very closely there, figuring the only thing they had to worry about might be Japanese trying to get aboard. They could spot them, but nobody would bother to count Canadians.

Morrie swore that if he got caught he would tell them he had stolen the uniform.

Ron and Stan talked to each other. They said if they got caught it could mean the brig. They would certainly lose their ratings and benefits. Morrie sat quietly, waiting for them to make up their minds.

"Oh, what the hell," said Ron. "I'll do it. At least it will mean that I've accomplished something good out here."

Morrie breathed a deep sigh of relief.

"If I live to be a hundred," he said, "I'll never be able to repay you fellows. You are saving my life. I'd die if I had to stay here another few months."

Morrie had a few honest tears in his eyes, out of relief and gratitude. He hugged his friends and they hugged him back.

Now things moved swiftly for Morrie. What had only been a dream before, a possibility, an outside chance, now had overnight become a fact. He had a thousand things to do and only a few days in which to do them.

First, he had to make his plans for getting to Yokohama. He had earlier decided that it would make no sense to attempt to stow away here in Vladivostok because the Canadian authorities would be checking everybody going aboard the ships in Vladivostok. Many Russians, among others, might want to get out and the Canadian ships offered a tempting escape route.

Second, if he was discovered between Vladivostok and Yokohama, they would put him ashore in the Japanese port. Morrie imagined that if he were discovered on the way to Canada or at the first Canadian port, he would at least be out of Siberia. He would do anything to get away from the Russian craziness. Yokohama would be his next destination. Morrie wandered around the docks, an area which by now was familiar territory to him. He asked some of his dockside friends about ships headed for Yokohama. They pointed to one, a rusty old Russian tub that carried timber. The *Simbirsk*, said the huge white cyrilic letters on the hull. Morrie could translate cyrilic characters into English sounds by this time, and he could say the ship's name, *Simbirsk*.

He went to the harbor master's office. Morrie was a familiar figure there. The harbor master had been a big customer, but no more, and he looked at Morrie warily.

"No money, Georgie," said Morrie, holding his hands up in the air to indicate he wasn't there on business. "Just came by to say hello. It's been too long."

"Da Alex. Chai?"

As they drank their tea, Morrie had time to study the blackboard that listed all the ships in the harbor, with their dates of departure.

April 30, 1919 was the date when the *Simbirsk* would sail out of Vladivostok harbor, en route to Yokohama and then to several ports on the South China coast.

April 30. That was two days away.

"Thanks for the tea, Georgie. Good to see you."

"Any time, Alex. No more money, okay?"

"Okay."

"See you soon, okay?"

Morrie waved. He hoped he wouldn't be seeing Georgie or anybody else in Vladivostok soon.

He would be on the *Simbirsk* when she sailed. Morrie ran back to his room and took inventory of what he owned and what he would take with him. He would take a small bag, plus his wallet with his hoard of dollars, and as much bread and sausage as he could stuff into his pockets.

The next two days passed swiftly. Morrie wanted to say good-bye to his many friends—the Markovs, Carl Ackerman, and his fellow journalists—but without actually telling them he was going. He didn't want anybody to know.

He spent some time with all of them, but he carefully skirted any talk about leaving, and shook all their hands warmly. He could do no more.

Morrie didn't sleep the night before the *Simbirsk* was due to sail. He dressed in dark clothing. Fortunately, it was spring again, so he wore enough to keep warm, without restricting his movements. He was fortunate. One of the occasional Vladivostok fogs had rolled in off the ocean. It was as thick as any he had seen and he had some difficulty finding the right pier. Foghorns moaned through the heavy mist in the harbor, as other ships groped their way toward shore. Here, however, all was quiet.

Morrie walked to the foot of the ship's gangplank. He knew from experience that all the ships in the harbor left their hatch covers open at night, with only a tarpaulin across the opening. He had wandered casually past the *Simbirsk* the day before, noting what cargo was being loaded in which hold. He suspected that Hatch Number 1 was almost fully loaded. That was what he wanted, a hold that few people would bother with the next morning, one where he could hide.

He saw someone at the top of the gangplank, and froze. As soon as the shadowy figure vanished, he dashed up the wooden incline. He clutched his bag, his wallet was tied tight around his waist and his pockets were bulging with food. He had a bottle of water tucked into his belt. As he had anticipated, the hatch was covered only with a tarpaulin. He lifted a corner and felt inside for the top of the iron stairway that he knew would be there. He found it and hastily lowered himself through the opening, climbing down the ladder. He descended only three rungs until his feet felt something solid. Good. He had been right. This hold was virtually full, loaded with timber. He carefully explored with his free hand and established the possibility that there was a space for him to sit, perhaps even to lie down.

After about an hour, he heard voices. He recognized that they were speaking in the Chefoo dialect. The tarpaulin was pulled back and sun streamed into the hold. Morrie cowered against the side of the hold, praying that none of them would look down. They quickly did their job, hauling the heavy steel hatch cover across the opening and making it fast.

Morrie was sealed into the tomb, black and quiet and totally alone. He knew he would be there for two days, and he hoped that Hatch Number 1 would be opened soon after the ship arrived in Yokohama. It would depend on the availability of longshoremen and the need for the timber, the weather, and all sorts of other variable factors.

Hours went by before Morrie felt the vibration of the ship's engines and the rocking motion that told him they were underway. He was finally leaving Russia. It was a year plus one month since he had been deposited on the cold, forbidding shore of Murmansk. Now he was off on another journey into the unknown. He celebrated with a bit of sausage and a small sip of water, but he was going to be very careful and ration himself severely.

He identified the sounds topside, the two toots of the tug boat whistle, indicating that the pilot had come aboard and then, an hour or so later, another pair of toots to indicate that the pilot had left. They were now on the open sea. He knew they had a days's sail, southeastward across the Sea of Japan, and another day making their way through the channel that separated the Japanese island of Kyushu to the south from Honshu and Shikoku to the north. The ship would be steaming up the eastern coast of those islands in the Pacific to Yokohama.

Morrie tried to relax. It was far from comfortable, but the thought that he was finally away from Russia was almost intoxicating. So too was the smell of the wood in the hold, newly-hewn. Its sap had an aroma that was almost like perfume. Morrie,s thoughts were on the one part of his plan that would have to be spontaneous: getting off the *Simbirsk*.

If they did things in Yokohama as they had done on the docks at Vladivostok, it could be done. In Vlad, when a ship docked, and the dock-workers decided it was time to unload it, they would open all the hatch covers at one time, put the tarpaulins across the openings, and then wait for the arrival of the longshore crew. If they followed that routine, Morrie was home free. He would wait until dark, crawl out as he had crawled in, wait for a moment when no one was around, and run for it. He didn't know for sure if they did things the same way in Yokohama: The Japanese were different about a lot of things they did and maybe they unloaded ships differently, too.

Morrie had expected to be seasick. He thought the combination of the ship's motion plus being confined in a dark place without much fresh air would certainly make him very queasy. He was pleasantly surprised to find that he felt perfectly well.

Morrie had plenty of time to think. He thought about home, and he realized that now he was practically half a world away from London. Would he ever see his family again? Probably not. Wherever he went, because of being a deserter, he would never be able to revisit England. He would never again see his mother, father, or sister.

That sad thought put him to sleep. He woke with the immediate realization that something—and almost certainly that something was a rat—was crawling down his arm. It was huge, cat-sized, and he could feel its weight. That particular arm was the one clutching a piece of black bread, which he had been in the process of nibbling when he fell asleep. Now the rat was interested in some nibbling. Morrie threw the bread as far as he could, and he shook his arm vigorously. He heard the rat scurry off.

He didn't allow himself to fall asleep again for the balance of the voyage. He sat there, clutching his knees with his arms, eating and drinking a bit, and carefully stuffing the food back under his clothing.

Eventually he heard the ship's whistle blow, the toot-toot that told him that the pilot had come aboard, and he felt the ocean's pitch-and-toss diminish to a gentle roll. He knew that the *Simbirsk* was coming into Yokohama.

He translated all the sounds and feelings into messages. The nudge of the tug, the thud of tying up at the dock, and the squeal of the gangplank being lowered. He heard the heavy- booted footsteps of what he suspected were Japanese naval authorities, checking the ship for stowaways, contraband, smuggled goods, or whatever. Then, silence.

Suddenly the hatch cover was slid back. Brilliant sunlight splashed into the hold, as though a spotlight had been turned on. Morrie was sure that whoever was up there had actually turned the beam of a huge spotlight right on him, and he was certain that he had been discovered. But it was merely daylight, and apparently none of the workers bothered to look down. They just shoved the hatch cover aside and moved onto the next one.

For the first time in two days, Morrie looked at his watch. It was five o'clock. Good—it would soon be getting dark. His legs had fallen asleep and he tried to move them, but it was only with great pain that he managed to stretch out.

He slowly maneuvered his weary, aching body into a reasonably comfortable position. He then froze, not daring to move, for he realized that he was very vulnerable, lying out in the open in broad daylight. Should anybody happen to look down into the hold he could easily be spotted. He knew that just a slight movement might be enough to attract the attention of someone on deck. So he waited and, ostrich-like, shut his eyes tight.

As he listened he heard the deck sounds gradually diminish. The men outside were speaking Japanese, of course, but Morrie imagined he could hear them saying good night to each other and making jokes as they finished their day's work. Suddenly there was total silence. He opened his eyes and saw the blackness of the night sky overhead.

Morrie waited another fifteen minutes or so, to be sure there were no stragglers left on deck, and then he slowly pulled himself upright. Assorted parts of his body had fallen asleep in the cramped position he had assumed, and he had to wait until circulation brought feeling back to his total body. He took his first clumsy step and accidently kicked the small bag he had brought with him, which contained his reserves of clothing and food. He heard the clatter as it made its way deep into the hold.

He felt the security of his wallet, tied tight around his waist. That was now the sum and substance of his worldly goods. But it was stuffed with money, so it should be sufficient.

He scrambled awkwardly to the top of the pile of timbers, reached up for the edge of the ladder and slowly pulled himself up and onto the deck. He crouched low behind some structure on the deck and only gradually did he look around the corner to survey the ship. There was nobody to be seen, only a few shadows from the clouds, which skittered across the surface of the full moon.

Morrie inched his way to the railing, peered over, and located the gangplank. He made his way there and then waited and watched for several minutes. Morrie had cursed his luck at having a full moon, as he would be too visible. He could not, however, see anyone on the dock; there were apparantly no guards around. The Japanese had seemingly come to the logical conclusion that a boatload of heavy logs was not a prime target for thieves, so they had not bothered to leave any guards on the dock.

After he had assured himself that there was no one below, Morrie dashed down the gangplank to the shelter of a small building he had seen from the deck. He then looked around, deciding to head in the direction of some distant lights. Presumably that was downtown Yokohama, and that was where he wanted to go. He was finally away from the British soldiers in Vladivostok, and he was tired of being called Alex Chernofsky. He took his father's anglicized first name, Barnett, and changed it to his last name. He would now be known as Morrie Barnett. He had no more to fear in Japan. He walked into the Japanese city trying to look as though he belonged there. He was looking for Yamashita-Cho.

His memory had dredged those syllables up from somewhere. He had heard somebody in Vladivostok talking about Yokohama, about the section called Yamashita-Cho, where the foreigners lived. It had meant nothing to him when he had first heard the name Yamashita-Cho, but now, when it might be valuable to him, he remembered it.

He stopped two elderly Japanese, with long white beards and gray kimonos.

"Yamashita-Cho?" he asked.

They pointed off to Morrie's left. They said a few words in Japanese and then bowed. Morrie bowed in return and said "thank you" in English, then went in the direction they had indicated.

After a walk of perhaps twenty minutes, Morrie knew that he had reached Yamashita-Cho. No longer were all the signs in Japanese, which was totally indecipherable to Morrie, they were in English as well. Hong Kong and Shanghai Bank, one said. Yokohama United Club, read another. He came upon the Oriental Hotel, and across from it the Grand Hotel. Both hotels looked too posh and expensive for Morrie. He wanted something smaller, and he found such a place as he turned down a side street. The sign read Matsuda Hotel, Prop M. Tanaka. It was small and, presumably, inexpensive.

He went inside and smiled at a small Japanese gentleman behind the front desk.

"Good evening, sir," said Morrie.

"*Konichi-wa,*" replied the Japanese gentleman. "Good evening. May I be of service?"

The man's English was heavily accented, but understandable. Morrie asked the price of a room, and the clerk said that the rooms were eight yen. Morrie wanted to know the price in American dollars, and the clerk said about four dollars.

"You come from ship?" he asked.

"Yes," said Morrie, taking four dollars from his wallet and giving them to the clerk. The man held up his hand. "Not necessary now. You please pay in the morning." In the room Morrie fell asleep on the tatami mat without taking off his clothes. He slept for ten hours without stirring and it was the clop-clop of wooden sandals on the street that finally woke him. He looked out of the window and saw Japanese men throwing buckets of water on the street, then scrubbing it down vigorously. He knew he was no longer in Russia, where the only time a street was cleaned was when it rained.

He was served a cup of tea by a blushing Japanese girl, then went out and found a shop where he bought a razor. That and other necessities had been in the bag that was lost as he made his way off the ship. He then changed some money. Each American dollar bought two Japanese yen. He went to a shop and bought some clothing to replace what he had lost.

Morrie quickly made friends with Tanaka, the owner and manager of the hotel. Mr. Tanaka was curious about him, but Morrie was, by now, the master of evasive autobiography, so easily fended off the curiosity. Tanaka was able to tell Morrie where the office of the Canadian Pacific Railroad's shipping division was located and Morrie found his way there without too much difficulty.

Once inside he asked to talk to whoever would know about the arrival of ships from Vladivostok. In a few minutes, a man came out of an inner office.

Morrie introduced himself and said that he was a friend of Ross Owen of Canadian Pacific in Vladivostok. That was the magic name. The man smiled and waved Morrie into his office. His name was Rick Bennett.

After some talk, Morrie got down to business. He said he knew that there would be three ships taking the Canadian troops back to Canada, stopping off first in Yokohama. He said he had some good friends among the Canadian forces, and he wanted to see them as they passed through. He wondered if Mr. Bennett might have the schedules and their arrival dates in Yokohama.

"No problem," said Bennett. "The turn-around dates have been fixed. I have all that information. First, tell me how old Ross is doing over there in Vlad with the Russkis."

Morrie told him everything he knew, but he tried to get Bennett back to the dates on which the Canadian-Pacific ships would be arriving.

Apparently it wasn't often that Bennett had a chance to gossip, and he loved the opportunity. It took Morrie an hour to get the dates.

The *Monteagle* was the first of the ships due. She would be sailing from Vladivostok on April 21, which meant that she would be arriving in Yokohama on the 23rd, a week from today. The *Empress of Japan* would be docking here on May 11 and the last of the three, the *Empress of Russia*, on May 21.

As he walked back to the hotel, Morrie looked at the paper that he had written the dates on. He had no way of knowing which of the three ships his friends would be arriving on. He could be making contact with them in a week or, if they were on the last of the three ships, in a bit more than a month.

Still, he had enough money to last him even if it was the *Empress of Russia*. Tanaka had given him a good weekly rate, so he could afford to stay at the hotel. Food, he had discovered, was very inexpensive. He walked along the street, looking at the wax models of the foods served in each tiny restaurant. People shopped for bite-sized portions, each costing pennies, and made a dinner by stopping at five or six different establishments.

He settled down to wait for the ship that carried his friends.

Chapter Fourteen

Naturally Morrie was eager for the arrival of the ship or ships, so he could get on with his odyssey. He was torn between fear that his plan wouldn't work and excitement over what turn his life would take if it was sucessful.

If it didn't work, what then? It was one thing to be stuck in Vladivostok, where at least he looked like he belonged but it was quite another to be in Yokohama, where he would be one of only a handful of occidental faces. He had learned enough Russian to get by, but he knew absolutely no Japanese. He had been able to make a living by his wits in Vladivostok, but that would be virtually impossible in Yokohama, where his fate was restricted by barriers of language and appearance.

If his plan didn't work,he would be lost. There was simply no alternative. It had to work. During the week until the *Monteagle* was due to dock, he restlessly walked the length and breadth of Yokohama. One evening, he even walked back to the dock where the *Simbirsk* was still tied up. He looked at the old tub now, as the timbers were being unloaded by a huge crane, and felt a pang of affection for the dirty battered ship. It had done the job for him.

After he had been in Yokohama for four of five days, Tanaka seated him at lunch next to a man who appeared to be an American. They were the only two in the dining room, and Tanaka had apparently thought that they would enjoy each other's company.

"Good afternoon," said the American. Morrie acknowledged his greeting. "You stay here often, at this hotel?"

"No," said Morrie. "First time. As a matter of fact, it's my first time in Japan."

"Sounds like you're an Englishman, right?"

"Right. Morrie Barnett. I'm from England."

"Glad to know you," said the American, extending a large, eager hand. "I'm Harry Dickstein, from Seattle in Washington state. Over here on my annual visit, buying Russian furs. You know you can get better Russian furs in Japan than in Russia. Took me a dozen years to learn that, but my competition still doesn't know it. So I'm ahead of the game.

"What's your line, Morrie?"

Morrie had met enough Americans on his recent travels to realize that they always wanted to know what you did for a living.

It was a question that Englishmen would never ask, at least not until they knew you very well. But it was practically the first thing to pop out of an American's mouth. Morrie was prepared for Dickstein's question and said he was involved in shipping. True enough, after a fashion.

They talked through lunch, and Dickstein volunteered to show Morrie the city, since he knew it well after coming here annually for the past eight years.

"It'll be nice to have some company," he said. "I have to be here two weeks, and in all that time I may work a total of ten hours. That's the way it is here in the fur trade.

"Gets mighty lonely, I'll tell you that. The Japanese are lovely people but, after all, it's good to be able to talk the King's English, especially to someone who talks it as good as the King himself."

Dickstein said that he had an appointment in the afternoon, but he suggested the two get together again for dinner, and then, afterwards, "I know a great little place over in Blood Town I'd like to show you."

"Blood Town? Blimey, sounds grim. What's that?"

"It's what they call their Chinatown," said Dickstein. "Would you believe a Chinatown in a Japanese city? It got the nickname of Blood Town years ago. Used to be a fight there all the time but now its very peaceful. Okay with you?"

It was fine with Morrie. He welcomed the company.

As Morrie waited for the first of the Canadian troop ships to arrive, time was hanging heavily on his hands. The evening out with Dickstein, who seemed a pleasant friendly sort, would be a nice diversion.

After their dinner, Dickstein led Morrie across the Maita Bashi Bridge into Blood Town. It was just like Limehouse in London. Morrie realized that Chinatowns were Chinatowns, in London or Yokohama. Dickstein pointed out houses with dim lights. "Rumors have it they are opium dens." There were a few bars and Morrie saw French, English, and American sailors inside. The American led him to a small bistro, almost Parisian in atmosphere.

"Great little place," Dickstein said. "The drinks are good, the prices are fair, and they have a great little singer. You haven't lived until you've seen a Japanese chanteuse."

"Lead the way," said Morrie.

They found a table near the back and ordered drinks. An American was playing the piano. The spotlight then pointed to a pretty girl who came out from the side and made her way to the piano.

"I'm a little Japanese," she sang.

"I come across the sea and my name is little Tootsie Wee.

Sing a ling ling high, sing a ling ling low.

Have a Japanese cup of tea, I'm a little Japanese and I came across the sea and my name is little Tootsie Wee."

Silly words, but she sang in a husky voice, and evidently she was trying to capture the flavor of the French chanteuses. It was only partially successful as art, but it was fun to watch her try to be a Parisian-style singer while looking very Japanese, and it was a laugh to hear silly English words done by a Japanese girl trying to sound French.

That was only the first of several nights that Morrie and Harry spent together. They found that they enjoyed each other's company, and Morrie thought that Yokohama night life was exciting. There were places catering to the tastes of any person, from very conservative bistros where there was merely tasteful entertainment to wild and wooly clubs where virtually anything could happen.

During the days, when Harry had some time off, they explored Yokohama's more conventional sights. They found a section of magnificent homes, and other areas where the houses were merely some rice paper supported by bamboo- pole beams. Through their mutual wanderings, Morrie came to know Yokohama intimately. But his mind and his eyes always drew him to the waterfront, to the pier where the Canadian Pacific's big steamers moored.

"Why are you always hanging around the pier?" Harry wanted to know. Morrie couldn't tell him that he was planning to stow away on one of the ships, so he merely said that since he was in the shipping business, it was good for him to look at various ships. He wasn't sure if that explanation satisfied his friend, but Dickstein didn't pursue the matter.

The day then came when the *Monteagle* was due to arrive. Morrie arose before dawn, dressed quickly, and made his way to the pier. There was no one there. Then he realized that it was only five o'clock, and the big ship wasn't due until eight. Still, he had felt that it might be early and so he had better be there. He was so excited he couldn't have slept anyway.

Morrie waited in the cold and foggy Japanese morning, and gradually the sun came up and burned off the fog. A few longshoremen straggled onto the pier and then, suddenly, it was eight o'clock and the pier was jammed with onlookers. The arrival of a troop ship from Vladivostok was a major event.

"There she is," someone called and Morrie strained to see. He made out the silhouette of the *Monteagle* against the slate- gray horizon. A couple of tugs pushed and pulled, and the the ship was at the dock.

The railing was lined with Canadian troops getting their first glimpse of Japan. Morrie searched the faces for the familiar ones of Ron Perry and Stan Churchill. He didn't see them, but the troops were at least three and four deep.

He waited at the base of the gangplank while the Japanese customs men boarded the ship for the inevitable and interminable official procedures that always hold up any ship's landing. The vessel got its clearance, and at last the men began filing down the gangplank for a few hours of shore leave.

The *Monteagle* was carrying slightly more than a thousand troops, and Morrie looked at every face as the men walked down the gangplank. Ron and Stan were not there.

His new friend, Harry Dickstein, was due to leave in a few days, so once again Morrie would be alone. Morrie and Harry had a few days and nights of fun, and, during one of them, Morrie stopped in a store on Silk Street and bought a gift for Harry to take home to the girl he had said he would soon be marrying. It was a small vase, brightly colored in red, white, and gold and decorated with a small but spirited dragon. Morrie said it was a gift to bring Harry and his Ruthie good luck in their marriage.

Harry sailed to Canada on a passenger liner, the *Empress of Australia*. Morrie saw him off, and ached to be with him.

There was nothing to do now but wait. The days dragged by slowly, until the day came finally when the *Empress of Japan* was due. Once again, Morrie was at the dock before dawn. He saw the ship nudged into its berth by the tugs, and he quickly began to scan the faces along the railing. There they were!

He couldn't believe it. Ron and Stan were actually there, and they were waving at him and giving him the thumbs-up signal. They were going to go through with it.

The three men had made specific plans as to how things would go in Yokohama. They would not recognize each other once the two soldiers disembarked. Morrie was to stand by the gangplank, and when he saw them begin to come down, he was to start walking and they would follow him. He would have already picked out a safe place for them to rendevous and talk.

It worked perfectly that way. Morrie led Ron and Stan over the Yato-Bashi Bridge to a section of the city known as Camp Hill, where they would be safe from any authorities. When he reached this spot, Morrie turned and raced back to his friends and embraced them.

"Oh, you two look good to me," he said.

"How have you been, you old so-and-so?" asked Ron.

Stan handed Morrie a duffle bag, and inside was the spare Canadian uniform they had collected. Ron and Stan said they had to be back on board the ship by two the next morning. They had a bunk for Morrie.

"We'll go back with you and take you to the bunk," said Stan. "When you get there, stay there. Play sick. Don't go out for anything, especially not for inspection. We'll bring you food when we can. It won't be a pleasure cruise, but we'll get you to Canada, that's the important thing."

"You two blokes are really special friends," said Morrie and he almost had tears in his eyes thinking of the risks they were taking for him. "I promise you this. If anything goes wrong, and if they find me, I won't bring you into it. I don't know you at all. So you're safe."

Morrie took his duffle bag and said he had to go back to his hotel to settle up. He told them of places for them to visit and offered suggestions to them on where they should go to have a good time during their one day in Yokohama. He arranged to meet them again in front of the Yokohama United Club at 1:30 in the morning. It was only a ten- minute walk from the Club to the Pier where the *Empress of Japan* was berthed.

Morrie went back to the hotel, got his things together, paid his bill, and told Mr. Tanaka that he would be leaving. He then waited, impatient as always, for the adventure to begin. He had a leisurely dinner in Yokohama, buying himself the little treats that had become his favorites from the little food stores.

Morrie went back to his room and put on the Canadian Army uniform: heavy boots, shirt, jacket, trousers, tie, hat. The trousers were a little long, the shirt a little tight, and the boots were at least two sizes too big but he wasn't complaining. He hoped the uniform would do the job.

He then put his wallet, still stuffed with money, into his jacket pocket, crammed his other belongings into the duffle bag, and walked out. He was careful not to be seen by anyone at the hotel as he left.

"*Sayonara*, Yokohama," he said.

There was no one on the streets. He knew his way around by now, and he walked swiftly to the Yokohama United Club. Ron and Stan were already there.

"God bless you fellows," said Morrie.

"Let's go," said Ron.

'Walk between us, Morrie," said Stan. "Just act like nothing is bothering you.

And don't forget to salute when you get on board. They didn't give out passes when we got off, so they won't be looking for them when we get back. When we get on deck just follow us. Don't say a word."

There was a Canadian military policeman at the foot of the gangplank, but he merely looked at the three men and waved them aboard. No problem. Still, for Morrie, the walk up the gangplank—as he worried that at any minute he might hear a whistle blowing and a voice calling out, "Hey you there wait a second!"—was one of the longest walks of his life.

Ron led the way up and smartly saluted the officer on the deck. Morrie followed, imitating Ron precisely, and Stan brought up the rear. Ron led the way left along the deck, into a hatchway and down some carpeted stairs. They walked down three more companionways, finally reaching a deck where their stateroom was located. It was small, with four bunks. Ron said they had originally been given a room with a porthole, but it only had two bunks, so they swapped their cabin for this one, because it had room for Morrie.

"That upper bunk is yours, Morrie," said Ron. "Remember, you're going to be sick for the whole trip, so get in that bunk and stay there. We'll bring you food on a tray. If anybody comes in, turn toward the wall and start groaning. Not too loud, or they'll take you to the doctor."

"Look," said Stan, "it'll be tough, but it's the only way. Keep the door locked. We'll knock a special knock, two raps, then a pause, then a third rap, okay?"

It was late, so they went to bed. When they awoke the *Empress of Japan* was underway. Morrie couldn't see anything, of course, but the rolling motion was evidence enough. Ron and Stan went out for breakfast, coming back with coffee and some toast and a piece of fruit. It was enough for Morrie.

They fell into a routine that seemed to work for all three men. During the day, Ron and Stan were usually away from the cabin. They had some assigned duties, but they also felt it would be best if they were mingling with the others. Morrie was alone in the cabin.

He wondered over and over if he would be able to get off the ship all right. And Assuming he got off the ship, what next? He would be in a Canadian uniform, so it certainly would be the smart thing to ditch that quickly and switch to civilian clothing. But where? He had the money to buy the clothing, but where would he be able to change?

And what next? A job? They might ask for papers or identification of some sort.

The idle mind can conjure up problems where none exist, and surely Morrie's mind was going through a period of enforced idleness. He invented a myriad of problems. His friends pooh-poohed them, saying that anybody who had done as much as Morrie had done would find getting along in Canada a cinch. He was finally going to be in a country where he spoke the language, so that should make things easier.

In the small room, the only way Morrie could tell it was daytime was when Ron and Stan were absent. At night his subconscious dredged up nightmarish glimpses of the past—jail in Vladivostok, or the Bolsheviks attacking the train—and he would wake up moaning. Fortunately, his cabin-mates were sound sleepers and Morrie's nightmares never disturbed them.

After each meal, Ron and Stan would come back to the cabin with a tray. They would tell the mess sergeants that their friend was still sick down in their cabin, and they were able to bring the food back three times a day. Morrie knew that on the last day he would have to come up on deck, because the troops would be marched off the ship.

"Won't they check the names off?" asked Morrie. "No, not then," said Stan. "Everyone will be so glad to be getting home that it will be one big party. I'm sure there will be relatives on the dock in Vancouver and a lot of excitement. We'll just march down the gangplank and then run to find our folks or whoever. You come with me, Morrie. You'll stay with my folks a few days, until you get on your feet."

"But won't...."

"Stop worrying. You're home free now."

On the next-to- last day of the voyage, Morrie had begun to believe his friends. Even his pessimism was giving way to optimism and excitement. He was almost free. It might not be London, but it would be a place where English is spoken, and a place where he could make a new start, where he could find a new life for himself.

The two soldiers had brought his lunch tray, and then left the cabin according to their habit. Morrie sat down and put the tray on the bunk. It smelled good. He ate it hungrily and then, as he picked up his coffee cup, he noticed that there was a piece of paper neatly folded under the cup. He smiled as he unfolded it, expecting to read some funny note from his buddies.

"We're wise to you. Put all your money what ever you have, under this plate, or we'll tell, and you'll never get off this ship. This is no joke."

Morrie was stunned. Who could possibly have learned about him and his whereabouts? He doubted that Ron or Stan would have told, because discovery could have had serious consequences for them.

It must have been somebody who got suspicious about the "sick buddy" who kept getting food all of the time, and perhaps followed Ron and Stan and listened at the door.

When the two soldiers came down with Morrie's dinner, he showed them the note. They were furious, and they thought that the culprits were probably a couple of the mess cooks, who had suddenly become very curious about the sick friend who required a tray every meal. Ron was all for going back to the mess hall and confronting them but Morrie and Stan said they couldn't do that. If there was such a confrontation, the truth would inevitably get out, no matter what happened.

"No," said Stan. "I'm afraid you're just going to have to give them the money, Morrie, and hope they keep quiet."

"You're right. I have no choice. The money isn't as important to me as getting ashore safely. I made it across Siberia without any money, so I imagine I can get along in Canada. Give them their bloody money."

"Don't worry about it, Ron. I'll get along. Here, take this tray up, like you always do."

Morrie held back ten dollars and, for their souvenir value, a couple of Japanese yen and a few Kerensky rubles. He put the balance of his money under the plate, as the note had instructed. Ron and Stan brought the tray with the money up to the mess hall. They didn't even wait to see who picked it up.

The Empress of Japan docked in Victoria on Wednesday morning, May 21, 1919. Some of the troops, who lived in the area, disembarked there, then the ship sailed on to Vancouver. It docked there at four o'clock that afternoon.

Morrie had his last lunch alone in his cabin. He was ready, dressed in his uniform. They went up on deck together. The brilliant sunlight hurt Morrie's eyes, but he felt his spirit soar as he saw the sun and the sky.

"Remember," Stan whispered "We line up, double file, and march down the gangplank. Keep your eyes straight ahead, and pull your cap down as low as you can on your face. I'm sure my folks will be there, and I'll take you over to them. I'll try to get them moving as quickly as possible. I know you want to get away from here, to where you can change into civilian clothes."

Ron was going on to his hometown, Calgary, and it meant that those two close friends, Ron and Stan, would be separated. So it was going to be an emotional few moments all around.

The ship finally stopped moving, tied up at the pier. Morrie stood with his friends. He heard some orders barked from far away, and the double line of soldiers began shuffling toward the gangplank. There was a band playing in the distance, and its music grew louder as the file of soldiers drew steadily closer to the gangplank.

Morrie marched ashore with the others. Stan's family was at the dock and after introductions they invited both Ron and Morrie to their home. The next morning Stan's mother showed the men the *Vancouver Daily Sun*. It described the arrival of the *Empress of Japan* in Vancouver at 4:00 P.M. on Wednesday, May 21, 1919.

The article also mentioned, to Morrie's surprise, three officers and five other ranks of the Czech Army aboard the ship.

Morrie also read that the ship carried in the hold 450 tons of flax and flax seed. He wondered if that had been shipped by the flax merchant he had met along the way.

Epilogue

Morrie came to Canada with the troops who had left Vladivostok. He arrived in Vancouver at 4:00 P.M. on Wednesday, May 21, 1919. The Bolsheviks, at the time, controlled only a small fraction of Russia. The Treaty of Versailles was signed in June 1919, ending any thought that Germany posed a threat to the Allied stores and ammunition in Russia. The tide then turned favoring the Bolsheviks in July.

The British Middlesex Regiment was withdrawn from Vladivostok in September 1919, and by the middle of October the British withdrew from Murmansk and Archangel, having suffered almost a thousand casualties and over three hundred dead.

General Deniken's armies were in full retreat by November 1919. Deniken continued his retreat until April 1920, when he reached Constantinople, where he boarded a British warship and sailed to Malta.

Admiral Kolchak gave up his headquarters at Omsk in November 1919, and retreated to Irkutsk. By then the eight hundred thousand men who once composed the Kolchak forces numbered less the twenty thousand. Some crossed the Chinese border, and some joined the forces of Semenov. Kolchak's train arrived at Irkutsk on January 15, 1920, and was surrounded by armed workmen. He was taken to Irkutsk prison and was shot on February 7, 1920.

The Czechs, in the meantime, began leaving Vladivostok in December 1919, and by June 1920 all of the them had left Siberia and were transported across Canada en route to Europe.

General Graves received a message from the War Department, late in 1919, that he would soon be ordered to depart Vladivostok with his American troops. Secretary of State Lansing announced the decision to withdraw on January 9, 1920 and the last American troops left Vladivostok on April 1, 1920.

General Horvath, head of the Chinese Eastern railway for so many years, fled Harbin on April 6, 1920, and on February 15, 1921, the Chinese flag was raised over the government of Harbin. The Japanese remained as the last of the Allied forces, until they departed on October 25, 1922. The Far Eastern Republic was absorbed into the Russian Soviet Republic on November 14, 1922. Siberia was fully Sovietized by January 1923.

Semenov decided by the spring of 1922 that he had no future in Siberia. He sailed to Vancouver in March 1922. He entered the United States and left immediately for France. Semenov spent the inter- war years in Europe and returned to Manchuria during World War II, where he became the puppet ruler under the Japanese. In 1945, The Red Army captured him and he was executed.

Author's Note

This story, essentially, is a true one. Morrie Kotler was my father. He told me, in lieu of fairy tales, the saga of his trip across Siberia.

He did go home to Stan's family, after disembarking from the *Empress of Japan*, and he stayed with them for a few days. He got a job at the "Tip Top Tailors" on Hastings street in Vancouver, and he worked there for several months. He had written a letter to Harry Dickstein, the man he had met in Yokohama. Harry wrote back, enclosing an invitation to his wedding in Seattle.

My father had no passport or any other official papers. He showed the wedding invitation to the American Immigration official at the border and was waved ahead.

He simply stayed in the United States after the wedding and migrated to Los Angeles. He opened the Empire Cleaners and Dyers in downtown Los Angeles and eventually married my mother, and they had two children, my sister and me. There was always the fear that he would be apprehended, and that fear made him lead a very quiet life.

A general amnesty was declared for people like him before the beginning of World War II. He became a citizen on November 14, 1941.

His plans to return to England were postponed because of the war. My father later became a vice president of my company, R.A. Barnett & Co., importers of steel products. It wasn't until 1959 that he made that emotional journey back to England. He saw his father and his sister again, his mother having passed away. He walked down Picadilly with his old friend Willie. It had been forty-two years since he had last set foot on English soil.